# DO YOU KNOW ME?
## & OTHER ABERRATIONS

## BRUCE ELLIOTT

### Introduction by Nicholas Litchfield

**STARK HOUSE**

**Stark House Press • Eureka California**

DO YOU KNOW ME? & OTHER ABERRATIONS

Published by Stark House Press
1315 H Street
Eureka, CA 95501, USA
griffinskye3@sbcglobal.net
www.starkhousepress.com



ISBN: 979-8-88601-143-2

Text design by Mark Shepard, shepgraphics.com
Cover design by Jeff Vorzimmer, ¡caliente!design, Austin, Texas
Proofreading by Bill Kelly



First Stark House Press Edition: May 2025

**Do You Know Me?....**

Staggering, he tottered to his feet. Like a man coming out of ether, he rotated in slow motion. The pattern of his movements was so stereotyped that he might have been doing a macabre dance.

Forcing the door open he kicked the rumpled papers out of his way. He had not even seen the message he'd scrawled on the wall near his bed in the girl's lipstick.

*Since you can't catch me, and since I don't want to kill again, I'm going to kill myself.*

Sprawling, each letter larger or smaller than the rest, the scrawl, red as the lipstick, redder than the girl's blood, remained after he closed the door, remained as a message of despair from a long-lost soul.

It was forgotten as he had forgotten so many things.

His hand in his pocket cuddling the knife that was his only beloved, he made his lonely way down the dirty steps of the stairs that led to the street.

# Table of Contents

# "Do You Know Bruce Elliott?"

by Nicholas Litchfield

Bruce Walter Gardner Lively Stacy Elliott (1914–1973) was a versatile writer known for his contributions to science fiction, crime stories, comic scripts, television scripts, and nonfiction books about magic. He excelled in writing novels and editing the works of others, and for a time, he managed a book publishing imprint, where he often revised large portions of numerous manuscripts to meet editorial standards. In total, nineteen of his manuscripts were published, with his noir novel, *One Is a Lonely Number*, being the most well-known.

Elliott began his career in fiction with the sale of his first story, published in Street & Smith Publications' *Doc Savage Magazine* in June 1944. Shortly after, while he was writing Nick Carter stories for *The Shadow Comics*, his friend and fellow magician, Walter B. Gibson ceased adapting *The Shadow* pulp stories for the comics due to a fallout with the new editor, possibly over financial issues, leading Elliott to take over the writing responsibilities. Under Gibson's pen name, "Maxwell Grant," Elliott wrote fifteen of the last novels featuring *The Shadow*.

Without question, his most popular piece of short fiction is the lycanthropy-themed "Wolves Don't Cry," first published in *The Magazine of Fantasy and Science Fiction* in April 1954, edited by Anthony Boucher and J. Francis McComas. In this unique tale, Lobo the wolf transforms into a human and wakes up in his cage, finding himself in a new body. Elliott offers no explanation for this transformation, instead presenting numerous questions that ultimately give the piece more depth. In her analytical critique of the piece, fiction writer Doris V. Sutherland states: "Elliott's main intention appears to have been simply to tell a humorous story that examines the human world through the eyes (and nostrils) of a very confused wolf, and the story succeeds on this level; but the intertextuality adds another layer of appeal—and demonstrates how the werewolf theme had become familiar enough to warrant a revisionist take" (Sutherland, 2022). His much-admired story has been anthologized many times in volumes edited by notable figures such as Rod Serling, Bill Pronzini, and Douglas Hill, who was one of my favorite childhood authors.

Personally, I think "The Man Next Door," a science fiction story exploring the theme of writer's block, is an even finer story. Here, the prolific storyteller Bennet Barlay—who has "sold millions of words to the pulp science-fiction market"—has become oblivious to the world beyond the page. Having long neglected his wife and son while toiling at his typewriter, he finds one day that he is unable to "force his weary brain to conjure up a single story idea." He remains unaware of his wife's infidelities or his son's experiments, leaving you wonder if the truth would affect him anyway. The remedy for his block is masterfully executed by Elliott, whose exquisite prose and wonderfully tongue-in-cheek humor provide a glimpse of just how talented a writer he was. The elegant sentences and intelligent observations make some of his other stories seem as if they were penned by different authors.

Elliott also sought to showcase his versatility by attempting fantasy, even though this genre did not come naturally to him. Hugo Award nominee Steven H. Silver described "The Devil Was Sick" as "eminently forgettable," and yet he did admit that it contained "interesting ideas" (Silver, 2022). While book critic Everett F. Bleiler considered "So Sweet as Magic . . ." to be "of some small interest for conveying the atmosphere and personalities (in disguise) of the modern world of legerdemain, but as a story, weak and erratic" (Bleiler, 1982). Some of Elliott's fantasy stories may have lacked form and cohesion, but they remained readable nonetheless.

It's unclear whether he preferred crime and mystery stories over science fiction and fantasy or simply found more success in those genres. However, one thing is certain: he excelled in crime and mystery storytelling. The titular story, "Do You Know Me?", showcases his brilliance. In it, Elliott depicts chaos erupting on the streets of New York City, where a dangerous individual suffering from a severe mental disorder systematically removes the faces of various victims, ostensibly to eliminate fake personas. No one is safe, and the tension is so palpable that it feels as if it could be sliced with a razor-sharp blade—just like the one the killer carries.

You can't help but admire how the writer offers a compelling examination of the culprit, the victims, and the witnesses, revealing their desires, fears, obsessions, and peculiarities. The depth of the backstories is so well-crafted that you feel intimately familiar with each character, especially the culprit, making you want to jump out of your seat and flee before his blade reaches you. As noted in a recent review, the author presents a diverse cross-section of society, unafraid to explore a wide range of themes while unsettling and provoking the reader (Paperback Warrior, 2023).

"Death Lives in Brooklyn," another quality piece, first appeared as a novelette in *Thrilling Detective* in April 1953. The suspenseful crime story follows Max Farrell, a down-at-heel former lawyer who makes it his business to retrieve crucial evidence hidden in a restroom after witnessing a murder at a dive bar. The plot-driven narrative with an emphasis on action and tension—typical of a *Thrilling Detective* tale—holds your attention throughout. While Farrell's motivations for getting involved in the drama might be seen as questionable, Elliott develops his character's desire for redemption, providing a plausible reason for his interference. The story is further enhanced by vivid descriptions that bring to life the cold, grim setting and the gritty characters that inhabit this bleak, wintry environment.

As with Max Farrell, the protagonist in "Vengeance is Not Enough" is a broken man grieving the loss of a loved one. Henry Timms' life has been cruelly shattered, and the shock therapy he undergoes to treat his partial amnesia ultimately leads to even more suffering. Although the story begins intriguingly, Elliott chooses not to delve deeply into Henry's psychological torment, opting instead for a sensationalized, action-packed scenario with a rather predictable conclusion.

Interestingly, despite his successes as a fiction writer, it is his nonfiction work that brought him distinction. *Magic as a Hobby*, published in 1948 and containing a foreword by Orson Welles, *Classic Secrets of Magic* (1953), *The Best in Magic* (1956), and *Professional Magic Made Easy* (1959) have all been translated into many languages (New York Times, 1973). Magic was his passion from an early age, and he dedicated much of his time and energy to learning, performing, and cataloguing tricks and techniques. His home in Manhattan served as a weekly gathering place for magic enthusiasts (Wasshuber). During the 1930s until 1941, he assisted the respected mentalist Ted Annemann with editing *The Jinx*, a revered journal for magicians and mentalists. From 1942 to 1954, he was Assistant Editor of *The Phoenix*, a bi-weekly trade journal for magicians that spanned 300 issues.

He shifted his focus from magazines about magic to editing *Playcraft*, a popular publication centered mainly on the hobby of model making. He subsequently became an editor of numerous men's interest publications, starting with *Tempo*, a digest-sized magazine that featured pin-up girls, crime stories, sports, current events, and celebrities. This was followed by *Dude*, *Gent*, and *Rogue*, which were part of a clutch of "skin magazines" similar to *Playboy*, thriving on semi-nude pictures of women.

*Gent*, subtitled "Home of the D-Cups," was an adult magazine focused on women with large breasts, while *Dude* stood out for publishing fiction from renowned writers like multi-Pulitzer Prize winner Robert Penn Warren, James Thomas Farrell, and William Lindsay Gresham, the author of the noir novel *Nightmare Alley*. The highly profitable *Rogue* contained a wider array of fiction than its competitors and boasted an impressive roster of well-known contributors, including Hunter S. Thompson, J. G. Ballard, Brian Aldiss, Graham Greene, Fritz Leiber, Richard Matheson, Frederik Pohl, William Saroyan, Philip Wylie, Steven E. de Souza, Robert Bloch, and Fredric Brown.

In his fanzine *El*, the distinguished Earl Kemp, an American publisher, editor, and critic, shared his experiences with publisher William Hamling's staff of writers and editors at *Rogue* and its various paperback imprints. He recounted legendary boozy lunches at their local hangout, The Dark Place, where work often felt like a distraction from their fun. Kemp wrote: "It took Bruce Elliott to bring drinking as a participant sport out into the open for real. It was nothing to have a three-hour, three-martini lunch and take extras back to the office with us in paper cartons to go. I know I was really out of it for the rest of the day following one of those frequent lunches. It was almost all I could do just to sit there and sip at my extra cocktail of the day, whatever was in style. Editing was impossible...." (Kemp, 2003).

Writer David Stevens, who briefly worked at *Rogue* before moving to *Playboy*, where he stayed for over thirty years, corroborated stories of their indulgent workdays and shared interesting observations about Elliott: "My fondest memories are the three-hour lunches that we used to take at The Dark Place with Bruce Elliott where everyone got juiced on martinis and took a to-go cocktail in a paper cup back to the office with us. How did we ever get an issue of *Rogue* out? I remember that Bruce tried to edit a magazine called *Rake* that may have come out once or twice. Don't have any copies. I also remember Bruce being on the radio one night to be interviewed and he was fried and made a total ass of himself. Came into the office the next day and kind of apologized to everybody in that snarly way he had" (Stevens, 2003).

According to various memoirs, many who worked at *Rogue* enjoyed a reckless and untamed lifestyle. Among them was Elliott, the life of the party, though his tenure at the company was relatively brief.

"Unknown to most of us, Bruce had become a really heavy using alcoholic. Most of the days he would go around the office in a total stupor, not knowing even where he was, much less what he was supposed to be doing there. I saw him take reasonably good manuscripts, rip whole sections of them apart, and spend days rewriting the portions the way they should have been written in the first place. Days . . . at a time when our hurried schedule didn't even really allow for hours.... In 1963 Hamling finally called a halt to the boozing, eased Bruce and Bonnie Elliott back to New York City, and gave the job to Earl, who had been doing the work for a while anyway. And, at the same time, he made some major revisions within the *Rogue* staff, cutting it considerably" (Schieskopf, 2003).

Following his removal from the position of Executive Editor, Elliott was reassigned to Blake Pharmaceutical, a company associated with Hamling's more risqué business ventures. By December 1965, *Rogue* magazine ceased publication.

The confession industry was thriving in the 1950s, and "Macfadden blazed the trail with *True Story*," a publication launched in 1919 that stuck to "the same trite-and-true formula: first-person stories of subjective sex that are more often fiction than fact, and read like supercharged soap operas" (Time, 1957).

Elliott eventually took on editorial responsibilities for several other magazines, including *True Love Stories*, which claimed to "accurately portray the lives and loves of young America today," and the romance novel magazine *True Experiences* (New York Times, 1973). These publications and others under Macfadden's banner were sold off in 1975. However, Elliott's editorial career was cut short in 1972 when he was involved in an automobile accident, passing away four months later, in 1973, at the age of 58.

In 2012, Stark House Press reignited interest in Bruce Elliott by reissuing *One Is a Lonely Number* alongside Elliott Chaze's *Black Wings Has My Angel*, as part of a paired novel collection. This compilation offers a mixed selection of Elliott's earlier works and sheds light on his contributions and significance in the publishing industry.

—January 2025
Rochester, NY

Works Cited

Bleiler, Everett F. *The Guide to Supernatural Fiction*, p. 203. Kent State University Press, 1982.

Kemp, Earl. "Fear and Loathing in Evanston." *El*, Vol. 2, No. 6, December 2003. URL: efanzines.com/EK/eI11/index.htm

New York Times. "Bruce Elliott, Mystery Writer: Author of 14 Novels Dies—Edited Pulp Magazines." *New York Times*, Mar 25, 1973, pg. 70.

Paperback Warrior. "Do You Know Me?" *Paperback Warrior*, August 24, 2023. URL: www.paperbackwarrior.com/2023/08/do-you-know-me.html

Schieskopf, Francine. "Midnight Readers on the Nightstand." *El*, Vol. 2, No. 6, December 2003. URL: efanzines.com/EK/eI11/index.htm

Silver, Steven H. "Random Review: 'The Devil Was Sick' by Bruce Elliott." *Black Gate*, December 29, 2022. URL: www.blackgate.com/2022/12/29/random-review-the-devil-was-sick-by-bruce-elliott/

Stevens, David. "This Ain't No Foolin' Around…" *El*, Vol. 2, No. 6, December 2003. URL: efanzines.com/EK/eI11/index.htm

Sutherland, Doris V., "Werewolf Wednesday: Wolves Don't Cry by Bruce Elliott (1954)" DorisVSutherland.com, February 16, 2022. URL: https://dorisvsutherland.com/2022/02/16/wolves-dont-cry-by-bruce-elliott-1954/

TIME. "The Press: Tin from Sin." TIME, March 25, 1957. URL: time.com/archive/6611615/the-press-tin-from-sin/

Wasshuber, Chris. "Bruce Elliott." lybrary.com. URL: www.lybrary.com/jinx-p-29013.html

...............................................................................................

Nicholas Litchfield is the founder of the literary magazine *Lowestoft Chronicle* and editor of twelve literary anthologies. His stories, essays, and book reviews appear in *BULL*, *Colorado Review*, *Daily Press*, *The MacGuffin*, *The Virginian-Pilot*, *Washington Square Review*, and elsewhere. He has authored three novels: *Swampjack Virus*, *When The Actor Inspired Chaos and Bloodshed*, and *Hessman's Necklace*. He has also written introductions to numerous books, including twenty-three Stark House Press reprints of long-forgotten noir and mystery novels. Formerly a book critic for the *Lancashire Post*, syndicated to twenty-five newspapers across the U.K., he now writes for *Publishers Weekly*. You can find him online at NicholasLitchfield.com or Twitter: @NLitchfield.

# DO YOU KNOW ME?
## & OTHER ABERRATIONS

## BRUCE ELLIOTT

# Do You Know Me?

## I

In the small room just over the huge, ever-flashing electric sign, slightly east of Broadway, on West Forty-seventh Street, the man nobody knew sat on the edge of his unmade bed and felt life return.

New York autumn was crisp, outside his window, but the comfort-giving coolness did not penetrate into the room with door frame and windows stuffed with newspapers. The first harsh clanking in the radiators proved that even the landlord of this fifth-rate rooming house knew that summer was gone. The dry acridness of the dusty radiators as the heat forced its way through the long unused pipes showed that. Next to the radiator, the dirty stove squatted, its two burners coated with rank-smelling grease.

Sweat poured down from the man's armpits. Sitting there on the edge of the bed in his shorts, his thin, hairy chest heaving slightly with the effort of getting some of the overheated air into his lungs, his hands knotted on his lap, his lumpy, unfinished-looking face set with the hurt of concentrated thought, he forced his brain through the tortuous patterns that filled his days and his nights with agony.

Statue-still he had sat poised like that for twenty hours. Night had gone, the day had gone, twilight had come and gone, the glimmering flashing lights of Broadway so near him in reality, so far away from him as he was, had flickered on and off, and now, as night fell again, slow-moving life was returning to him.

The plastic shell that surrounded him was slowly dissolving. Not that it ever went away completely, but sometimes it was soft enough so that he could move inside it, like a deep-sea diver inside his suit. And sometimes it froze solid so that he could not move a muscle. That was what had kept him immobile for so long. It had caught him just as he was sitting down on the bed.

Now the gelatinous mass was so soft that he could lift his broken-knuckled hands a trifle. The hurt, as the ability to use them returned, was something he was long acquainted with, and the pain was in some odd way not connected with him.

Staggering, he tottered to his feet. Like a man coming out of ether, he rotated in slow motion. The pattern of his movements was so stereotyped that he might have been doing a macabre dance.

He worked his mouth, making it gape like an open wound. His dry lips were sandpaper-rough as he pushed one lip against the other. Water, he thought dully, water would help.

The glass was full of bubbles, the water long stale, but it was enough, it would serve. He gulped at it greedily and some drops dripped down from his mouth across the hair on his chest, down toward his waist.

He was not hungry, not for food. He never was when he came back to life. Instead, there was that other hunger, that desperate need that drove him despairingly, the desire to be known, and loved.

Only if he were recognized, only if he were loved, could he feel that he had indeed come back to life. Without that recognition he was nothing and less than nothing.

It was difficult getting his worn slacks onto his stiff legs, and his dirty shirt tore as he forced it into place on his thin, high shoulders. The leather jacket he donned last was worn and hung almost pathetically from his skinny body.

There was a knife in the jacket pocket. The blade that snapped out into view at the pressure of his forefinger was almost as lean as he. Six inches long, and razor-sharp, it was the solution to many of his problems.

He whetted it on his callused palm. The light caught on its edge and almost held him, but he shut his eves to it. He would not he forced away from life again. Not now, not when he could feel the hot baked air of the room surging in and out of his wheezing lungs.

Closing the blade of the snap-knife back into its pearl handle, he dropped it into the one whole pocket in his slacks.

Uncomprehendingly he looked at and was puzzled by the newspapers he had earlier so carefully stuffed into the cracks of the windows and the door. It seemed like an odd thing to have done, before the plastic froze him in, but then he did so many odd things.

Forcing the door open he kicked the rumpled papers out of his way. He had not even seen the message he'd scrawled on the wall near his bed in the girl's lipstick.

> Since you can't catch me, and since I don't want to kill again, I'm going to kill myself.

Sprawling, each letter larger or smaller than the rest, the scrawl, red as the lipstick, redder than the girl's blood, remained after he closed the door, remained as a message of despair from a long-lost soul.

It was forgotten as he had forgotten so many things.

His hand in his pocket cuddling the knife that was his only beloved, he made his lonely way down the dirty steps of the stairs that led to the street.

Meeting no one on the stairs, he stood for a moment in the narrow doorway. The cool air of autumn dried the sweat from his long unwashed body. But he did not feel it. Sweet and fragrant, a wisp of air that had not yet been curdled by the smell of the city, that had not yet been defiled by the exhausts of the cars, met his flaring nostrils. It contained the sweetness of the winter-dying trees in Central Park, not fifteen blocks away. But he was not aware of it.

The eddying crowds of hurrying people who darted back and forth across the streets were quite unreal to him, as they would be to anyone who had to look through a thick layer of translucent plastic. Distorted, the faces of the masked people wove in and out of his consciousness. Why, he wondered hopelessly, did they insist on wearing masks?

If only once one of them would remove the mask, so that he could see them the way they really were!

He thought, God knows I've tried to get them to take off their masks. But somehow, when he cut the mask away, that which remained, the bloody pulp, was never what he expected to find.

And, too, they were so unfair. That girl, the last one. She'd lied to him!

He walked the street, silent, cold as the grave, and he could see it happen again. Not a girl, not really, but a woman. Broad in the beam and heavy in the breast, face painted with a representation of youth, big purse hanging heavy at her side. Night, long past midnight, nearly four A.M.

Hopelessly he asked her his question. "Do you know me?"

"Sure, honey. What's new? How ya?"

Delighted, unable to really believe that it had finally happened, he asked, "You do know me? You recognize me?"

"Surest thing you know, Good-looking. How about it?"

Then the walk down the silent streets, a few paces behind her because she'd said, "Let's not louse around with the cops, baby. Just follow me."

Through the streets where the garbage collectors were the only ones still hard at work, past the scrawny cats that infest Eighth

Avenue, that wait till late night before they come out and scrounge for the scraps that feed them, and fight for the love they need, past the bars which were closing now, he followed her heavy, slow-moving hips. Her too-high heels made her teeter ridiculously, but what did that matter?

She knew him!

Delight was like a live thing. He could taste it in his mouth, feel it in his throat, his heart sang with joy.

Then up the long white tile stairs to the room.

Crowded with junk, with baby dolls that had long spindly legs, and souvenirs of Coney Island, and the smell of an unclean woman, she'd sat on the edge of the bed and moaned as she kicked off her too-tight shoes, from which the fat had bulged upward at the instep. The springs of the bed had jangled loudly when she had slouched down on it.

Then he'd asked, "Where do you know me from?"

Massaging her sore feet, her bulky dead-white thighs showing above the slatternly stockings that bisected the meat of her upper leg, she had said, "C'mon, honey, we're alone now, so cut out that crap, will ya?"

Puzzled, he had stood over her, looking down at the balloon softness of her fish-white breasts that rested now on the protuberance of her jelly-soft belly and he'd said, "But—but—don't you know me?" Unbelieving, not wanting to accept the fact that he'd been lied to, that she really didn't know him. "Didn't you recognize me?"

"I reckernized a guy who needed what I got," she'd said and smiled, a horrid caricature of mirth that had made the coldness come back into his bones.

It was so unfair. Of course, he wore a mask, too, but his was plastic and you could see through it to his real face underneath. It was distorted, that face, distorted by the thick layer of soft ooze, but you could see his face. His mask was semi-transparent. But all the others wore those flesh masks through which you could not peer.

She'd patted the dirty sheet next to her and, still with that false smile on her puffy mask had said, "C'mon, baby, this is the last trick I'm gonna turn tonight. I'm tired."

Bending over her he had tried to look through the skin to her real face that he knew was in hiding under the mask. He could not make his eyes penetrate that far.

There had been only one thing to do.

It was a pity that you had to kill them, he thought as his shoulder and one hand brushed against those others in the lonely, lonely crowd that throngs Times Square.

Such a pity that they had to die before you could peel off the mask. Just once, he'd like to be able to cut and rip off the mask while breath still coursed through them. But that was almost a hopeless dream. He knew that even while he wished wistfully that his dream might someday come true.

Looking about him, seeing and not seeing the happy, sad, lonely, extroverted, introverted humans who hurried by him, each intent on their little errands, he thought, I'll walk over to the pigeons.

They at least did not wear masks. No animals did. That, he thought proudly, was lucky, for it was the one thing that kept him from going mad.

If animals wore masks then there would be nothing to live for.

**II**

Stopping at a gigantic white store where animated dummies of men in the shape of peanuts advertised that goobers were for sale, he bought food for his only friends.

Through the vast expanse of glass that made up the store's window he could see his destination.

Duffy Square.

In the center of Broadway where the triangle of the Square that is not a square comes to a point at Forty-sixth Street, in the very middle of the coexisting arteries that are Seventh Avenue and Broadway, on a plot of land so valuable that its price would be astronomical, if it were for sale, there is a little island of ground. On it stands a statue of a gallant chaplain who died in what was to have been the war to protect democracy.

Father Duffy stands there always, covered with pigeons, and facing downtown. On the west there is a bus stop, on the east, if he could turn his head he would see the Palace, home of a dying art form called vaudeville. Behind him there is a building in which, during the second war, which was to have been the last one, servicemen were given free soft drinks and coffee.

Now that the world is waiting with baited breath for the next, last war, servicemen do not seem to be quite so highly regarded. So the big store that faces Father Duffy's statue is empty but for some ads for the soft drink that was formerly given away.

Nearer to the statue, on the island, are two of the only existing admissions that New York makes that humanity has to do something with that which it eats and drinks.

On the west side is the men's room, down a flight of stairs, under the surface, hidden away from prying eyes, and on the east is the ladies' room, just as hidden, just as far underground.

Over all the island and over the statue there is a coating of white, since there is no doubt in anyone's mind that pigeons must do something with what they eat and drink.

He spent his last dime for food for his friends, then ducked through the ever-present traffic to the statue. He liked to think that the pigeons knew him. He was aware of the fact that they smelled the hot-roasted peanuts, but he tried not to realize that this was what attracted the tame, sophisticated birds.

Covering him like a feathered blanket, the birds poked inquisitive beaks into his pocket till he smiled and took out the bag for which they were searching. They clustered on his shoulders, rapped at his hands with their hard beaks as he teased them and alternately proffered and withdrew the offer of food.

But too soon the peanuts were gone and when he was empty-handed, the birds left him, and with them went the only warmth he ever felt. The cold was back.

Leaning his tired body against the iron bars that keep interlopers at a respectful distance from Father Duffy, he looked about.

A cluster of people were waiting at the iron sign that said this was a bus stop. Hurrying by were office girls, living in their odd manless world, sticking together out of fear, going to restaurants in groups large enough so that if a man dared to try and single one of them out from the crowd they would be able to hide their hunger from each other by sneering at the man who had dared to try and rescue them. Gulping down their tasteless food so that they could hurry equally fast to a movie where they could swallow down the predigested stuff of which dreams are made. Scurrying from the movie to soda fountains where they could snare their sexual appetites with food, and blackjack their desire into submission by the lethargy of a too-full belly.

Separating at last, they disappeared into the different subways that would return them to their various homes. There they would fall into bed so tired that they would be able to go right to sleep instead of being tormented by the tumescence caused by the titillation of the movies. Or by men, more arrogant in their need, eyes moving restlessly, almost sickly as they feasted on the visual aphrodisiac that is New York's woman. The men singly and in pairs, like gaunt wolves who tried to cut out a woman or two from the herds where they traveled for self-protection against that which they did not really want to be protected from.

The man no one knew crumpled up the empty paper bag which had printed on it a picture of a peanut shaped like a human, wearing a top hat. He smashed the paper into a hard ball, pressing it harder and harder as the need in him grew greater and greater.

He would have to ask his question again, and soon!

Throwing the ball of paper over his shoulder, his hand darted to the pocket where the knife lay waiting as he heard a voice squawk, "Hey, what do you think you're doing, throwing things at me?"

She was young and she was pretty and she was in a hurry. "I get out of work," he'd said, "at eleven-thirty. Meet me in front of Father Duffy's statue. It's right across from the Automat where I work."

Such terribly hard work he had to do. He was a busboy, and it meant being on his feet for six and a half hours, clearing off the tables, bringing the dirty dishes into the kitchen—but that was at night. In the daytime he went to school, and next semester was the last one he'd have to work, for he had a scholarship coming up that would allow him to concentrate all his energy on his schooling.

But there had been a slowdown in the subway and before that the inevitable fight with her mother about going out at, "Such an ungodly time of the night! What'll the neighbors say? The idea of a young girl like you meeting a man at this time of night."

No point in repeating it over and over again, no point in telling her mother that this was the only free time Danny had. No point at all. So she had set her young face and squared her lovely round shoulders and walked out of her house while her mother had yelled, "If your father was alive you wouldn't be actin' this way, young lady. No indeed! He'd have walloped your behind good, the way he used to, and you'd have obeyed me."

But then the door had cut off that shrill voice and she had hurried down the rickety stairs, almost run the three blocks that separated her from the subway station, and then relaxing, she'd caught her breath as she sat in the train, and held her skirt. Of course, she'd seen the man across the way slump down in his seat when she'd first sat down. She knew that trick, she knew he was trying to see up under the hem of her dress, knew it, and without anger and almost without being aware of it, because it happened so often, she'd grabbed her willful skirt and held it down.

The man had grunted and picked up his newspaper and had read the so-called comics with a set, angry face. It seemed to get angrier and angrier as he read each strip, every one more filled with blood and violence and sorrow than the last.

Then consciousness of the train had faded away. Sitting primly and stiffly, her purse on her knees, her back straight, she listened again to what Danny had said the last time they were together.

"It won't be long, darling, honest it won't. It just seems that way. Then we can be married and have each other for always."

For always. How wonderful!

But then the train had slowed down, come to a stop, and the lights had flickered. Some kind of momentary power failure, the conductor had roared out in a brogue that filled the ear with soft, slurred consonants.

But it hadn't been a short time. It had taken half an hour before the stuffy train had again begun to move. And that had made her terribly late.

She'd rushed out at Times Square, run up the steps past the soft drink stands and the stores that sold souvenirs, and the magazine stands that sold magazines from all over the world and in every language, and in a mad rush up and out onto Forty-third Street, past the out-of-town newspaper stand, where every smalltown paper in America is represented. Then, without a look to the left where the flashing marquee of the Paramount advertised a mammoth stage show and an even more mammoth feature picture, she had rushed up Broadway past the Bond Building where the artificial waterfall on top of the roof roars like a miniature Niagara, up past the stores and the other movie houses toward the little triangle of empty land where Danny waited.

Or did he?

She strained her eyes trying to see across the two remaining blocks but it was in vain. She could not make out his familiar, beloved shape, let alone his features.

Hurrying on, she almost scampered past a man who looked at her and thought, "So clean, so sweet, so pretty. I'd like to kiss her from the tips of her little feet to the top of her red hair." But when he spoke his voice was harsh and he muttered, "Hey, honey, don't I know you?"

She didn't even bother to answer, and he cursed her aloud even while he silently wailed, I could make such beautiful love to you. Honest I could.

Then he, too, was swallowed up as she breathlessly ran on and, pausing on the street corner nearest the triangle, she looked for Danny.

There he was, and he was furious. She could tell that from the way he threw his cigarette butt on the street and ground it out with his heel.

But what did that matter? He was there, and he'd get over being angry. Then they would be together for their one hour in all the other lonesome, miserable twenty-three hours of the endless day.

He was there and as soon as she could wheedle him out of being angry and had explained what had happened, then they would go to the little delicatessen on Sixth Avenue—she never thought of it as the Avenue of the Americas, any more than any other New Yorker ever does—and they'd get bagsful of good food and a couple of ice-cold cans of beer for him, and then they'd hurry, feeling like guilty children, to his little furnished room that was so horrible for him except when she was there.

And then—and then—

They'd make love just as if they had a right to.

Just as if they were really married; just as they were so soon going to be in reality.

Rubbing her finger on the five and ten cent store wedding ring that she'd slipped on her left fourth finger as soon as she'd left her mother's house, she truly felt married and that made it all right.

The angry north eye of the traffic light was red and that meant it was safe for her to cross the street.

He was lighting another cigarette and looking up at the clock on top of the Paramount building and she knew he was thinking, "I'll give Rosie another ten minutes and then the hell with it!"

Racing the last ten feet that separated them, soft, sweet face aglow, she smiled her greeting. But he was still angry. She could hear him let out the anger in an expostulation as a ball of paper hit him in the back of the head and he spun around, away from her and her outstretched hands that reached for him.

She heard his voice and to her love-tuned ears, even the harsh, brusque anger of it was good to hear as he snapped, "Hey, what do you think you're doing, throwing things at me?"

She smiled a secret smile and was rather glad that he was being able to take his anger out on someone else. This meant he'd get over being peeved at her that much faster.

She waited for the little flurry, the burst of words to end, knowing that as soon as the other man apologized that Danny would turn and welcome her, take her in his arms and kiss her. Then and only then would she be able to forget her nagging mother and the dullness of her job and the horror of her too crowded Bronx apartment where her mother insisted on never throwing anything out.

Oh, she'd forget everything and be happy! So happy, just to be with her beloved. And how happy he'd be when she told him the news! She almost hugged herself. Of course it would mean they'd have to get secretly married, but who cared? They'd meant to anyhow.

The other man, the lean one who'd thrown the paper hall was turning around now, facing Danny.

**III**

New York is people. More than eight million of them, plus the odd million or so who daily pour in and out of town from Jersey and the suburbs, from Long Island and Staten Island, from New Rochelle and Mount Vernon. Every weekday without fail, coming from their bedrooms to the workroom that is New York.

He'd left his big white house in Mount Vernon late that morning, later than usual, for he'd known that at the end of his day at the advertising office he was going to have to go to his analyst. Three visits a week, and so far it had cost him as much as a new home, and he'd be damned if he could see what good the analysis was doing him.

He'd sat all day behind his big blond desk, looking at the back of the little triangular wooden stand. He knew that there was a brass plate on the front of the stand, and he knew, too, that his name was on it in big letters.

Thomas C. Berring. "The Third" was not lettered on the sign, but it was in his head as he always thought of it, the way it had looked in the headlines:

Thomas C. Berring III in Trouble Again

Of course that was one thing that the analysis had done. It had been four years since any scandal had been printed about him.

But that wasn't why he was lying on that damned couch, not just to keep out of the headlines. That was just part of it. No, he wanted peace, and escape from that hag that rode him always.

Most of his life nowadays was spent between commuting to town, his trips to the doctor, and the return to the big house he hated and the woman he was married to whom he hated, and the squalling, too-white-faced son that he was supposed to love and cherish, but whom he hated even more than he hated its mother. For it was the proof that he was a man.

The hell with her and the kid, and the damned doctor and the probing questions, and forcing himself to remember his mother, lovely and serene and not the way the doctor tried to make him see her at all.

And he had never had any desire to do to his mother what that sneaking, sniveling doctor was always suggesting he had. The hell with the whole bloody mess of his life!

He'd left the doctor's office on Park Avenue and walked slowly across town west of Fifth Avenue where he rarely went except to the theatre. Tonight he'd forget the whole shabby pretense, the sham of normality within which he'd been hiding for these four years. And most of all he'd forget what the doctor was trying to make him say about his dear, sweet mother.

The foul-minded, lecherous slob! He wished the doctor would die. Horribly.

He'd forget women altogether. He'd go back where he had come from.

To men.

It had been a long time since he had cruised. But not so long that he had forgotten the belles on Forty-second Street between Seventh and Eighth Avenues, the love for hire, with the bleached hair and the plucked eyebrows, and the pancake makeup, and the tell-tale holes in their arms, and in their thighs.

He'd never wanted that, not even when he had taken it because he could not get what he wanted.

No.

Tonight he wanted a man and he didn't care if it was dangerous, and he didn't care if rough trade sometimes turned on you and beat you up, and sometimes even killed you. He wanted a real man.

But while he trod the streets, and flirted with the truck driver types for whom he would have given his soul, he knew that the homosexual paradox was going to defeat him once more.

When he had been young and had just "come out" an old aunty had said, "Do you know, dear, why straight, normal people are called jam?"

He'd said no, while he'd tried to keep his skin from crawling as the old man's hands molded his young thighs. The aunty had tittered and said, "Because there's an old Tibetan proverb that says 'You can have jam yesterday, and you can have jam tomorrow. But you can't have jam today.'"

Yes, he thought disconsolately, that was the paradox. For the men he wanted, if they allowed him to do to them what he wanted to do would cease to be the men he wanted.

Rubbing his forehead tiredly, he wondered if perhaps the analyst might not be right. Perhaps he had stayed forever in a narcissus-like state through which normal men passed. Perhaps that was all homosexuality was—delayed, continued adolescence. But then as the hunger surged through his veins he said no, it could not be true, and his hands itched as he passed a tall, rather lean, rather dirty-faced man in a torn leather jacket who was leaning against the railings in front of that simply foul statue of some long dead chaplain.

Forcing his face into the semblance of a smile, he watched as the masculine man rolled a paper bag into a tight ball and then threw it over his shoulder.

Now, now, now he told himself, as soon as that paper bag lands on the ground, I'll speak to him. He must come with me—he must. I've got to have him! And the strength of his desire was like bile in his throat.

He thought, as soon as the paper bag lands, I'll speak to him. The worst he can do is refuse me. But he looks poor and I'm rich. I can buy him clothes, and I can love him—cuddle him, cuddle him. Oh, please, he thought with anguish, let him be nice to me!

The paper did not land on the ground. It hit another young man on the shoulder. Thomas C. Berring the Third waited while the other man spun around in a passion and roared out, "Hey, what do you think you're doing, throwing things at me?"

This little squabble would soon end, Berring thought, and when it did, he'd approach the man and say—What would he say? No sense in frightening him. If he was straight, maybe he didn't even know about the gay life. In that case better go slow. Offer to buy him a drink. Something like that.

Gritting his teeth, he waited impatiently for the little flurry to end. Good God, would they never get it over with so he could make an attempt to know the dark, sullen-faced beauty?

But wait! Was that a knife that flashed in the air?


Not everyone races away from Manhattan at work's end, or at play's end. Some live there. If you have been on your feet all day for fourteen or sixteen hours, and if you're not as young as you once were, then it's worth a little extra, he always said, to live close by the shop.

Besides, he thought, as he looked down at her bent back, it was easier for her. If only the little candy store made just a couple of dollars more so he could afford to hire someone, so she would not have to work, waiting on the insolent ones, pretending to smile at the ones who were thoughtlessly cruel, scooping up ice-cream, cleaning the malted milk machines that soured so easily, unwrapping the heavy bundles of newspaper, picking up the fat magazines and putting them in the racks.

If only they could afford to hire someone! For himself, he did not care. He was a man, and if no longer young, still a man. But she was a woman and a mother and a grandmother three times over.

He sighed.

He thought, it is hard, very hard, to have run from Russia and the pogroms, and to have settled in Germany only to have Germany turn into a trap, and have to run from the gaping teeth that were called Dachau and Buchenwald, only to end up one's years working in a candy store.

Not that he was ungrateful. Never! But it was such a little thing he wanted. A dry store. If he could have a dry store, he thought, then life would be good. A wet candy store is one that serves ice-cream and soft drinks. A dry one is a stationery store selling only newspapers and the like.

Maybe someday, he thought, as he held her arm tight and helped her across the street, across Broadway, toward the bus stop they always waited in front of for the trip home. Maybe someday they could get away from the wet store between Eighth and Ninth Avenues, away from the tough people and the bad children, to a nice neighborhood. Maybe in the Bronx on the Concourse.

Almost unconsciously, he squeezed her thin old arm to give her reassurance, as though she could read his mind, and his hand could tell her that all he wanted out of life now that they had their children and the grandchildren, were good things for her.

She felt him squeeze her arm and it was a *mechaye*, and she almost knew what he meant by it. But tomorrow was Friday, and at sundown it would begin the Sabbath, the day she liked best. She was looking forward to getting up early in the morning and chopping up the fish, and boiling the chicken and mincing the carrots for the *tsimmis*. Perhaps tomorrow, on the Sabbath, she would surprise him and put both" *luckshen* and *knoedlen* in the chicken soup; maybe even *kreplach*, too!

What a surprise that would be! The chicken liver chopped up fine with the warm, golden-rich chicken fat running over it, and then the soup with three surprises in it, then the gefilte fish made as he loved it with plenty of freshly ground horseradish ready to be spooned over it. Then the chicken.

But best of all, she thought, was the white tablecloth, and the lighting of the seven candles. That was when she really felt that she was partaking of the sacredness of Shabbos. For the men folk was the *schule* and the *dovenning*—the praying. But she felt closest to Him-who-must-not-be-named when all the food was ready, and the sun was almost gone, and she lit the candles.

To *bench a licht*, that was the holy part of the day to her.

Her raddled old face turned to him and she said softly, "My dear one."

He barely heard her, but then his ears had not been right since that awful night in Berlin. Better not to even think of it. Thanks to Him on High that all was over, and they could live and die here near their children and the grandchildren.

So what, she thought, if Moishe had changed his first name to Maurice? It still meant Moishe and her love was just as great. So what if the children had strayed a little from the faith? Wait till they got a little older. They'd come hurrying back. She knew they would.

Perhaps this Sabbath they would all come and visit, and she could really enjoy the glory of being a grandmother. How she'd spoil the little ones, and tell them *bubemeises!* Grandmother stories. Sure they were grandmother stories, but that didn't mean they weren't good ones. Stories about the wonder-rabbis who could do miracles, and about the wise old men who—

But there was the bus stop up ahead.

A warm wave of gratitude welled up in her that another week's work was done and that now on Friday and Saturday she could again be what she had been made for—a cook and a housewife. She loved the Sabbath so much that she was a little worried for fear it might be sinful. Perhaps she had better ask the rabbi about it.

Arm in arm they waited near the iron sign. Behind the old couple there was a loud voice, raised in anger, and they turned slowly to see what was wrong.

"Mama," he said in Yiddish, his voice heavy, "we have seen so much violence, I hope there will not be trouble."

"Shah, old woman," she snapped, "a young man raises his voice and right away you fear! For shame. It was not thus that you carried the children across the border in the dead of night! Where is your manhood, old woman?"

He smiled, and it made his tired old face warm. The fact that she was snapping at him meant that she was worried, too.

His eyes were not as good as they had been and he had to peer to see what was going on. Pushing his glasses closer to his eyes than the ear-pieces held them, he squinted at the scene in front of the statue. A knife?

It was, and it had, just been buried in a man's stomach!

He grabbed his wife and turned her away, pulling her head down on his shoulder, he shielded her eyes and said, "Don't look, mama, is trouble. Bad trouble."

His old eyes looked sick as he saw the blood rush out of the outraged stomach.

"Where are the police?" he demanded loudly.

The cossacks! When you didn't want them in the store, eating up all the profits, tearing the magazines, then you couldn't get rid of them. But when you wanted them, where were they?

Pcha! A black plague on them! But still he wished that one of them would appear.

She shook him free of her. She snapped, "Since when I have to close mine eyes? Since when I am afraid of what is to be seen?"

But she held onto his arm with a death-like grip as she turned slowly and looked at the man who rolled over and over on the ground, watched grimly as he tried to hold the pieces of his stomach together, and the looks of his *kishkes* hung out over his straining fingers.

Her old eyes went up from the scene to the man who still stood with the wet knife in his hand and chanted, "Don't you know me? Don't you recognize me? I asked you and I asked you and you wouldn't answer me. Why wouldn't you answer me? Why won't anyone answer me?"

Then, the knife outstretched like a wicked elongation of his finger, pointing out in an arc that passed in turn each of the people who stood in frozen horror, he gasped, "Do you know me? Any of you, do you know me? Please, please, do you recognize me?"

The old woman thought, The poor sick boy—he's in agony. That's why he did it. He can't help himself. How could he get so sick in the head? Did no one love him?

Before she could think any further, he had leaped over the fallen body of the man he had stabbed and now, horror of horrors, the old woman thought, he was running straight at them!

## IV

Patrick Murphy, detective second class, felt lousy. He always did when he had to make the pickups. Damn and blast all crooked cops, he thought, and most of all his immediate superior who was too far above graft to dirty his own hands with it and made him, Pat Murphy, an honest man, do the picking up of the filthy, rotten money.

Was it for this he had strained a gut, he thought, passing the patrolmen's examination, lifting weights, running a mile, straining his brain to remember things he had never needed to know once he donned a uniform? Was it for this that he had grabbed a holdup man barehanded and at imminent risk to his life and limbs, and so been promoted to plainclothesman?

No, he answered himself, it was not for the likes of this. The poor little guys who owned the stores from whom he got the graft on various pretexts that ranged from violation of an obsolete ordinance against stores being open for business on Sunday all the way up to outright violations of the law at which he had to wink, just so his lousy crud of a sergeant could wax fat on the petty, dirty, rotten dollars!

Oh, and he was in a fine mood for a fight was Pat Murphy. He prayed obscenely for something to happen. He looked about him as he crossed the street from Broadway over toward Seventh Avenue. If only some holdup man would come along who could be impressed with the power and majesty of the law in the person of one Patrick Murphy!

He felt a little better when he saw, perhaps forty feet away, Mr. and Mrs. Ginsberg, the old couple from whom he got his newspaper when he was swinging his shift. A nice old pair they were, and how pleased and proud they were at the little Yiddish and Hebrew he had picked up in the course of living in Manhattan most of his life. Of course it was funny, he thought, for someone like him, as Irish as Paddy's pig, to be after speaking a little of their language.

But they were flattered by the fact that he had bothered to learn at all. That was nice, for he liked to make people, especially old people, feel good. And, too, there was the odd fact that Mrs. Ginsberg, despite the difference in backgrounds, did remind him a lot of his old granny.

Walking a little faster and feeling some of the anger in him ebb away, he prepared to pass the time of clay with the old people.

But then—

Mother of God! That shriek! It was like his old granny keening at a wake. And the words—the skin on the back of his neck felt strange as he heard the old woman scream; *"Me schlugt der Yidden!"*

He knew enough to know that it meant, "They're beating the Jews!" And he knew, too, that it was a cry that should not be heard in America.

Loosening his gun in its holster he ran through the maze of waiting cars toward the little island in the center of the street in which

Father Duffy, Mary bless his name, stood in all honor.

He was closer now, and there was enough light cast by the flashing signs on Broadway for him to see that there had been trouble. Bad trouble.

Two men were on the ground, and one stood holding a bloody knife, and he was waving it at the other people who stood in front of Father Duffy!

Murphy was a good Catholic, and it made him feel strange to hear the old woman chant the words He in his weakness and suffering had cried out on the cross that meant, "Why hast thou forsaken me?" The thin voice of the old woman trailed off in the silence that followed Murphy's running toward the man with the knife.

Patrick Murphy saw at a glance that old Mr. Ginsberg was done for, another glance showed that a younger man was near death. His gun out, he said, and his tone was pleading, "Just make one move, you rotten bastard, and I'll cut you in half!"

But the man no one knew was not concerned. With the railings behind his back and his knife in his hand and death at his feet he was as alive as he ever was.

He could feel the soft plastic hardening and he knew that he did not have long now. If he were to get an answer to his question it must be soon, very soon, before the plastic was as stiff and unyielding as glass.

Making his voice low, for he knew that sometimes people seemed to be afraid of him for some reason, he beseeched the people in front of him, "Do you know me, any of you? Doesn't anyone know me?"

And then a miracle came to pass, and it held the plastic for a moment, prevented it from freezing up as quickly as it usually did. A well-dressed, quiet man whose mask was not as impenetrable as most people's was coming toward him slowly and there was recognition in his face. The mask was fading, fading away and the man with the knife wondered wildly if he had finally found the person whom he had been seeking all the days of his life.

Thomas C. Berring III, eyes wide with excitement, pushed the puzzled, heavy-shouldered man with the gun, who was so clearly, a police officer, out of his way.

Stepping over the vapidly pretty little girl who was crouched over the dying man whose stomach had been ripped open, Berring came closer to the man no one knew. Berring paid no attention to the little old woman who cradled her dead husband's head in her lap, and who was now making a rather disgusting public display of her emotions over the corpse.

The man no one knew lowered the hand with the knife as the other man came closer. How long would the plastic stay soft? That was the question on which his sanity depended. For the man who was coming to him had fallen to his knees.

Thomas Berring III, on his knees in public for the first time in his life, unashamedly looked up at the man with the knife.

The man no one knew looked down at the other and asked his question. His voice was plaintive as he repeated, "Do you know me? Do you recognize me?"

The answer came plain and true. "I know you. I recognize you."

"Who am I?" Could it be that he was finally to find out the truth? Was it possible that after the long-continued nightmare he was to have escape and peace? "Who am I?" he asked again.

"You are death, and I love you."

Wild jubilation surged up in the man with the knife. How could he not have known? Of course that was the answer, of course that was why he was always cold, cold as the grave, cold as—death. In the wild ecstasy of the knowledge he dropped the knife.

Berring picked it up and handed it back. Berring said, "Death, take me."

Someone, someone in the whole lonely world who knew him and loved him, who wanted the boon that was his to grant! Smiling as he had never smiled in his whole life he took the knife.

He would give his greatest gift to this man who knew and loved him.

But then the agonizing ecstasy faded, and he knew love and recognition had come too late. The plastic was solidifying.

It was perhaps the very fact of the killer freezing where he stood and then suddenly falling over like a tree chopped down, stiff and immobile, that freed Patrick Murphy from the state he had been in. Never had he been faced by anything similar to this. Too astounded even to pull the trigger on his gun, he had stood like a fool, he thought, with his fat face hanging out, and had made never a move.

The man who was on his knees suddenly crumpled inward on himself and began to cry. "Too late!" he wailed. "Too late!"

It had taken him sixty seconds too long to know that death was the goal of all his days. And now it had been taken from him. And the horror of it was that he knew himself too well, knew he was too much of a coward to do to himself what he had tried to make the madman do.

Murphy looked about wildly. There had come a sudden cessation in the city's noises. When he had been a kid, he thought incoherently, he had looked at the clock to see if it was wearing a mustache, for that had always seemed to be the signal for a sudden incomprehensible period of quiet.

The city's silence was broken only by the sound of three people crying. The heavy, racking, self-pitying sobs of Thomas Berring III almost drowned out the sounds the young girl and the old woman were making.

Then the roar of traffic was back and Patrick Murphy came back to life and began to do that which he should have done earlier. He went through the prescribed sequence for taking care of murderers.

First the ambulance and then the meat wagon and then the patrol wagon. That was the proper order, and that was the way he took care of the situation.

The faceless mob that gathers anywhere in New York at scenes of violence was pushing closer now and the island was being overrun. But reinforcements were coming, and Murphy was finally able to do what he had wanted to do in the first place.

Dropping down besides Mrs. Ginsberg, he put his arm around her thin shoulders and said, "*Macushla*, I can't tell you how sorry it is that I am."

Burying her face on his chest she cried—little, old woman's tears— and the agony that was in her seemed to come from her bowels. She had ripped the front of her dress and she was mumbling over and over, "Why him? Why not me? A poor woman am I, and I would not question your decisions. But how am I to live without him?"

"Hush, honey," Murphy heard himself saying. "We'll get him back to you, and you'll sit *shiva*, and before you know it, you'll be waitin' to be after joinin' him. Now don't take on any more, please, Granny."

And it was as if he was holding his long dead grandmother in his arms and trying to comfort her. It made him feel both older and younger than his years.

When his sergeant did finally show up at the scene, bad cess to him, there were tears in Murphy's eyes, and he didn't give a damn that the lousy scut could see them.

Ambulances in New York no longer have internes riding in them. In a wave of economy and man-shortage during the last war that was to have been the last war, the city decided to send out orderlies instead of medical men.

It was just plain luck therefore that Dr. Aaron Bedrick happened to come out of the newsreel theatre that faces Father Duffy's statue in time to see the ambulance roar up. Hurrying to the scene, he was just in time to see the white garbed orderly reach down to a disemboweled man and attempt, with the aid of a cop, to roll the man onto a stretcher.

The doctor found that his voice had risen too high when he yelled, "Don't move that man, you idiots!" So he lowered it to a more dignified tone when he said, "He must be treated here. Any movement may be instantly fatal."

When you are young and have been in practice only a short time, and you have cultivated a heavy mustache in order to make you look older, it does make you feel a little silly to find that you have shrieked in what almost amounts to a falsetto because of excitement.

The orderly looked at him in annoyance and said, "Who the hell are you, Buster?"

"I'm a doctor." It still sounded good, just hearing the word. "I will treat that man here. You must have some of the sulfanilamides in the ambulance. Bring them to me. You—" he called to a big, stupid-looking, insensitive-seeming red-faced man who must be a plainclothesman. "There's a five-and-ten over there. Run and get me some needles and thread. That is—" he felt a wave of embarrassment come over him—"if there aren't any on the ambulance."

The orderly snarled, "Sure there are. Whyncha ask?"

But he hurried to get the things the doctor ordered.

**V**

If there were only some way to perform a blood transfusion why then the scholarly looking young man who lay gasping his life away might have a shred of a chance, the doctor thought. Impatiently he made the young girl move away from the dying man.

She said, "Doctor, is there—any chance?"

He might have snarled at her that he wasn't God, which is what he was tempted to do, but the emotion was so plain on her face that he couldn't. Instead, he said, "I don't know, my dear. I'll do what I can."

Danny, she thought. He couldn't die. Not this way, not futilely by the hand of a maniac. If he died now, in front of her, there would be nothing left for which to live. She and the life in her belly would have to die too. Young she might be, foolish, but she knew that she could not go on living with him dead. Live—to face the taunts of her mother? Live—to bring up a bastard? No, death was much easier than that.

"Doc," Patrick Murphy said, "when you get a chance, see what you can do for the little old lady, will ya?"

"Sure, sure, but don't bother me now." The fool, the red-faced dolt!

Couldn't the man see that he was busy?

The doctor sprinkled the sulfa drug into the gaping cavity of the young man's intestines, then bemoaning to himself the fact that there was no time for surgical sterility, he dusted his hands with the sulfa powder and found, rather to his surprise, that he was praying that what he was doing was the right thing.

Gently picking up the looped intestines he replaced them in the gaping unbelievable cavity that is a man's heritage.

The man, the doctor thought, was almost completely exsanguinated. He must have blood. That was all there was to it.

The orderly returned with the curved needle and a length of catgut. The doctor stitched as rapidly as he could, hoping that he would not have to disappoint the frightened girl who stood and watched what he did with her heart in her mouth.

The uniformed cops were busy pushing back the mob.

Patrick Murphy stood over Thomas Berring III and said, "You better get up outta here, Mack, or you're gonna go right straight to the psycho ward."

Berring heard the words, but it took a long moment for them to penetrate. Pushing himself upright, he looked down at the man who might have given him release.

Frozen stiff, like a side of beef, the man who had held death in his hands was curled up in a position that Berring had seen before. His knees tucked under his chin, his arms around his calves, he looked like—a fetus—an unborn child, Berring realized with a little falling of the stomach and a feeling of infinite disgust.

Dusting the dirt off the knees of his Brooks Brothers suit, he looked around wildly. Had he been momentarily out of his mind? What had ever possessed him to make such a public spectacle of himself? Good God, if anyone he knew ever heard about this—his wife, his business associates, his analyst— He must have been insane!

Melting back in the crowd that surrounded the scene he thought with a slight return to normalcy, "If there were a couple of more bodies strewn around this'd look like the last act of *Hamlet*."

But just when he thought he'd made good his escape, a plainclothesman spotted him edging away and sent a uniformed cop after him.

Berring drew himself up and demanded, "By what right are you taking me into custody?"

Before the officer could answer, Murphy, the beefy red-faced plainclothesman called out, "Book him as a material witness." And then went back to watching the doctor who was hard at work over the young man, who lay so still, whose breathing had become so stertorous that it hurt the ear just to listen to it.

The young doctor was getting desperate. He had sewn together the gaping raw edges of the wound, and he knew from things that medicine had learned at the battlefront that there was a sporting chance for the young man to recover, if the sulfa drugs prevented peritonitis. But that still left the biggest problem of all.

He looked up at the girl who hovered nearby, whose hands were so tightly pressed together that the knuckles were dead-white, and asked her, "By any chance do you happen to know what his blood type is, miss?"

It was the last question in the world that Rosie was prepared for. Blood type? She racked her brains. She put out of her mind the wild prayers she had been repeating over and over again. Blood type? That time that both of them had gone down to the Red Cross and donated blood.

Bending over, she slipped her pallid hand into his back pants pocket. His wallet. Opening it she found a card that the Red Cross gave out to all donors.

The doctor glanced at it and grunted. "Most common type of blood. That's good."

Then he looked up at the police officers who were pushing and yelling at the crowd that alternately surged forward and slowly retreated, as the policemen threatened and pleaded with the people that made up the mob.

Surely one of them must have the proper type blood. The doctor now had one more big problem. He needed the apparatus for a transfusion. It was simple and that was one good thing. All he needed was— Would the ambulance be likely to have it?

He asked the orderly the big question, and found he was holding his breath as he waited for the answer.

"Nah. We don't carry stuff like that. But the hospital's only a few blocks away. I can rush back and get it."

"Then hurry, man, hurry!"

The doctor wondered whether it was worth the trouble as the orderly hopped onto the ambulance and the car drove away. The young man who lay so quietly on the city's property gasping away his life was so nearly dead that he had begun that awesome sound that is called Cheyne-Stokes breathing. He was, as is known in medical parlance, in extremis.

But looking up at the pale face of the girl who loved the wounded man, the doctor knew that he would have to continue trying. Under the prodding of those eyes he could not quit.

Patrick Murphy said, "Doctor, the old lady—"

Anxious to let out his helpless irritation on someone, the doctor snapped, "Send her home in a cab, tell her to get some—No, wait a minute."

Taking out a prescription pad he scribbled a request for some nembutal. That would let the old woman sleep, would force her to sleep, he thought. And almost anything in the world seems a little less had after a full night's sleep.

How had Shakespeare put it? The young doctor was proud of his classical knowledge. "To sleep, perchance to dream—" No, not that. "Let sleep knit up the ravelled sleeve of care." That was the quotation.

"Doc," Murphy said, "what about the screwball?"

Leaving his patient, for whom he could do nothing until the transfusion apparatus arrived, Dr. Hedrick rose from his kneeling position and went to where the murderer lay curled up in the foetal position.

Psychiatry was out of his field, but even a first-year medical student or a psychology major would be able to spot this one, he thought.

Looking down at the man's frozen features, at the uncomfortable rigidity of the psychopath, the doctor said, "He's in catatonia. He may not move from that position for days."

"No kiddin'?" Murphy was astonished.

"No kidding." The doctor's tone was almost surly. Where the hell was that ambulance? "Yes catatonics freeze that way, and some of them will stand poised on tiptoe, or bent over about to open a door, just the way they were when it hit them. He's probably a paranoid-schizophrene." Let the cop try to figure out what that meant!

There was the clanging of the ambulance's bell. They were no longer allowed to sound their sirens for fear the public would confuse the sound with that of the special sirens that had been installed to alert the population in the event of an A-bomb attack.

Fear, the doctor thought, piled on fear, A-bombs and H-bombs and eight million people pressed into a city that had never been meant to contain that many humans. No wonder, he thought, as he walked away from the madman, that people cracked under the strain. No wonder at all.

Then he was calling for volunteers and found that the ambulance orderly had forestalled him by bringing blood plasma of the proper type from the hospital.

The transfusion took almost no time at all.

Rosie asked timorously when the doctor was done:

"Now"—she gulped and repeated herself—"now will he live?"

The doctor wished he could give her the promise she wanted, but he couldn't. He said, "Now he's got a sporting chance. That's all I can tell you, dear."

It was enough, it was flimsy straw, but a straw to which she could fasten all her hopes.

She watched and waited and prayed as at long last Danny was placed on a stretcher and put in the ambulance. Now it was in the lap of the gods. But she would pray. Oh, how she'd pray.

The doctor looked around. He'd given the girl the address of the hospital so she could go and sit in the corridor and wait there as he had seen so many others wait, and hope.

Patrick Murphy watched the calloused men from the meat wagon pick up old Mr. Ginsberg's body and drop it in the big wicker basket.

He was grateful that he'd sent Mrs. Ginsberg home before this so that she'd not have this memory.

The dead man was gone now, the wounded man, too. The killer was the next to be taken away and a tough job that was, Walsh thought, watching the orderlies as they struggled with the statue-stiff body of the madman.

Then it, too, was gone.

The crowd was ebbing away. They watched silently as Thomas C. Berring was escorted to the patrol wagon. Then he also was gone.

No more show.

The doctor glanced at his watch. Good Lord! His wife would be worried about him. He waved to Murphy and then hurried away.

Then Murphy was alone with the pigeons, and Father Duffy and the bloodstains that scarred the pavement in front of the statue. But, Murphy thought, the rains would wash that away, and the scurrying feet of the crowds and the pigeons would cover the stain that remained. Soon there'd be nothing left to tell you that an old man had died there.

Nothing at all.

New York is people. Eight million of them. And they are born and live and die, some peacefully, some violently, just as if they made their homes in the tiniest of whistle stops.

Patrick Murphy, detective second class, walked off into the night and left Father Duffy staring sightlessly down at the heedless, sleeping pigeons who surrounded him.

But the maniac's question haunted Murphy for days. "Do you know me?" When you come right down to it, he kept wondering, who knows anybody?

# Vengeance Is Not Enough

Despite the fact that the doctor had just turned off the current, the big man on the couch continued to roll and retch. His muscles convulsed so that they stood out like ropes on his thick neck. It seemed that his spine must snap from the force with which his head jerked back. From his taut mouth there came garbled syllables like the sounds man must have made before he learned to talk. His body heaved so that the springs in the couch seemed ready to burst through the upholstering.

The small, dry-looking doctor watched. His face was lined with sympathy. His eyes were full of compassion. He said, "What day is it, Henry?"

The man on the couch lurched till he was half up, his arms moving aimlessly. The doctor pressed a gentle hand against the man's chest. It was enough. The tortured man fell back onto the couch.

"What day is it, Henry?" the doctor asked. Next to him on the cluttered desk a wire recorder spun on with mindless efficacy. "What day is it, Henry?"

The man on the couch rolled over. Thick stands of saliva drooled from his split lips. The rubber gag was out now, lying on the desk. The gentle voice asked tirelessly, "What, day is it, Henry?"

What day? Why it was Saturday. *The* Saturday. The day he'd been looking forward to all summer. The day he and his son, Jimmy, were to go fishing. Sure. Saturday. Gotta get a good early start if you want to catch anything but crabs. They'd kidded a lot about who was going to catch more fish. They'd eaten a hurried breakfast, promising themselves that they'd eat again at some roadside diner. Now there was nothing to do but get the brand-new sparkling tackle into the back of the battered convertible.

The sun had washed the dirty city streets with a kind of lambent magic that made them sparkle. His son had been bemused by the way the gold made even the garbage cans look like some kind of ancient treasure. Funny kid. Be peculiar if his son were a poet. Didn't know whether he'd liked that or not. Oh, well, maybe it was just a phase boys went through. Adolescence did odd things.

They had the tackle stacked fairly neatly and were standing next to each other. Jimmy had been almost bouncing with excitement as he'd said, "Gee, Dad, thanks a million. I know it's hard for you to get away from the office. 'Specially now that the mayor's been sick." Thoughtful kid, grown up in a lot of ways.

Jimmy had nudged him in the ribs. Said, "Dad, isn't that Mr. Vincent?" They'd waved, and Ben Vincent, portly, self-important, had waved back with a tired flip of the hand. They had watched him leave the back entrance of the big apartment house and walk around the corner.

"Must be hard for Mr. Vincent, being acting major," Jimmy had said.

Hard? That was a question. He made it look hard, that was true. But this was no day to worry about the city, or the office or any of the people connected with it. They'd waited too long for this fishing date. He'd slapped Jimmy on the back and said, "Let's go, Son. If there's no traffic, we should be able to have our hooks wet inside of an hour." Then he'd gotten into the car. His head had been bent forward as he put the key in the ignition.

That was why he hadn't seen it, just heard it. Heard that despairing scream as his son died. Leaped from behind the wheel in time to cuddle Jimmy's broken head in his lap. Been blinded by horror so that he hadn't seen the car that had stolen his son from him. Hadn't even been aware that there must have been one.

He had just sat there in the middle of the street with his dead son in his arms. Crying as he hadn't when his wife, the mother of his child, had died of cancer. Cried for all the things he had wanted for his son. Cried till something, somewhere inside of him let go.

Now someone was saying, tonelessly but insistently, "What day is this, Henry?"

He said tonelessly, "Saturday."

"Good work. Who are you?"

"Who are you?" What a question. As if anyone could ever answer it. He was a man. A hard-working man who'd loved a woman and lost her. Who'd fathered a son and lost him, too.

The black clouds swirled back.

The doctor sighed. Rapport was broken again. However— He looked at the wire recorder. The reel still looked fairly full. There was enough there for an hour's recording

"What day is this, Henry?"

"Saturday."

"Who are you?"

Time passed. The reel of wire ran on and on. The low hum of the motor was the only sound. Outside the office darkness fell.

"Who are you?"

"Henry," thick tongued, the heavy voice went on, "Henry Timms."

The doctor smiled. Some of the strain fell from him. His voice was a little louder now. He asked, "What do you do?"

"I'm in politics. It's a job."

"And—" the doctor paused for a second; this was the test— "why are you here?"

"I—I think someone brought me here—or an ambulance. I—" There was great hesitation, then: "It's all muddled. I think you're a doctor and you're going to help me. You—you said something about shock therapy." The big man got panicky. "You're going to give me electric shock."

The doctor killed the building panic. He said, "Relax, Henry. It's over. You've had the treatment. This partial amnesia is the result of it. It will pass quickly, now that you know who you are."

The big man on the couch said, "I don't remember getting anything. Has it—am I—"

"It's worked. You're better than you were when you came here. In a sense, you were already in shock because of your son's death. The electric shock has helped you over that other, greater shock. But you'll be all right now. In a way, you've had the equivalent of battle fatigue. You've been overworked, and then—this other—it was too much for you. You escaped from life, from everything. You blanked out.

"But that's over now." The doctor made his voice more positive. Patients were at their most suggestible at this point. Now was the time to impress the message. "The treatment has given your brain a rest, given you time to make at least a partial adjustment."

"I see." Timms sat up, looked around the office wonderingly. As far as he was concerned, he'd never seen the room before. The books— that was the thing that you saw first. Hundreds of them. Thousands of them. He looked from the ceiling to the floor. Textbooks, books on mathematics. Books. Then the crowded desk—the wire recorder— and behind it, the little wizened, tired-looking doctor.

"Why the recorder, Doctor?"

"So that I can play it back to you. So that you can see how the treatment works. So that this partial amnesia you are undergoing will not frighten you in the future."

"I see." Things were beginning to come back. Little things. Like the nurse who had helped him untie his tie. He looked around, wondered where she was.

He swayed as he rose. The doctor leaped from his chair. "Steady, now. You shouldn't have done that, it's too soon."

The doctor almost fell, trying to keep him from falling. Their bodies spun in a grotesque waltz. They reversed their relative positions.

It was then that the bullet crashed through the window and plowed deep into the doctor's back. Timms, faint, almost falling, tried to grab the doctor's body in time to keep it from falling. He failed.

Two more things happened almost simultaneously. There was a bigger crash of glass, and the door of the office slammed open.

Timms looked stupidly at the window. On the floor, shards of glass made a pattern around the gun that had been thrown through the broken window.

The nurse screamed. "Doctor Welles! What's he done?"

She turned on Timms, and words bubbled out like the blood that was coming from the doctor's back. "Why did he do it? Why did he insist on treating you lunatics all by himself. I tried to make him let me be in here. But no, he never would. He didn't want anyone else to hear what was said."

She fell to her knees. Instinctively she did the professional thing. She felt for his pulse. The hysteria left her. She said flatly, "So you've killed him! Killed the finest man I ever knew. Killed him. For what? Why did you do it?"

He fought off the black clouds. That was the easy way. He'd tried that, and it hadn't worked. This was no time to escape. There was no escape. He had to find out what was behind this seeming madness before it claimed him.

It was hard to get the words out. His tongue was still thick. His jaw ached. He saw the rubber gag, saw his tooth marks in it, and realized why his jaw hurt.

He said, "I didn't."

She looked at the doctor's body, at the gun, and then at him. Her hand dropped on the phone. She said, "Oh, of course. No. You didn't do it. Why don't you sit down on the couch. You still look pretty rocky."

That was a temptation, too. All his muscles hurt the way they had in the old days, when he'd been a fullback, after a hard game. But no. If he sat down, he might never get up. He saw the nurse pick up the phone. Her lips formed the word police before he really realized what she was doing. He lurched toward her, knocked the phone out of her hand.

"No."

She backed to the broken window. It was only then that the darkness outside made him know that night had fallen. A whole day gone. He didn't know what had happened to it, and that frightened him terribly. He shook all over. Night. The last thing he remembered, really remembered, was seeing his son die. Twelve hours ago, at least. His mind jumped around; he couldn't force it to work the way he wanted it to.

He said, "I won't hurt you. I just want to get out of here." He backed to the door. He had to go someplace, and sit. Think. Try to find out what had happened. For one thing, he knew—no matter how muddled he was, no matter how scrambled his brain was—he knew that the shot that had come through the window had been meant for him and not the doctor.

Whoever had fired the bullet had fired just as he lurched. He and the doctor had spun around so that their positions were reversed. That's why it was the doctor who lay on the floor and not him.

Who would benefit by his death? Not his political enemies, for he wasn't that important. Besides, it was easier to kill a man at a committee meeting with a few well-chosen words, or in the newspapers with a smear campaign, than to use a gun.

He ran, almost fell, through the door and slammed it behind him. There. Let her phone the police now. But— He looked around him. The doctor's waiting room had three doors. Which one led outside?

The first opened on a closet. He didn't bother to close it but lurched to the middle door. He gasped for breath. Yes, this was the one. Out in the hallway he didn't wait for an elevator. He went down the fire stairs. No point in taking a chance on getting bottled up in a little car. Smarter just to walk downstairs.

Or was it?

One flight, two, three— How high up was the doctor's office? His knees were shaking when he reached street level. There, right ahead was the door. A thought hit him like a blackjack. Suppose the door were locked as doors so often are. If it were, he might as well give up. He knew he could never go back up the stairs.

He put his hand on the knob timorously, turned it. When the door gave, the wave of relief that went through him left him as exhausted as had the stairs.

He looked through the partly open door. The elevator indicator was on nine. That showed where Dr. Welles' office was. The nurse must have sent for the elevator in an attempt to stop him. Or had she phoned down? Alerted someone to grab him?

He shook his head, tried to clear his muddled brain. Only one thing he could do. He boldly walked through the door. Out on the street he saw a cab. He was in it fast as he could move.

Through the glass door of the building he could see activity. The nurse ran out of the elevator. A man at the desk leaped to his feet and ran toward the door.

"Get moving!"

The hackie had the car in gear and on its way before he asked, "Where to?"

A good question. A very good one indeed. Where could he go? Whom could he see? Vincent? Yes, it had to be Ben Vincent. There was no one else who could tell him what had happened since he blanked out.

He said, "Nine-thirty Fifth Avenue." If Vincent weren't there, the butler would know where he could be found.

A butler answered his ring. He knew where his employer was, all right, but he was amazed that Timms didn't know.

"Mr. Vincent? But—" It was first time Timms had ever seen the flat-faced servant nonplussed. "I thought you knew, sir. He's in the hospital! His wife is there with him, at his side."

"What happened? I've . . . I've been out of town all day."

"He was in an auto accident, sir. Not too badly hurt. Cut up a bit. The doctor says he'll be all right after a rest."

Dare he go to the hospital and see Vincent? Risk being seen? Surely the police must have radioed his description all over town by now. He hoped they'd been to the doctor's office. Once they'd seen the setup, seen the broken window, they'd know that the shot must have come from outside. The hole in the window and the radiations would show that.

He felt good for having thought of that. Sure, the lab could prove that with no trouble at all. But— He deflated. The thrown gun had shattered the area where the bullet had penetrated. No, the police lab was not going to prove that he hadn't shot Dr. Welles.

He pictured the doctor's office. The body, the gun—and the broken window. It would look as if there had been a tussle which had smashed the window. That's what it would look like.

He suddenly realized that the butler was looking at him curiously. He wondered how long he had stood there, lost in thought. Aloud he said, "Too bad. I'm sorry Mr. Vincent was hurt. What hospital is he in? I'll go see him."

The butler told him and closed the door—closed the door on the warm, relaxed intimacy of Vincent's living room. The deep carpet, the comfortable chairs, the ease— If only he could just go somewhere and sit and think.

His home? The very thought of it, with its wealth of reminders of his son, made him ill again. His stomach lurched. He wondered idly, as he fought down the nausea, when he had eaten last. It must have been that snack he'd had with Jimmy.

Easy. Better not think about that.

Out on the street, he looked around him like a blind man who has regained his sight. The familiar buildings looked like a stage set. He got no warmth from them. They frightened him. This was no place for him. Even the beat cops knew him.

East. That was the way to go. To the small bars on the side streets. One of them would serve as sanctuary till he could get hold of himself.

The heat of the summer night made the spilled beer smell good. Queasy as he felt, it was good. He almost fell through the door. The bar was lined with men. Some talking, some brooding. He worked his way down to the end of the bar, past an interminable baseball discussion, right through an embattled argument on world affairs, till he came to a booth.

He let his battered muscles go slack. He was in the seat before he saw the woman who sat across the table. Discs of rouge stood out like patches on her swollen cheeks. Her bust cascaded onto the table dangerously near a puddle of spilled liquor. Her brazen hair hurt his eyes. Fat bulged under her arms.

She manufactured a delighted tone and said, "Hello, honey."

When he failed to reply, she said, "Gonna buy little Betsy a drink? Come on, honey, you won't regret it. I know how to treat a man. 'Specially a big feller like you." She narrowed her mascaraed eyes in an attempt to look lascivious and succeeded only in looking ludicrous. She said, "The strong, silent type, huh? I like them."

The bartender, annoyed at having to leave the bar to serve the table, stood over them. He said, "We don't serve drunks, mac. Why doncha go back where you got that load?"

Timms bit his tongue, forced air deep into his lungs, grated, "I'm not drunk. I'm sick. Get me a boilermaker. And hurry about it. Get one for the lady while you're at it!"

It worked. At least, the bartender shuffled away. The blonde preened herself. She said, "That's the way to talk. Them bartenders think they're king—"

He said, "Hold it a while. Like a good girl. I just want to think."

She eyed him a little more closely. A little less invitingly than she had. She said, "You *are* sick."

He nodded. The bartender slammed the glasses down in front of them. Timms wondered frantically if there was any money in his clothes. If he could only remember these things. His hands fumbled at his pockets as though he had never used them before. There—his wallet.

He opened it, still wondering if there were anything in it. Even if he had been blind, he would have known it was full from the way the bartender changed his attitude. He said, "Is there anything, else, sir? Can I get you anything?"

"You showed him!" the blonde said. Then she was silent. She sipped at her drink as if anxious that no one guess how fast she wanted to gulp it down.

Twelve hours. Where were they? What had happened in them? The papers. Why hadn't he thought of that? He said, "When you finish your drink, would you get me the evening papers?"

"Sure, honey. Anything you want. Any little old thing." Now that she had an excuse for hurrying, she poured the drink down her throat so fast, it hurt to watch her. He threw her a dollar bill.

Alone. At least, until she came back with the papers. Watching her walk down the length of the bar, watching the fat sway, he wondered if she'd just keep on going with the dollar.

It couldn't matter less.

All he knew was that Jimmy was dead, that someone had tried to kill him and had killed the doctor instead. The liquor burned as it went down. He gulped the beer to wash away the taste and feeling of the raw fire. Maybe he had better eat. Maybe some food would chase some of the rats out of his stomach, drive away the black from his brain.

The sandwich the bartender brought him was as appetizing as dead owl, but he managed to force it down. The beer helped it on its way.

He was halfway through it when he saw the blonde coming back with the papers pressed against her bulging front. She plowed through the men at the bar like a steamship coming into harbor. Her smile dented the make-up as she plopped the papers and herself down.

She said, "Bet you're surprised, honey. Bet you thought I was never comin' back, now didn't you?"

He ordered her another drink to shut her up while he thumbed through the papers. Vincent's accident had made the front pages of the night final. Pictures showed where his car had skidded, and made contact with a lamp post.

The leader said that the mayor was flying back to resume his duties, now that his assistant was laid up. A dope ring had been broken up. Three children had been burned to death while their mother got drunk in a barroom. A sexy looking redhead named Janice George had been found strangled in her apartment. The international mess seemed even messier than usual. An actress had lost a half million dollars' worth of gems. The usual news.

He pushed the papers to one side and ran his hands through his thick hair. Nothing. Not a single blasted thing to put his finger on.

She said, "You got trouble, haven't you, honey?"

He nodded.

"Wanna come to my place? Oh, not for that! I mean, you wanna come and just take your shoes off and drink some beer and think?"

He nodded.

The barflies grinned when he walked out, holding onto her fat upper arm. As the door was closing, he could hear the bartender say, "Well, I'll be damned. That's the earliest Betsy ever picked anything up. Generally she can't connect till it's real drunk out."

The door closed on bawdy laughter.

Her room was as blowsy as she, but it was a place to sit. He pushed some confession magazines off an overstuffed chair and took their place. They'd brought back some beer and some food. She busied herself getting things ready. There was a sickeningly sweet calendar picture of a boy and a dog pinned haphazardly to the wall. He averted his eyes from it.

Maybe that was the reason he couldn't think clearly. Maybe the answer was hidden back there somewhere. Perhaps he *should* think about his son, instead of ducking it as he had been doing.

His fingers pressed deep into the arms of the chair as he thought back. There was no blood in his face at all. The blonde looked at him while she poured the beer and wondered if he had passed out. But his back was straight, his head was upright.

When he opened his eyes, he had a different look about him. She handed him a sandwich and a glass of beer. She was wise enough to keep her mouth shut.

He said, "So now I know." Ridges of muscles jutted out at the hinge of his jaw. "You can't run away. Not ever."

She nodded, not knowing what he was talking about. She refilled his glass, murmured, "Beer'll help most anything, I find."

He wolfed down a sandwich, two of them. He needed fuel. This was not going to be easy. There were lots of angles. From some ways of looking at it, it didn't make sense. But then neither did the hit-run death of Jimmy or the shot that had killed the doctor.

A mangled boy and a dead doctor. All because he had wanted to get an early start in order to be sure of getting some fish—and because a redhead had been found strangled.

He got to his feet with surety. There was no sway now. The blonde watched him. He knew what he was doing. She asked, "You feel better, don't you, honey?"

He nodded. From his wallet he took a handful of bills. Knowing where the money would go, he still gave it to her. He said, "With this goes all my thanks."

She was silent. The door closed on him before she dared to count the windfall.

In a drugstore phone booth his mind went back to the scene in the doctor's office. He wondered, if the nurse had not come in on the heels of the shot, if he might not have picked up the gun and blown out his brains. Perhaps that had been what the killer wanted. Considering the state he was in, coming out of shock, faced with the corpse of an unknown man, it would not have been unlikely if he had picked up the gun and finished what the murderer had started.

His unseeing eyes roved over the counters of merchandise that faced the booth he was in. How was he going to work this? He wanted to get the killer dead to rights where there could be no out, no chance of anything going wrong.

Even when the coin dropped, he wasn't quite sure he knew how he was going to set it up. It wasn't till he heard the killer's voice that he knew how it had to be done.

He ripped the handkerchief out of his breast pocket and muffled his voice with it. "Wonderful invention, wire recorders," he said.

He waited. In the receiver, he could heat a strangled gasp. He said, "Sometimes a reel of wire can be worth lots of money."

"Where can I meet you? Pay you off?"

His smile would have been frightening had there been anyone to see it. He said, "I'm the handyman in Dr. Welles' building. I been snoopin' for years. Tonight's the first time I ever found something that was worth the trouble."

"Shall I meet you in the office?"

Would the police have a stakeout there? Well, he'd worry about that at the proper time. He said, "Sure, meet me there. And you'd better come loaded with loot. I'm retirin'."

The phone clicked. He wiped the sweat off his forehead with the handkerchief. This would never do. His throat was closed with the fury of his desire. This was no time for personal vengeance. He knew that. Yet with all his heart and soul he wanted to kill the man to whom he'd just spoken.

As he walked out of the drugstore, he thought wryly of what a shock the killer must have had when the bullet had missed him and hit the doctor. It was a little surprising that the killer hadn't tried again. Unless he'd figured that he had more important things to do at the moment and had meant to kill again as soon as he was able. He must have fired and then thrown the gun almost in one motion. After all, he couldn't very well have stayed put.

On the fire escape of the doctor's building, Timms waited impatiently. Through the broken window he could barely make out the wire recorder, the phone, the jumbled mass of odds and ends on the desk.

His luck must be wearing pretty thin. He'd ducked three patrol cars on the way. He wondered how the papers were handling it. He was no big-time politico, but after all, his name was not unknown. Probably something about how he had run amuck after the death of his son. Then a follow-up of the nerve strain induced by modern politics. The papers liked to dwell on that.

He wondered if the killer would follow his trail up the fire escape or if he'd brazen his way into the office.

The light clicked on. He blinked. He saw the chalk outline on the floor. The doctor's body contour. It seemed pathetic for that to be all that was left of the doctor. He'd seemed like a good man.

Then he heard the uniformed police officer, who had opened the door, say respectfully, "This is irregular, but seeing as you—"

"It will be perfectly all right, my good man. I know what I'm doing!"

The cop left, closing the door behind him.

The pompous, portly man looked around the office. His eyes flicked to the window. Blinded by light, he couldn't distinguish the darker shadow that Timms made. He saw the wire recorder. His hand turned the rewind lever. The machine worked noisily at first.

From the fire escape, Timms could see the busy little arms that worked the rewind. Its function was like the moving arm of a fishing reel that forced the line to wind on the spool smoothly.

The machine stopped automatically when the reel was rewound. Ben Vincent turned on the playback. On the fire escape, Timms cringed a trifle when he heard the doctor's voice ask, "What day is this, Henry?"

This was repeated three or four times, then Timms heard himself say, "What day? Why it's Saturday. *The* Saturday." He hadn't known he'd said all that out loud.

The machine droned on. He heard himself describing how he and

Jimmy had seen Ben Vincent come out of the apartment house, how Vincent had waved to them.

In the doctor's office, Vincent's too big face grimaced. He bent over the wire recorder, looking for the button that would magically erase the wire, rearrange the molecules so that the recording wire would be blank as though it had never been used.

Only then did Timms step through the broken window and face the man who had murdered his son.

He asked, "You can clean the wire, but how can you erase what happened from my mind?"

Vincent's face blanched. He said, "But I thought—"

"You thought I was a blackmailing handyman. Yes, I know."

"I thought you'd gone crazy, that I had, nothing to fear. Why didn't you call cops after I—"

"After you ran down Jimmy, you mean?" Timms' voice was flat.

"Henry, I didn't want to! It was such rotten luck! Why did you have to be there on the street? Why did you have to see me leave her apartment house? I had a perfect alibi all rigged. And then you saw me. You and your son! Why couldn't you have been there five minutes earlier—or five minutes later?"

Five minutes, and Jimmy would still be alive. Timms began to shake. The black— He shook his head like a wounded bull trying to clear the blood from its eyes.

"I didn't want to kill anybody," Vincent was saying. "I didn't even want to kill *her*. But I couldn't stand the stink. The papers would have— My wife would have— Janice wouldn't let me go. She threatened a scandal that would have blown me out of politics.... Henry, listen to me. Understand the spot I was in!"

"Sure, I know the spot you were in. You killed your mistress, and we saw you leave the house where she lived. I forgot that. It was wiped out of my mind—with blood. With my son's blood. Then not content with that, you tried to kill me before I remembered. It took me all this time to remember that you were leaving the wrong house early this morning."

Vincent whispered, "Henry, don't look at me like that. I'm not a killer. I didn't mean to— But one thing led to another."

"Then after you ran over Jimmy, you had to cover up the blood on the car so you ran it into a lamppost, bled a little yourself so your blood would hide my son's."

"Henry, you don't know the hell I've been through! If you did, you wouldn't look like that."

"Yes, I know, it must have been terrible, sneaking out of the hospital, getting a gun, coming here, shooting at me, missing and killing the doctor. I feel for you." Timms paused, then asked, "How did you know I was here?"

Vincent looked startled. "Don't you remember? Why, Henry, I brought you here. I hoped the shock would wipe your mind clean so l wouldn't have to kill you. Then I went out, cracked up my car, was taken to the hospital, got out without being seen and came back here. I— I didn't shoot till I could see that you were starting to remember. Henry, believe me, I didn't want to kill you. Why, I've always been fond of you."

Timms retched. He said, "I'm glad you didn't hate me, Ben."

The sarcasm was lost. Vincent was too concerned with trying to justify his actions.

"Henry, I'm a rich man. Let me give you some money. Leave town, start over again somewhere. I'll make it up to you somehow. Look, Henry, with the mayor ill, away all the time, I'm getting to be a big man here in town. I can do a lot for you."

The same old routine. The palaver they handed out in the local political clubs. Just a ward heeler at heart. It was inevitable, of course. Man works by mechanisms, and Vincent was using one that had always worked for him.

"Shut up." Timms voice was louder than he meant it to be.

Vincent was shocked into silence. Timms locked eyes with him, wondered when he would try again to kill. The tension built in the silence of the room. The waves of fury that racked Timms were held in control only because he wanted Vincent to suffer his penalty lawfully. That is, he wanted it with his mind. But his muscles ached to kill the man with his bare hands.

Timms' feet were on the chalked outline of the dead doctor's head. Vincent stood on the chalked knees. They were that close together. The blood drained out of Vincent's face.

He said, "You're a fool, Henry."

His hand went to his pocket. Timms let him get that far. Then he exploded into action. His hand clenched on Vincent's wrist. The barrel of the gun picked up glinting highlights from the lamp. They stood chest to chest, frozen into their pose.

Vincent's muscles cracked as he tried to force the muzzle around so that it would face Timms' stomach. Suddenly Timms let go. The violence of Vincent's gesture brought the gun high in the air as the tension of his muscles was allowed too sudden release.

It was then that Timms hit him with all the hate, all the frustration, all the futility that he felt. Vincent's lower jaw slipped sideways, broken, and the sounds that came from him were like those of an idiot child.

The door slammed open. The young cop's face was frightened. He gasped, "Did I wait too long. Mr. Timms? I could hear through the transom. It was open."

Timms let his hands hang at his sides. He said, "No, you didn't wait too long."

The reaction was too much. He couldn't even feel gratitude that the policeman had heard they whole thing. He just felt empty. Empty and useless. Vengeance was not enough. It wouldn't bring back Jimmy. Wouldn't reanimate the doctor.

All his fury, all his desire for vengeance were gone. They had vanished when he hit Vincent.

He watched while the policeman put the cuffs on Vincent, listened while the policeman phoned Homicide. He walked along quietly when Vincent was led from the building.

He said, "I'll be down later to give my story."

The cop nodded. "Anything you say, Mr. Timms."

He walked off into the night. A big man, almost burly, with empty hands hanging uselessly at his sides, with bent back and heavy heart.

The cop watched him shuffle off out of sight in the darkness of the night.

# The Darkened Room

## Chapter I

There were electric light bulbs in the fixtures on the walls, but they were colored and didn't cast much light. Some were deep red, some dark green; what little illumination filtered down to the people who crowded the double hotel room was enough to show their outlines but not their features.

At one side, a phonograph, its volume turned down low, was making one of the only two sounds that could be heard in the room. A husky-voiced vocalist on a record was singing:

*"When your throat gets dry, you know you're high."*

Below that could be heard the whispered sound of smoke being pulled into avid lungs. Fingers curled around the precious reefers as the men and women in the room got their kicks.

Near the door an incense burner was busy trying to camouflage the smell of marijuana by superimposing the sickeningly sweet smell of incense on the already heavy atmosphere.

The reefer lights around the room were there because bright lights are a "bring-down," and when a tea head is getting high he wants to stay there, not get brought out of his condition by any violent contrasts.

The voice on the record chanted:

*"—then you're a viper."*

In one corner a low-voiced man was making time with a girl he had brought. He was saying, "That's it, baby doll, hold it down, don't let it out of your lungs till you have to."

The eighteen-year-old girl was trying desperately to obey directions, but the acrid smoke hurt her throat, and the crowded room, the air breathed and rebreathed by many lungs was combining to make her feel queasy.

A man who held an eighth of an inch of thin cigarette between the callused ends of his forefinger and thumb, and who, from time to time placed his cupped fingers and the "roach" into his mouth and dragged at it, moved across the room, stepping over the couples on the floor. He made his way to a dark, sullen-faced man whose two-day growth of beard was visible even in the heavy shadows.

The man sucked the last possible bit of drug out of the dinch and asked the sullen-faced man, "What about a couple of broads, Mac? Some of these squares are getting lonesome."

"Yeah."

The dark man eased the door open and left. In the other room where three women sat, the lights were a little brighter. The man with the heavy beard said to a tall, too slim blonde whose hair color hurt the eyes because of its chemical harshness, "Let's go. Maybe you kids would like to meet some new guys."

Blondie said, "Yeah, we've wasted the best part of the evening already." Turning, she spoke to the other two women. "C'mon, Betty. Pick it up, Louella."

Louella, who was as stocky and heavyset as the blonde was thin and light, said, "This was the night I was gonna get home early. I swore to the babysitter I'd get right back."

The only remotely pretty girl of the trio, Betty, said, "Cut the squawking. To meet a few new guys, it's not bad."

The blonde girl looked at herself-appraisingly in a compact mirror and said as they all walked toward the door, "Sometimes I think I'd rather play tag in a poison ivy patch."

The door closed on them.

Downstairs on Forty-seventh Street near Broadway, a man detached himself from the lamp post he had been supporting. He was close to thirty-five and looked older. Thin-faced, long-nosed, with worry lines around his eyes, he hunched his narrow shoulders so that his overpadded jacket would sit more correctly as he walked toward a little tubby man who was reading a horse sheet avidly.

The thin man said, "What room's the tea pad in tonight, Morry?"

Without raising his eyes from the tip sheet, or moving his lips discernibly, Morry answered, "1214, Garrow. Why you wanna know? You're no viper."

"Ya never know, I always say," said Garrow.

Then Morry focused all his attention on the longshot he was trying to handicap.

Bill Garrow turned away from Broadway and walked toward Sixth Avenue. In the middle of the block, identical with all the other hotels that line the street, was the one he was looking for. He didn't pause in front of it but, walking more rapidly he went up the three dirty steps that formed the stoop and into what passed for a lobby in the hotel that called itself the Elite.

The ratty lobby was full of what had once been overstuffed chairs. The padding had long since dribbled through tears in the cloth and now the chairs were as misshapen as the elderly, lonely people who sat in them.

Clustered near one poorly dressed seventy-year-old woman were five asthmatic Pekinese. They looked almost as old as their owner, and their fur was matted and dirty.

Not looking down Garrow came too near the dogs and stepped on one. It snapped and tried to tear at his leg. Unthinkingly he bent down and cuffed the dog. It skittered across the lobby howling in pain.

The old woman yelled for help, and before Garrow quite knew what had happened he was the center of attention.

The old woman said, "You fiend!—poor little Ming Toy, come to Mother! Diddums bad man hurt little Ming?"

The dog somehow managed to jump from the unwashed tile floor up into its mistress's lap.

The old woman glared at Garrow.

The house detective said, "Be more careful next time, huh?"

Garrow bit his lip. This was the last thing he wanted to have happen. He wondered if, since he had now been noticed by everyone in the lobby, including the dick, if maybe he had better put off what he had in mind.

But his plan was all set, and it would be another week before there was another pad in this particular hotel. It was a rotten break, but possibly not a fatal one.

Stalking towards the elevator he entered it and when it was in motion, said, "Twelve."

Leaving the elevator he kept his hand in his pocket on the key he knew would open any door in the hotel. Almost unconsciously, he waited till the sound told him that the elevator had gone, then hurried up two flights of stairs.

He walked down the torn carpet that covered the narrow corridor, his eyes busy, looking for the room in which Madigan was waiting for his cut.

1420. There it was. Right ahead of him. He slipped the skeleton key from his pocket and then pausing for just a moment, went over in his mind the various details of what he had to do.

Then he slipped the key into the lock and softly, ever so softly, slid the door open. The unshaded single bulb in the ceiling cast its raw light down over the small room. An unmade bed in one corner almost filled the closet-sized room. A chair, a dresser and a wash basin the management felt filled the requirements of what they called a single, at two dollars a day.

On the rickety dresser a cheap alarm clock ticked time noisily away.

Madigan wouldn't have left the light on unless he had just gone down the hall to the bathroom, Garrow knew, and took advantage of it. He stepped to the right of the door so that he would be momentarily unseen when it opened.

Heavy footsteps warned him that the room's occupant was returning.

Garrow's hands went to his own neck and he loosened his tie. Holding one end in his right hand he looped it around his fingers. He did the same thing with his left hand. About eighteen inches of heavy silk hung between his two hands.

The door opened.

When it closed, Madigan saw his visitor. He said, "Bill Garrow! It's about time you got here! I need the dough for getaway money."

But then he saw the length of cloth in Garrow's hands and his voice died down. For just an instant fright showed on his face, then it was washed away by anger as his hand dived for his hip pocket.

Before it got there, Garrow had leaped, and the cloth was around Madigan's thick neck and it got tighter and tighter.

Almost no sound at all escaped from Madigan's throat. That, Garrow thought, was one of the big advantages to garroting. The man he was strangling fell to his knees. His thick trunk was arched, his hands tore at Garrow's but they were getting feebler now.

Eyes wide, Garrow stared down at his victim's face. It was changing color fast. Garrow liked that. He loosened his hold a trifle so that death would not come too rapidly. Madigan managed to get a gasp of air into his lungs before the hand tightened again.

The oxygen kept him alive perhaps thirty seconds longer than he would have lived without it.

When Garrow was sure that he had succeeded in what he was doing, he pulled the tie from the folds of flesh that had held it, then flipping the tie out, he tied a slip knot in it and carefully replaced the loop around the corpse's neck.

A broken piece of wainscotting up near the ceiling had caught his eye the last time he had visited Madigan. He used it now. Muscling the unwieldy body onto the bed, he forced the corpse upright.

It took him a little longer than he had figured to tie the free end of the cloth around the break in the wainscotting, but he managed it at last. Stepping down from the bed he moved back from the corpse and considered it.

Then he went to the bed and arranged Madigan's big feet so it looked as if he had arched his body out from the bed, his feet the base of the bow, his neck the top of it. Held by the tie, his face becoming bloated, Madigan looked enough like a suicide to satisfy his murderer.

Garrow reached into Madigan's back pocket and removed the gun that the man had tried to pull. No sense in leaving it. The cops might wonder why a man would choose so painful a death as strangling, when he had a bullet handy to blast into his brain. Only one thing left to decide. Garrow wondered, if he were killing himself, would he do it in the dark? Or in the light? Hard to tell. But he'd better leave the light on, he decided, because otherwise the cops might wonder how Madigan had been able to see in the dark to catch the silk tie on the wood.

## Chapter II

Locking the door after him, Garrow looked up and down the long, narrow corridor. If he were spotted now he'd be in real trouble. He had to get to the fire escape at one end of the hall, and he had to get there without being seen.

Tiptoeing, he made his way towards the window that led to the fife escape.

Pausing often, eavesdropping at the doors as he went, he was prepared for violence at any moment. He'd shoot anyone who spotted him.

He didn't let the pent-up air out of his lungs till he was safely out on the rusting iron of the old fire escape. Then he looked down, straight down, fourteen floors to the ground. He didn't care for the view much and found himself gritting his teeth to control the vertigo that always affected him when he looked down from heights.

No time for lousing around now!

He raced down the two flights of iron stairs and without pausing ducked through the window on the twelfth floor.

This was the next to the last danger he had to face. If he was seen coming in this window— But no one was in sight.

He knew Room 1214 was nearby, but first he had to find an empty room. Again listening at doors, he had to try four before he heard no signs of occupancy. Then, slipping the key into the lock he eased the door open. No sound, no light. It was safe. Lighting a match, he found the phone and asked the operator for a number. Waiting, he whistled tunelessly.

A harsh voice said, "Police Headquarters. Sergeant Kahan."

Keeping his voice down, Garrow lied, "Listen, this is Blacky. I'm one of Walsh's stoolies. Tell him there's a marijuana party going on at the Elite on Forty-seventh, Room 1214."

Without waiting for an answer, he returned the phone to its cradle and, crept out of the quiet room.

So far so good. The hard part was over now. Smiling a little he walked casually down the hall to Room 1214. Tapping it with a "shave-and-a-haircut" rhythm, he waited till the door opened a crack, then said:

"C'mon, lemme in. This is Garrow."

The sullen-faced, black-bearded man looked a little surprised. He said, "It's almost over, Garrow. Why waste a finski?"

"Ah," Garrow said, smiling, "Mac, what's money?"

Handing the man a five-dollar bill he entered the double room of what passed for a suite in the Elite Hotel.

None of the couples in the room even looked at him as he crawled over them and leaned against the wall, where he could see the people in the darkened room as clearly as possible.

Looking around, he tried to spot the stooge with the reefers. Some petting parties were going on.

Garrow finally managed to make out the faces of three girls he knew, but all of them were occupied with their dates. The heavy blue smoke that vipers say smells like a chicken dinner hurt Garrow's eyes. He needed a stick of tea.

The stooge with the stuff worked his way to Garrow's side and held out his open palm. On it was one of the thinly rolled handmade cigarettes that the others were inhaling so lustfully. Garrow took it and, lighting it, dragged the smoke down into his lungs and held it there for a long moment.

Then the atmosphere no longer hurt his eyes. He could feel his edginess begin to fade away. Three more drags and he could feel the cotton wool beginning to form around his fingertips. There, that was better.

But suddenly he remembered that he hadn't ditched the gun. The ease supplied by the drug vanished. No sense in taking a Sullivan law violation, that was for sure. Edging past the sprawling couples he made his way to the bathroom.

Inside the room he lifted the top of the water closet and dropped Madigan's pistol into the water.

Then looking at himself in the bathroom mirror, he wondered if his lack of a tie looked suspicious. Just for safety's sake he put his shirt collar outside his jacket. He was wearing a sport's shirt, and it looked all right. As he went back into the double room the outer door slammed open and three uniformed policemen entered. They had their guns out. One said, "This is a pinch. Don't anybody try to beat it. We got the place covered."

White lights clicked on, assaulting drug-heavy eyes.

The girls looked irritated more than anything else. It was the men who were really concerned. They looked guilty and shamefaced, Garrow thought, a thin sneer on his own face. The stooge who carried the tea on his person, swore a blue streak and as the others began to file out the door, he slipped an envelope to Garrow and said:

"You're near the window. Throw this the hell out, will ya?"

Garrow gauged how far away the police were and decided to take the risk. Holding the envelope of tea behind his back he moved backward to the window. It was open only about six inches but that was enough. He slipped the evidence out.

The stooge whispered, "Thanks, Garrow. I always knew you were regular."

"It's okay."

"No sense in me taking an extra rap, and they can't prove nothin' without the Mary Warner for evidence."

"Sure, sure." Garrow turned away. He wanted to get arrested and have it over with.

The male customers were leaving the room in single file. Garrow got on the end of the line. Two of the cops were pushing the dark man with the heavy beard toward the door. Through the open door into the other room, Garrow could see three girls struggling into their wraps.

Mac, the dark man, said to the cops, "What's wrong with you guys? I iced the cap'n on'y last week."

One cop shrugged his shoulders in irritation. "Who knows? Maybe' he's mad at you."

"Mad at me? After I been fixin' him for years?" Mac was outraged.

"What are you beefin' about?" the cop asked. "You can stand for a rap. So you get six months on the Island. It won't kill you."

"Six months, hell!" Mac swore again. "I'll get a suspended sentence or I'll know the reason why!"

Dispassionately the cop smashed his nightstick along the side of Mac's jaw. He said, "That wasn't a threat, was it, Mac?"

"Why'n'cha keep your hand to yaself? You coppers are all alike!" Mac had his hand to his swelling face. "I pay off and I pay off, and the next thing I get rapped."

The cop pushed him out the door after the others.

Load after load of arrested men filled the small elevator cages. Garrow was in the last batch to go down and so was able to see the way the policemen treated the girls. He was pleased when Betty smashed her pocketbook in a cop's face, and said, "Keep ya big hands off me, copper!" She spat, and said, "I hate cops!"

The policemen called her a few choice names and then rapped her across the buttocks with his nightstick.

She let out a yell, and the cop, surprised by the volume of sound said, "Shaddup! Or I'll close your mouth for good."

Her epithets were, if anything, even more unlikely than the ones the cop had called her.

The last thing that Garrow heard as the elevator door closed was the cop saying, "You better button your lip or I'll ram your teeth down your throat."

Garrow felt pleasantly excited.

The feeling persisted even when he had to cross the lobby and stand hearing the old woman with the five dogs say, "See! See! What'd I tell you! He's one of them! Just like I said!"

Outside the lobby Garrow saw the paddy wagon waiting and by the time the old woman finished shouting at him he was almost glad to get into the wagon with the other men. They sat in stony-faced silence. No man wanted any other to look at him.

The ride to the local precinct house did not take long. But it was enough time for Garrow to be able to double-check what he had done. He had been the last one into the wagon and his unseeing eyes looked out the rear door past the patrolman who stood on guard and passed incuriously over the crowd of people who as usual milled around on Broadway, going to, or coming from the movie houses.

But Garrow had seen it all too often to pay any attention even to the girls in their dressed-up best, or the men in their going out clothes. His mind was busy with himself and what he had done.

He had saved four thousand dollars by killing Madigan. It was in a safe place, one that the police would never suspect. The burglary had gone like clockwork right from the moment he had spotted the story about that Hollywood star in the papers and had decided that some of her jewelry must be legit.

As a matter of fact, he thought, the whole thing had gone off swell. He'd pointed out the news item to Madigan, they'd decided to do something about it, and the following night had seen them in the star's Park Avenue apartment.

When they rumbled the joint all they'd had to do was knock out one female servant and go looking for the loot. They hadn't found it. But the answer was obvious. The star must be wearing it. They'd waited patiently, drinking her brandy while they sat around. The one dangerous point in the whole night's work had been when the girl had come in roaring drunk with a guy.

But the guy had left when she got sick. Then Madigan and Garrow had come out of the closet in which they'd been hiding, ripped the jewels off the star, and left her, sprawled across the bed in a drunken semi-stupor.

Eight grand Garrow had received from the fence. Four apiece, Madigan had thought.

Garrow looked at his hands. They had saved him four thousand dollars and he was obscurely grateful to them. So now he had eight grand. It was no big deal, but it was enough to keep him going for a while. He had no expensive tastes.

## Chapter III

Thinking back, Bill Garrow went over the murder scene again. His necktie wouldn't give him away for there must have been tens of thousands of them made. He'd paid a buck for it in a store that sold nothing but ties, and where there were so many customers it would be impossible for a clerk to remember one buyer.

The patrol wagon came to a halt and Garrow could see the dull green lights in front of the station house. He had been seen going into the hotel, of course, but that was covered by his having been at the tea pad. He hadn't been seen on the fourteenth floor by anyone as far as he could tell and, with any sort of luck, Madigan's body shouldn't be found till long after he was arrested. It would be nice and tidy to be in jail when the murder was discovered. He liked that, for he knew full well that, detective stories to the contrary, it's almost impossible for a medical examiner to tell from a corpse at what precise time death had occurred.

Following the burly policeman into the station house he looked about him. The other men and women followed him in single file, most of them looking uneasy. Garrow could imagine what it would be like for those of the men who were married to try and explain what they had been doing.

The desk sergeant looked down at them over the high rim of the stained mahogany in front of him. He grinned, then turned to the arresting officers and said, "Quite a little batch of beauties you got!"

The men were giving their names as John Doe and John Smith. Just as automatically the women gave their names as Jane Doe and Jane Smith. It was as cut and dried as a well-rehearsed scene in a play.

Garrow watched with some amusement. He was the only one who was benefiting from the whole thing. Leaning against the wall he wondered if all station houses all over the world looked the same and smelled the same. Every one he'd ever been in had smelled this way.

It was an odor made up of unwashed bodies, dead tobacco, and fear.

Ambling over to the desk sergeant, Garrow asked, "What's going to happen to us, Sarge?"

The red-faced, heavyset man who could have stood the exercise of walking a beat, looked down at him and said, "You just an innocent bystander like these other slobs?"

Nodding, Garrow grinned. "Even more innocent."

"A night in the tank, unless you wanna see if you can get hold of a bail bond boy."

"And after that?"

"Umm," the red-faced man considered, "they generally call it disorderly conduct in court. Ten days or twenty-five dollars. That's about all." He pointed a stubby thumb at the girls, and Mac. "They're the ones who are in for trouble."

"Six months?" Garrow asked.

"Maybe more, depending on how the magistrate feels. Sometimes one of them gets real holy and throws the book at them."

Thanking him, Garrow retreated again to the wall, to watch what was going on. He wondered if maybe he should take the ten days instead of paying the fine. The island would be a good place to wait while the heat over Madigan's death died down.

Look at it from any angle, he thought, and he was in the clear. There was just nothing that the cops could fasten onto that would get him in trouble. Smiling, he congratulated himself.

It was just before twelve o'clock and the police were negligent. There was nothing to be feared from a group like this. As soon as all of them had been booked and thrown in the tank these prisoners could be forgotten.

Garrow watched Mac, the man who had put on the tea party. His face was turning black and blue and the swelling was bigger now. That had been quite a clout he received from the cop, Garrow though.

Mac must he real mad, he decided. To pay off for protection and then not get it, must be annoying.

Louella, one of the girls Garrow knew, walked to his side and said, "Can you go bail for me, honey?"

He asked, "Why?"

"My kid." She looked shaken. "God knows what the babysitter will do now. I swore I'd be home an hour ago."

No one was paying any attention to them. He dilated his nostrils and said, "You've been a bad girl, haven't you, honey?"

She snapped, "Oh, cut that out, will ya?"

He leaned closer and gripped the soft flesh of her arms. Maybe, he thought, it would be worthwhile to spring both of them and go home with her. He had a little fun coming to him after what he had been through.

She said, "Garrow, have a heart, will ya? Spring me. I'm broke and need dough bad."

Her compact body was close to his. He walked towards the desk, estimating how much it would cost him. He was riding high. He'd got away with murder. He was in the chips, and he felt great.

Then, right then, through the doorway of the station house came two uniformed policemen. They were having a hard time with their prisoner. She was drunk, noisy, and nasty.

A mink stole dragged on the dirty floor of the station house as the cops muscled her into the room. Her strapless gown had given up the struggle to do any covering at all. Her breasts which had carried her from a tenement in Brooklyn to fame in Hollywood were bare.

She said, "You can't do this to me! You know who I am?"

A cop said, "Yeah, sister, we know who you are. Now shut up and try to act like a lady, or is that too hard?"

Her long-nailed fingers ripped out and cut the edge of the policeman's eye. He swore and the other cop managed to grab her wrists before she could do any more damage.

"You can't throw me in a drunk tank! I'm too important!" She threw her head back and her long red hair whipped through the air in the gesture that celluloid had made immortal.

The desk sergeant groaned. "Not that one again! Movie stars! Bah! They save it all up on the Coast and then they come to New York and they get rid of it all in one big lump!" He shook his head and asked the arresting officers, "Why didn't you take her home? You know her press agent'll he down here in half an hour with fifteen lawyers!"

"We hadda bring her in," one of the officers said. "She made such a mess in the nightclub that the manager swore that this time he'd prefer charges!"

"Yeah, yeah, until the lawyers get around to him and buy him off. All right, let's book her and get it over with."

The Hollywood star drew herself up with drunken arrogance, shook off the restraining hands of the two policemen and said, "G'wan, take a good look!" Then in a fumble lingered fashion she managed to pull up the bodice of her gown till she was almost respectable.

Throwing the longer end of her stole about her bare shoulders, she waggled her head from side to side in a weak attempt at an imitation of sobriety and said, "What a hunch of punks!" She looked drunkenly into each face of the men who had been arrested in the raid and said to each one in turn, "I wouldn't date you, ya bum!"

And then she came to the end of the line and her reddened eyes were focused on Garrow. A limp forefinger pointed straight at him and she said, "I know you!" Pushing her celebrated face even closer to his she said, "I know you!" Outrage was plain on her face. "You—" Her brows drew together at the painful process of thought.

"There was another guy," she said slowly.

Of all the lousy breaks! The one person in all the world who could connect him with Madigan. He could see what had to follow. Her identification of him and Madigan as the jewel thieves, then the connection between him and the dead man would no longer be tenuous. The cops would not accept Madigan's death as suicide.

And then Garrow felt as if something had let go in his brain. There was an almost audible click, as if a too tightly wound spring had let go.

Behind him the open door of the station house gaped. Beyond it was the darkness of the street. All Garrow could think of was escape.

At first the police had been amused at the movie star's recognition of one of her fellow prisoners. But when Garrow, with no warning, suddenly spun around and raced for the door, the girl screamed like a fishwife:

"Don't let him go! He stole my rubies! Catch him!"

She was no longer as drunk as she had been.

That was the last Bill Garrow heard as his pelting feet carried him out of the station house. One leap carried him down the five steps and the soles of his feet stung as he landed and continued without a break to run with all his strength.

Ahead of him the sidewalk was solid with uniformed policemen. His brain reeled. It was too complete a nightmare to be real. He spun around. That direction was blocked by the bulky bodies of an equal number of cops!

Even as he spurted across the street his stunned mind told him why the cops were there. It was midnight. They were changing shifts. The men who had worked from four to twelve were going off duty and the men who had the twelve to eight grind were coming on.

To the rear of him a cop yelled through the door of the station house:

"Stop him!"

By then he was across the street.

Crouching behind a parked car he tried to make up his mind what to do. It was hard with the street blocked by blue uniforms but he would not, absolutely could not, give up this easily.

Ahead of him was a railing that kept people from falling into an areaway in front of an old brownstone house. He vaulted over it and down into the pitch darkness.

Just in time, too, for a bullet hit the iron railing and screeched as it ricocheted away. He had landed before he heard the shot.

Pain screamed up his leg to his brain from his ankle. He'd landed with one foot in a garbage pail the other on the uneven ground of the areaway. Clenching his fists till his nails cut into his palms he looked about wildly.

Above him he could hear the sound of pounding feet racing toward him and the cul-de-sac into which he had dropped. To his right there was an ornamental ironwork door, a remnant of time when this house had been respectable. Throwing his shoulder against it, he prayed for it to open. People, he thought, who live across the street from a police station shouldn't have to worry about burglars.

It gave and he tumbled on one leg through the iron-scrolled door.

## Chapter IV

Inside, the rancid smell of cats and garbage hit Garrow's nostrils. A flashlight was turned downwards from the street into the areaway he had just quitted.

He was in a section about four feet square. He had to stoop, for above his head was the underside of the stairway.

In front of him was another door. A wooden one. Scratching a match, he looked at the lock. Then he dropped the match and, still standing one-legged, he ripped his wallet out of his pocket and tore the celluloid square out of the wallet.

Pushing it in between the door and the frame he wriggled it experimentally. Then pushing against the door he turned the knob as hard as he could. The door opened as he heard behind him the sound of the police running down the wooden stairs that led to the areaway.

Slamming the door behind him, he dropped the celluloid and leaned against the wall for a moment, biting his lips at the torture of his ankle. Experimentally he put part of his weight on it. He couldn't decide whether it was broken or just badly sprained.

Hopping through complete darkness on one leg was dangerous, he found. He kept humping into furniture in the long hall through which he was making his way.

Perhaps ten feet ahead of him was a dim glow of light which must be coming in through a rear door or window. With all the noise he was making he was sure no one could be in the house, but he was wrong, for as he staggered to a dirty paned window through which some random light was pouring, he heard a little shred of sound, then the overhead, unshaded bulb went on.

Simultaneously he heard the police yelling, and pounding on the front door.

The little wispy old man who was revealed by the raw light was more frightened than he was, Garrow saw.

"Wh—" the old man gasped as he held the front of an old-fashioned nightshirt closed with a shaking hand.

"Shaddup!" Garrow was ferocious. "What does this window lead to?"

"A backyard." The voice trembled off into silence.

Slamming the window open, Garrow said to the old man, "C'mere."

Shaking in every limb, the man obeyed. Garrow pushed the old man out the window ahead of him.

Some inner surge of resentment made itself verbal and the old man said, "I'm in my bare feet, I'll catch my death of cold!"

As he went through the window, his bent back even further humped by the exertion, Garrow leaned over him and sliced at the thin neck with the edge of a deadly hand.

The old man didn't even grunt. His slack body hung half in and half out of the window. With no hesitation, Garrow tumbled the unconscious man out the window and followed as swiftly as his hurt ankle would let him.

He heard the front door crash open under the shoulders of the police.

The darkness of the yard was not complete. A slit of moon sent pale light over parts of the area. Other parts were in blackest shadow. So little time, Garrow thought almost despairingly. So little time.

Bundling the slight weight of the old man into his arms he hobbled towards some trash that was piled high in a rusting garbage can nearby, next to a fence that was on its last legs. Boards were missing from it and those that remained were rotten and soft.

Garrow arranged the old man behind the garbage can so that most of his body was hidden. Then lifting one frail arm he pushed it out into a little cold patch of moonlight.

If only he had Madigan's gun, he thought, he could prop it up in the old man's hand and leave him, as a decoy for the police. But he could waste no more time. The sound of the pursuers was loud in his ears.

With as much effort as he had ever expended in all his life he managed to squeeze through a space in the wooden fence. Then, his eye to a knothole, he waited.

The police streamed out into the yard, flashlights in hand.

The uniformed man in the lead had a gun and when the searching lights spotted the hand the cop said, "There he is!"

Garrow called through the fence, "Yeah, you got me, but I'm gonna take a couple of you with me!"

If they fell for his bluff it might cover him for some desperately needed time.

He waited, heart in his mouth, until he saw the police draw back uncertainly. If he had been behind the garbage can with a gun, he could have picked them off like clay pigeons.

Once he saw the police had realized their danger, he backed away from the knothole as best he could on one leg.

They'd have the whole block staked out by now, he knew. What was there for him to do? Where to go? How to hide?

If only he hadn't injured his ankle, he'd have given them a run for their money. But now— His eyes swept around the yard into which he had gone. It was a replica of the one he had just left.

Stumbling, hopping, grunting, he made his way across the yard and through the fence on the far side. The cops would not be halted by his dummy defender much longer.

At the far side of the fence he paused and looked about. The house that abutted on the yard was in a better state of repair than the ones he had just passed through. A fire escape ran up an outside wall.

It took his last bit of strength to make his way to an iron ladder, climb on a box, and then, hanging by his arms from the end of the ladder, muscle his way up to it. He clung there for a long moment gasping as though his lungs were on fire. Then, using just his good leg and his hands, he made his way up the ladder to the first-floor fire escape.

From his vantage point he could look across the two fences and into the yard where the police were now splayed out fanwise, and were closing in on the garbage can behind which the old man was lying.

It would be only a matter of seconds before they found out how they had been hoaxed. He lifted the window that faced the iron lattice work of the fire escape. It was locked.

Bunching up his coat around his fist he drove it through the window, timing the crash with the roar of rage that came up from the policemen as they discovered the unconscious old man.

Inside the room a quavering voice called, "Don't come in! Help! Police!"

A brunette girl, twenty-seven or twenty-eight years old, a faded robe clutched to her breast, screamed in fright as she saw him hobble through the broken glass of the window and ease himself onto the floor.

"One more peep out of you, sister, and I'll slit your throat."

She fainted and slid to the floor, her robe opening. Looking at her nakedness dispassionately, he thought, some other time, honey. But that was sheer bravado.

Hobbling around her he made for the door.

In the hallway a dim yellow bulb cast long shadows along the carpeting. Dragging one leg behind him, his arms supporting most of his weight, he pulled himself along the wooden banister next to the stairwell.

Getting downstairs was almost more than he could manage, but by half sliding on the banister, and hopping on his good leg, he managed to make it to the ground floor. Behind him, he could see some baby carriages stored for the night under the stairway.

His ankle hurt too much. Falling on all fours, he clumsily pulled himself along on his hands and knees. The pain was now almost all he could feel or think about.

Blackness was pushing against his eyeballs. But he got to the side of the nearest baby carriage and drew a packet of matches from his pocket. First he lit a cigarette and, dragging the smoke down into his lungs, felt some of the blackness fade.

Then, using the lit match, he set fire to all the other matches in the packet. When they flared up brightly, he dropped the whole flaming thing into the baby carriage. It smoldered for a while, and then burst into flames. Kneeling, he watched as the flames licked upward, higher and higher, then caught on the underneath part of the stairs. The old wood caught as though it had been drenched in gasoline.

Satisfied, he made his way on all fours towards the front door. The flames in the back of the hall were following him now. He couldn't tell if it was his imagination or if the fire was moving faster than he was and was catching up with him. That would be too ironical, he decided, to die in a fire of one's own setting. Drawing on some last unthought-of reservoir of strength, he managed to get to his feet.

Tucking his bad leg under him, he tried to hold it there with his hand and hop for the front door. It was tough, tougher than anything he had ever clone in his life, but he made it.

Forcing the door open, he screamed, "Fire!"

He was on the street below the station house. The yards had led him there. He'd not even been conscious of going downtown. Above him in the house he'd set ablaze he heard frightened voices, the tumult of people stirring in fright at man's most ancient fear.

A middle-aged couple ran down the stairs, their arms around each other protectingly, the fire searing them so that they had to leap the last four steps.

They surged in mad panic for the front door, and Garrow said, "Please, I'm crippled! Please help me!"

They were decent enough so that the plea penetrated even their fear. The man shook his head, his iron-gray hair frizzed from the fire, and said to his wife, "You go ahead my dear. There's the street and safety. I'll help this poor man."

"Don't be silly, dear. I'll help, too."

With the man on his bad side, and the woman on the other, Garrow managed to get out the door, down the stoop and onto the street. In the distance he could hear the barking sound of the fire engines' horns. Behind him the old house was roaring.

People were pouring out of the house now. Garrow thought idly of the girl who had fainted in the back of the house, the one he had scared. She'd look like a piece of old toast in a couple of minutes.

Then the fire engine sped into the street and he asked, "I wonder, could you help me into that taxi across the street? I know it's a nuisance, but I'm just a visitor here, and this excitement is bad for me."

The man said, "No trouble at all." He helped Garrow into the taxi and returned to his wife as Garrow mumbled his thanks.

The street was thick with firemen and policemen, but none of them were concerned with the taxi that was edging its way out of the street. If anything, the firemen were glad to see it go, for cars are the bane of all big city firemen, getting in the way, parking too near fire hydrants, being a general nuisance.

The cabbie asked, "Where you wanna go, mister?"

That was the big one all right—where to go? All he had on him was about ninety bucks. He had to get to the place he'd hidden the eight grand. With that in his hands he could see a doctor he knew who was not precisely a doctor, but whose lack of curiosity made up for the fact that he had lost his license.

When he'd hidden the money in his hotel room he'd never expected to have to grab it when he was on the lam. The cabbie twisted around and asked his question again.

Bill Garrow said, "Forty-seventh Street between Sixth and Seventh."

## Chapter V

Now the biggest danger was that his hotel was just across the street from the Elite where he hoped Madigan's corpse was still hanging. But what if the body had been found? That would mean more police.

Garrow had to take the risk.

The cab had to go east to Sixth Avenue, for Forty-seventh Street is one-way east to west. Cutting through traffic, it drove through the street. Garrow sat back in the cab, his teeth almost meeting through his bottom lip. The jouncing the cab was giving him was not doing his ankle much good.

The car went through the street past the shop that sold antique coins and the one that sold special shoes for dancers, and passed the shop that sold canes and umbrellas. It passed the bars where the young chicks hang out with sailors and soldiers, and the one bar where you could always be sure of being able to put down a dime on a number, a fiver on a horse, or find a contact for anything from marijuana to the white stuff.

And then it stopped in front of his hotel.

Hoping that he was hidden in the darkness of the cab, Garrow looked all around. So far there was no sign of police activity around the Elite. Garrow could see no menace there. Paying the cabbie he painfully made his way out of the cab. The lobby of his hotel was as empty as it ever got which meant that there were only about eight people sitting and standing, reading tip sheets, or talking idly or passing the time of day.

The one bellhop that his hotel boasted saw him hobbling in through the front door and hurried to his side. The bellhop said, "Hi, Mr. Garrow. Need help?"

Unable to speak, Garrow just nodded, and put his arm around the uniformed man's shoulders. Even though no one turned to look, Garrow knew that everyone in the lobby, from the loungers to the night manager was conscious of him.

In the elevator the bellhop asked, "What happened?"

"Car," Garrow managed to get out. "Clipped me as it came around a corner."

"Lousy luck." The bellhop went into the usual New Yorker's tirade about how bad traffic is in town and how little the police seem to do about it.

But Garrow wasn't listening. He had one objective and only one. To get his money. To do that he had to stay conscious. All else was washed away in a sea of pain.

The bellhop helped him to his room and left, his palm green from the bill that Garrow had placed there.

It took all Garrow's courage to keep himself from throwing himself on his bed and passing out. Hobbling to the bathroom, he emptied a half full bottle of codeine down his throat and then, using a chair as a crutch he got to the night table at the side of his bed.

He was afraid to sit down on the edge of the bed even for a moment. Instead he bent over and pulled the Gideon Bible that all hotels have in every room out from the lower level of the night table. He knocked a flock of magazines and empty cigarette packages onto the floor.

Then, clutching the Bible to his chest, he fumbled the phone off the hook. Giving the number he wanted to the hotel operator he waited numbly.

A voice asked, "Yes?"

"Doc," Garrow's voice was weak, "Garrow. Come right over."

"Where and what should I bring?"

Garrow tried to laugh but it wasn't much of a success. "My hotel, and it's not a bullet wound. I just hurt my ankle. Hurry will ya, Doc?"

Hanging up, he finally worked up enough courage to look at his ankle. Sitting in the chair next to the bed he eased his trouser leg up and pushed his sock down. It was worse than he had thought it would he, although the pain should have told him. A half-inch of white bone showed through his puffed skin.

So it was broken. He tried to be philosophical about it. Doc could straighten it out, put it in a cast, give him something to ease the pain and then, out of New York but fast. He knew just the spot. And it wasn't far. He'd used it to cool off in before. Staten Island. A mere ferry ride away, and yet for all the connection the fifth borough had with New York proper, he thought, you might as well be in Kokomo.

Consciousness was sliding away and he shook his head to try to keep awake. The Bible had almost slid out of his fingers. Better, he thought, take out some loot and have it ready for Doc. No sense in letting that vulture see how much money he had.

Taking a cover of the Bible in each hand, he ripped. The bills dropped out from the spine of the binding where he had secreted them. The torn Bible fell from his hands as he grabbed at the money.

Stacking it neatly, he tried to make himself feel good. Eight grand. It wasn't bad, at that. Say a C-note to the doc, and the rest for him.

Forcing himself erect he divided the big packet of money into smaller packets and was preparing to distribute them into smaller packets and put them in each of his pockets so no bulge would show, when there was a tapping at his door.

"Doc!" he called, then added, "Come on in. The door's unlocked."

It was, too.

That was why the detective kicked it open with one foot, and threw himself to one side, just in case Garrow had a gun and was ready to use it.

Garrow stood, his back to his window, his one hand clenched around the back of the chair that was supporting him, the other filled with the bills for which he had stolen and killed.

There were hundreds in that packet, fifties, twenties, and a lot of tens and fives.

Eyes blurring, Garrow wondered for a moment if it was the amount of codeine he had taken, or if the pain was trying to make him pass out.

There was no reality to the plainclothesman who faced him, in one hand a gun so big that it made the Police Positive .38 look almost like a toy.

"Wh' you want?" Garrow asked, and the room was spinning around and around.

"You, Garrow."

"Wha' for?"

"Lots of things, kiddo, lots of things. Some little, some big." The detective's harsh face was bleak, but Garrow couldn't see it very well. "Little things like jewel stealing, and big things like arson and murder. We got lots of things to talk to you about, Garrow."

"Ya' can't prove it."

Garrow tried to make it sound positive but he wasn't very successful. That was the one real tenet of his existence. Nothing was real or true unless it could be proved against him.

The detective was slowly coming closer. He said, "Don't make book on that, Garrow. We got you cold. The gal from Hollywood identified you and Madigan."

So they'd had time to find out about Madigan. That made it real tough. Eight grand wouldn't buy him a very good mouthpiece.

Garrow said, "Who's Madigan?"

"Just a guy you strangled across the street."

It was just a guess, Garrow knew. The cops must have figured that if he and Madigan had been in on the robbery together then he, Garrow, was the most likely murder suspect. They had doped it correctly, but proving it was something else.

The detective washed that solace away when he said, "If we don't get you for Madigan, Garrow, we got you dead to rights for a girl who died in the fire you set. We got enough witnesses. More than enough."

The old man he'd slugged, and the middle-aged couple who'd helped him out of the burning house.

"But," the detective said, and he was only four feet away from Garrow now, "I ain't got all night to spend barberin'. Let's go. Gimme the dough. That'll help to fry you, but good."

His head down on his chest like an old, old man, Garrow looked at the money in his hand. It wasn't fair. He'd worked too hard for that money. He wasn't going to give it up. And he wasn't going to go to jail and stand trial and get electrocuted. Not him. Not Garrow.

Without a warning of any kind, he threw himself backwards.

It surprised the detective who stood flatfooted for just a second, then leaped for the window. But he was too late. Garrow's feet flicked past him.

It was a long drop.

Fifteen stories.

Long before Garrow hit the marquee out in front of his hotel down on the second story, he had released his grip on the money. It fluttered down through the night air.

It was still alive with motion, flickering and scooting off in unpredictable directions long after Garrow hit the marquee, bounced on it, then rolled off and landed with a dull thump across the motor of a cab.

The cabbie jumped when he saw what was coming, just before

Garrow's body landed. Then he swore at the corpse. It had dented the front of his car.

The cabbie said, "Damn leapers, they never think of anybody else!"

Then he saw the green stuff raining down all around him and, greedy hands outstretched, he began to collect the bills that were nearest him.

A vagrant puff of wind drove some of the bills down Forty-seventh Street and out across Broadway. Some of them landed on the pigeons that sleep on Father Duffy's statue. The birds complained as the bills woke them, but soon went back to sleep.

The last fifty-dollar bill wasn't found till almost two months later. By that time Madigan's and Garrow's bodies, unclaimed by anyone, had missed burial in Potter's field because a certain proportion of the unwanted dead in New York are turned over to medical schools where they are used for dissection by internes.

Separated only by the width of the wall of the metal tanks they floated in, their cadavers were beginning to turn brown from formaldehyde. When that happened, it was as if he had never lived, except as a statistic in the crime files that yearly, the New York Police Department turns over to the FBI. But you could never have found Garrow in the midst of all those ciphers.

# Carnage in Calossa

Sun.

White heat pounding on a tin roof.

Tin-roofed native shack jam-packed with the limp stink of decaying copra.

A man.

Dried filth crusted on his torn mouth, the man moves uneasily. Torn T-shirt soaked with blood, his chest moves hesitantly as he struggles for air.

Blue dungarees bleached almost white, grubby with dirt ground deep into the fibers of the cloth. Pockets torn and gaping, the dungarees stir as the all-pervading heat makes the man moan.

Unconsciously grinding the egg-shaped protrusion on the side of his skull into the debris on the dirt floor, the man forces more dirt into the gaping split in the colored lump that disfigures his head.

Tears of pain have gummed his eyelids closed and it is this discomfort of which he is first dimly aware as consciousness returns.

Grinding his knuckles into his eyes, and gasping for breath he slowly lifts his head. More pain. Retching, grinding pain that begins in his head and shoots outwards and down, ending in the pit of his belly.

Waves of heat pound down at him from the underside of the broiling tin roof.

Fetid stench makes his nostrils flare as he tries to manufacture saliva in the sandpaper rough lining of his mouth and tongue.

And then, and then, reality returns.

Muddled, nightmarish, but now he knows that he is a man, someone named Tommy Winters.

And he knows that he has no right to be where he is.

Staggering to the aperture, that serves as a door, he sees across the almost blue whiteness of the sandy beach that faces the hut, far out on the horizon, a tramp steamer.

His ship.

Gone, left without him.

He's on the beach in Calossa, worst hellhole he had ever seen in all the tiny islands that clot the Pacific like leprous sores.

Hesitantly he puts his hands to his pockets. Feeling the torn cloth he knows that his money is gone, but worse, much worse, is the realization that his papers are gone too. His seaman's papers and his seaman's passport.

Retching he empties his stomach, and then he stands there, framed in the doorway of the stinking native hut and he remembers . . .

There was a girl.

Lean and lithe with a waist that was almost small enough for him to put his hands around, the full bosom and out-curved hips that undulated like all the lonely dreams he had ever dreamt on shipboard, with long straight legs and covering and revealing, revealing more by what it clothed than what it showed above and below, a strip of cloth, her only clothing, was like wet satin.

Animal face with slanting eyes, that were as heavy lidded as ancient sin, and hair like a tortured ebony midnight, she was brown as good coffee with just the right amount of cream in it, brown with the color that white women try futilely to achieve by endless hours of sunbathing, brown like velvet, brown that made the tips of his fingers ache to caress it.

And he had.

But first there had been liquor, lots of it, and singing, and talk, good talk with his shipmates, who, after twenty-two days on shipboard, were like new men at the feel of solid earth under their feet, and it had been fun.

But then, he pressed his bruised hands to the aching lump that nuzzled him but then, what?

The hut.

And then nothing.

No remembrance came. No knowledge of the hand that had struck him down, no memory of how he had passed out, no idea as to who had beached him.

None at all.

Even then, even with pain racking him with a hurt he had never had to endure before, the sight of her walking across the too white sand, walking towards him, smiling as she came, was enough to lift his spirits momentarily.

She said, "Tommee, what has happened to your poor head?" Her speech was slurred and no one would ever confuse her English with that of a Vassar graduate, but she was able to speak as well as most of the people on the island, white or brown.

"I don't know, honey, I was kind of hoping you'd be able to tell me."

Winters was concerned with the way he looked. The water down at the beach's edge, that was the thing for him. Keeping a distance away from her so that she would not be offended by the state he was in, he stripped off his torn singlet and his ripped dungarees. Slipping into the water, he floated for a while trying to draw strength from the bath tub of hot sea water.

She stood knee deep in the soft rollers that broke on the shore and rinsed out his clothes.

Twenty feet out, Winters called, "Was I all right when you left me?"

"A little drunk, but not too," she said, busy with her chore. "You were very funnee, you said you would marree me."

Oh, brother, Winters thought, whatever else had happened to him last night, one thing was sure, he had been loaded. The salt water stung the wound on his head, but that was all to the good. The pain did not lessen but at least some of the dirt would be washed out. He called, "What did your husband think of that?"

"He was not there when you say that." Head bowed, he could not see what the expression on her face was.

Paddling in to the shore, he flopped in a heap just beyond the reach of the water and let the sun bake out his shorts. He could almost see the moisture disappear as the heat hit them. He said, "Acquila, was I very drunk? Sick, or anything?"

"Noooo . . ." She drew out the monosyllable. "When I left, you were sound asleep with a sweet smile on your face."

"Oh great!" Winters made a sour face, and said, "I must have been a real live doll."

"You were cute." Now the smile that had been hovering at the corners of her full lips broke out in full, and her white, white, teeth flashed, and sick as he felt, he managed to fling out an arm and encircle her waist and pull her to him. Her soft lips were as exciting as he remembered them being.

Near them, his pants and shirt were almost completely dry when they rose and he forced himself into his clothes.

He asked, "What the hell am I going to do, honey?"

"You mean for monee?"

A nod brought the forgotten pain back in a full burst that made him almost double up in agony. Her face showed concern as she said "First you had better go to the doctor, no?"

"Doctors like money, no?" He answered. "Money is what I ain't got none of."

And papers, his passport, without them he was a man alone in an alien world.

She said, "Maybe my husband would have you work in his place."

That would really do it, he thought dully. Put the horns on the guy and then go around and beg for a handout.

He ran his hand around her firm hips and said, "What if he knows about the games we been playing?"

"Bah," the monosyllable sound on her lips, "He not know. And if he know, he not care."

It was hard to believe, Winters thought, looking down at her, awful hard to believe that any man, no matter how long he'd gone native, would ever get over wanting to possess her.

They were walking towards what passed for the main drag in Calossa. Three hundred feet long, the dirt of the road was rutted like corduroy; garbage and filth almost covered the area, and on both sides of the "street" were houses, stores, and what might in some other place he called barrooms. Here they were open fronted wooden frames, tin roofed places with tables and chairs.

"Madigan's" was the name scrawled on the place her husband ran.

The equatorial noon day sun beating down made ink black shadows inside the bar.

Staggering, Winters held onto the side of the frame structure as he passed from the whiteness to the blackness. It was only after a while that he could make his eyes see into the bar. A length of what might have been mahogany stretched back to the rear of the place. A cash register, rusted and incompetent looking was between Winters and the man who owned both the bar and the girl who stood next to Winters.

She called, "Mr. Madigan." That had struck Winters as odd the night before, even in his drunkenness, that she had called her husband mister. But it was none of his business then and it was none of his business now.

The oversized chair that contained Madigan's bulk creaked as the man leaned forward a little. Winters thought "your mother may have been named Madigan, buster, but your father's name was something like Sen-Kai," for the man was monolothically fat. Perhaps two inches shorter than Winters' six feet, the man called Madigan seemed to be made up of rolls of hard fat. Winters remembered an old automobile tire ad that he had seen many years before; in it a cartoon man was formed of rubber tires. That was the effect that Madigan gave. But the fat was not soft, it was like the pads that cover Japanese wrestlers, those eugenically bred mountains of men who are agile for all their size.

Madigan's padded eyes opened a trifle, and he said, "Ah, Mr. Winters, you have not found it possible to pull yourself away from our so salubrious climate?" The esses were definitely hissed.

"Somebody took care of that for me." Winters said and wondered what a drink would do to his head.

Even in the quasi-darkness of the barroom, Winters could see the oily sweat that cascaded down from the mountainous man's forehead in a never-ending stream.

Madigan asked, "Will you join me in a drink? Or are you one of those cowardly drinkers who insists on waiting till the sun is over the yardarm?"

Acquila might have been invisible for all the notice that the monstrously fat man took of her. In fact, Winters noticed, she was sidling around behind the man, slowly, as if to try and get out of his sight.

"Sure, I'll have a drink." He couldn't feel much worse, that was for sure.

No wheat had ever gone into the composition of the drink that passed in these parts for rye. Downing it at a gulp, Winters was sure that fermenting rice had been the base of the almost pure alcohol that filled the American brand name bottle that sat next to Madigan on the bar.

Now that his eyes were more accustomed to the lack of light Winters became aware of what seemed at first glance to be a bundle of dirty clothes under a nearby table. It took a second look to show him that the clothes were on a man.

Getting out from under the table took the man a long time. When he was finally standing spraddle-legged, wavering back and forth slowly, he whined to Madigan, as he wiped some cigarette butts off himself, "How about a shot, Madigan?"

"I thought I told you, Gilroy," the fat man said slowly and distinctly, as though talking to a child, or an idiot, "that you were not to speak to me unless I asked you to?" The voice was gentle, but Winters had to restrain himself from interfering when Madigan threw a shot glass of the raw liquor straight into the derelict's eyes.

No sense, Winters thought, in getting involved in this.

Gilroy's pigeon breast rose and fell fast, as he seemed to debate with himself whether to do anything about the action or not. Finally his narrow head fell forward on his chest and he whimpered, "But you promised."

Madigan's big foot shot out and caught Gilroy in the groin. The man fell writhing to the littered floor, and Madigan said conversationally, "Acquila, get him out of here before I kill him."

The girl reappeared from wherever she had been lurking and taking hold of the famine-thin man by the ankles she dragged him across the floor and out of sight to some back room.

Madigan turned his heavy face to Winters, his sagging double chins dancing as he said, more quickly than was his wont, "What can I do for you?"

"Is there any way I can make coffee and cake money till the next ship docks here?"

"Depends, much depends on how much cake you need with your coffee." Madigan's padded eyes were focused on the middle distance as though he could see right through Winters, out into the street, such as it was.

"There's no American consul on the island?"

"None for eight hundred miles."

"Then the first amount of cake I'll need will be enough to wire the consul about my passport being missing."

"That is possible. It can be taken care of."

"Some money for clothes, food and a bed, that's about all need."

Some money to move around on, to try and find out just what the hell had happened to him, Winters thought, that was what he needed. Nobody had ever pushed him around like this before, and as the liquor bit in and began to do some good, he thought no one's going to start now.

"Ten dollars a week." Madigan said.

It was a far cry from his union scale as a seaman first class, but it would have to do.

"What do I have to do?"

Madigan waggled a fat thumb at a mop in the back of the bar. "Swamp."

A swamper. The clamhead who cleans a joint. Washes out the spittoons, mops up the floor, you couldn't get much lower than that. Beggars can't be choosers, Winters thought sourly, and picked up the mop. "Can you advance me some dough?"

The big head swiveled in the rolls of fat. "No, I fear not. Too many men have found it easier to live on the beach off some native girl. I must have an example of your industry before I can feel that it is an act of wisdom to give you your salary."

Swearing under his breath, head aching, stomach heaving with what Winters realized was the beginning of hunger, he got to work. When you got right down to it, he found out, it wasn't much different from washing down a deck. A lot dirtier that was about all.

It was a rough week.

Dossing down in the back of the bar took care of Winters' sleeping arrangements, and Madigan had Winters share his meals with him. Acquila was always there, always in the background, waiting on Madigan, obeying his every command. That was what made it rough, not the work. Having her under his nose all the time, brushing by her in the semi-darkness, smelling the fragrance of her hair, touching her lithe body . . .

But it paid off, for when it got late, when the last few drunks had finally quit the bar and staggered off into the soft tropical night, then Winters was able to ease away from the omnipresent bulk of Madigan, and go down to the beach. It never took more than ten or fifteen minutes for Acquila to join him....

By the time the lump on Winters' head had begun to subside the week had ended.

"Mr. Winters," Madigan called.

"Coming."

"Your salary, sir." The dirty dollar bills were a welcome sight.

Madigan counted them out slowly and reluctantly. Ten of them. But then as Winters hurriedly reached out to scoop them up, Madigan's big hand came down over the thin stack. "A moment, please."

Winters felt his hands curling into hard balls. Instinctively, his thumbs retracted below his fingertips. He'd learned that early in the game. It was the only way to keep them from being broken if you landed a solid punch.

Madigan said, "I am not charging you for sleeping here."

"That's pretty big of you." Winters could feel fury beginning to build up inside him.

"However, I do feel forced to charge you for the food you have consumed." Madigan withdrew three of the limp, soiled old dollars from the slim pile.

Winters allowed his fists to unclench. That still left seven bucks.

But Madigan was spreading the bills on the grimy bar. The seven of them were now lined in a row. Madigan said, "Tuesday," and pulled a dollar bill away from the row. "Wednesday," another bill was withdrawn. "Thursday . . ." still another bill....

Puzzled, Winters watched as the grotesquely fat man chanted out the days of the week, and at the name of each day, took back a dollar.

When there were no bills left, Winters said, "Just what the hell do you think you're doing?"

Crossing his arms on his tremendous belly, Madigan stared at Winters, "I believe that a man deserves to be paid for what he does. Therefore, I have paid you the salary I agreed to give you. But I also feel that in all fairness, a husband should benefit from what his wife does." The bland face, the man's statue-like immobility, was unbroken as Madigan said, "You do not dispute my arithmetic?"

Suddenly and surprisingly, Gilroy, the pale wraith of a man who was always lurking somewhere in the background, began to giggle.

His high-pitched voice cackled, "Looka his face, Madigan! He's shocked!"

Backing away from Madigan, his hands clenching and unclenching at his sides, trying not to let the black rage that was welling up inside him come to the surface, and make him do something he would regret, Winters stumbled down the single wooden step outside the bar, and walked quickly away.

A week wasted. Seven days shot. And here he was, just as bad off as he had been when he woke up broke and without his papers. Worse off; for now even if he could contact the consul on the distant island that government employee would certainly want to know why Winters had so long delayed reporting the theft of the passport. Seven days. Two more days and his ship would be docking and paying off in San Francisco. A great town when you had a pocket full of money, and he'd been at sea long enough to build up quite a bank roll.

Winters wondered if he could prevail on the one lone radio operator on Calossa to take a chance and call his ship. Maybe that's what he should have done in the first place if he had not been befuddled by Acquila, bemused by her nearness, intoxicated by her body.

So the lady was a tramp.

No wonder Madigan had had no husbandly jealous pangs. No wonder at all.

That was the first night that did not find Winters reclining on the beach.

Instead he paced angrily through the night, past the few houses where the decent law abiding citizens of this back wash of civilization were sound asleep behind drawn blinds.

But the trouble with the island was that there were no long winding roads where a man could walk the fury out of his veins. Winters found himself getting, if anything, angrier than he had been as his feet brought him back towards Madigan's bar.

Once around the island barely tired him. Five miles had not

consumed enough time, or energy to ease the rage that he was tending carefully as a householder banks a fire for a long winter night.

The single yellow light from Madigan's was the only man-made illumination on the rutted road. The moon was high in the sky, but Winters was blind to that.

Wondering if taking a punch out of Madigan would help anything, Winters walked towards the bar. From inside it, he heard some voices. Madigan's, Gilroy's . . . and a third man's.... Whose was it?

Suddenly cautious, Winters crouched down, and made his way nearer the voices.

The unknown's voice was saying, "When do we slough Winters?"

"Patience, patience is a virtue, my quick-tempered friend." That was Madigan.

Winters was on his haunches now, peering into the room. He knew the third man, but only as a hanger-on at the bar, one of the few on the whole island whom Madigan allowed to sign chits at the bar.

Almost as gaunt as Gilroy, the man's flaring red hair, and broad-shouldered body was tense as he snarled at Madigan. "Patience!"

Behind Madigan and the red headed man, Gilroy was holding a battered kitchen spoon over a match. Smoke coated the bottom of the spoon. Whatever he was heating in the bowl of the spoon was evidently ready, for while Madigan and the redhead talked, Gilroy placed the tip of a medicine dropper into the liquid in the spoon.

Madigan said, "Everything is all set. The ship lands here tomorrow. Follow my suggestions as you have in the past, Smathers, and I see no reason why our business should not progress as admirably as usual."

"Words." The redhead, Smathers, made a gesture with his hand. "Words." He made it sound like a swear word. "Let's get it over with."

"You have replaced his picture with one of you?" Madigan asked.

Behind Madigan the single light made eerie shadows on the wall as Gilroy unbuttoned his work pants and dropped them. Picking up a rusty pocket knife, he hacked a gash in the inside of his thin thigh.

Smathers reached into a pocket and flipped out a passport. He showed it to Madigan. "There'll be no trouble about this."

His passport, Winters realized. The redhead had substituted a photograph of himself for the one of Winters.

The oppressive silence of the tropical night was lightly broken. Bare feet. Winters got down on all fours and eased himself to one side, out of the way.

Acquila stormed into the bar. "He did not come!"

Madigan snorted.

Gilroy shoved the tip of the dirty medicine dropper into the gash he had cut in his leg. Then he pressed the rubber bulb and paid no attention to the drops of blood that welled up from the cut in his scrawny thigh. The blood dripped down on the other suppurating sores that defaced his skin.

Smathers said, and he was mimicking Madigan's heavy, almost pompous tones, "Oh, no, don't worry about Winters, he's safe. He's with Acquila." Then his voice his own, he snarled, "I said we oughta clobber the slob, but oh no, not you! Let's put it off till the last minute!"

Through a rip in the battered wood that served as a wall for the barroom Winters could see Gilroy pull up his pants. He could see Acquila's face and she was frightened and angry and . . . somehow a little excited.

Gilroy threw back his thin shoulders and said to Madigan, "You want me to take him? I'll rip him apart with my bare hands! I'll chew his throat out . . . I'll . . ."

"You'll shut up, while I think," Madigan said, and as maniacally hyped-up as the hophead was, he drew away from the cold anger in the fat man's voice.

Throwing back her head made Acquila's hair flare out like a wild horse's mane. She said, "Talk, always talk, think, always think, will you never act, fat man?"

Using the side of his hand, Madigan cuffed her across the jaw, as you might an impetuous puppy. "Shut up."

"Where would Winters be?" Madigan asked aloud. "Angry at my charming wife, what would he do? Where could he go?"

Still immobile, he looked about him. Winters hunkered down for it was almost as if the fat man's flat eyes could see through the wooden wall.

Behind him, Gilroy reached out, put his hand on Acquila's waist, caressed her. The woman was standing as though frozen, her hand still on her jaw. Smathers had taken a .38 out of his back pocket and was looking at it.

Madigan said, "Put that away. It would sound like an atom bomb in the silence of this island."

"Shiv?" Smathers asked.

"Of course. And then dump him in the inlet." Madigan's eyes were still the only part of him that moved. "I would not be too surprised to find that we have an eavesdropper, gentlemen."

Acquila was the first one to move. Making a fork of her forefinger and middle finger, she darted the tips of her fingers into Gilroy's eyes. As the man screamed in pain, she said, "I told you not to touch me."

Palms of his hands pressing into his assaulted eyes, Gilroy fell to his knees.

The redhead left the gun on the table between him and Madigan. This time when he took his hand out of his pocket it held a snap knife. Pressing the button, he waited till the spring whipped a razor-sharp blade into sight. Then like all knife fighters, he put his forefinger under the back of the blade and holding his hand in front of him, he asked, "You figure Winters came back here and is getting an ear full?"

"It would seem like a sensible course of action," the fat man said.

It was not too surprising, Winters found, to discover that here were the people who had broken his skull and robbed him. Then too, their reason now seemed obvious. But all that was washed away in a wave of berserk rage that threatened to break its bounds before Winters could make the best use of it.

Straightening up from his crouching position, he flattened his body against the warped boards of the bar's wall and waited, his hands aching to come to grips with the men who had assaulted him.

The sick yellow beams that came through the cracks were the only light. In that pale illumination, Winters could see the crouched form of Smathers. Like an animal with a single fang, the man came closer, the hand that held the knife projecting out in front of him.

From inside the bar, Madigan called out, "Any sign of him? After all, my hypothesis may not be correct."

"So far I don't see . . ." Smathers answered, and then his voice broke off as Winters, who was behind him, whipped his arm around the man's throat and pulled tight.

That left Smathers' arms free and his knife hand came up and back, jabbing at Winters' face. Twisting his head from side to side, avoiding the darting jabs as best he could, Winters continued to apply pressure on the man's throat. In another minute he might have had control of the situation, but for the fact that Smathers did the only thing that could rid him of the strangling arm. He fell forward to his knees, and as he fell, he pulled his head into his chest. Winters was catapulted over Smathers' body and landed on his back, the breath knocked out of him.

At the same time, the light inside the bar was turned out.

The waning moon cutting through some palm trees was now the only aid to vision and it was so weak that Winters had to squint his eyes in order to make out the blurred form of the man who was now stalking him on all fours.

"Don't forget," Madigan's flat, completely unemotional voice broke the silence, "that there's a hundred grand involved. Get him!"

A hundred thousand dollars was a hell of a spur, Winters found as Smathers leaped from his animal like position in a flat dive that caught Winters in the groin. The pain was enough to make a groan force its way out of Winters' throat, but knowing that there was no time to waste in anything but fighting to the death, he gritted his teeth, and his head swimming with nausea, he chopped down with the side of his hand on Smathers' neck. The blow made the man go limp. The spring knife shot out of his hand and landed four or five feet away.

Not waiting to see if Smathers was playing possum, Winters gambled everything on reaching the knife first. His hand was closing on it, when from behind him, from the doorway of the bar, Madigan said, "Drop it, Winters."

Duly aware that Madigan now held the gun that Smathers had left on the table, Winters stood irresolutely, the knife laying across his palm. Madigan said, "It's a big gamble, Winters, unless you are a fine knife thrower, I wouldn't try it."

One hand pressed into his groin, trying to assuage the pain that was sending fiery jets through him, his other hand occupied with the knife, Winters considered the odds.

Madigan said, "Given that you can throw that knife well enough to get me, it is highly improbable that I will die immediately. And unless I do, I shall certainly shoot you to death."

Winters turned his hand over and allowed the knife to drop to the ground. Gilroy popped into view behind Madigan and lurching to the knife, he scooped it up, and then stood crooning to the deadly blade.

"Inside," Madigan said, and turning his head slightly, he called, "Turn on the light, Acquila."

The hophead dragged Smathers into the barroom by the heels disregarding the way the man's head bounced and jolted from side to side. Releasing Smathers' legs, he again took out the knife and ran his thumb gently across the shining blade.

"Very little," Madigan said relaxing again into the oversized chair that Winters was used to seeing him occupy, "had been accomplished by your little feat of derring do, Mr. Winters . . . Very little indeed."

"I had very little to lose," Winters said. The nose of the gun in the fat man's hand was pointed directly at Winters' navel. He did not like to think of what it would feel like to get shot in the gut. The pain in his groin was letting up, and he found that he could again think fairly coherently. He was due to die, unless he could somehow turn the tables on the fat man and the hophead. Considering his own fate, his eyes drifted over Acquila's body. At that moment, he was only dimly aware of her charms. The puzzle that concerned him was what her position in this deadly game consisted of, would she throw in with any winner, or did she have any loyalty to the fat man? She stepped directly behind the chair that held her husband's gross body. All Gilroy's attention was on the knife.

Madigan was speaking, but Winters was not concerned with that, for he could see Acquila reaching out and picking up the ever-present liquor bottle that always sat near Madigan. Her tapering fingers closing around the neck of the bottle.

Her savage face was completely impassive. It signaled no message to Winters at all.

The bottle was over Madigan's head now.

"It is obvious of course," Madigan was saying, "That you have had the bad luck to be selected for the role of pigeon in the highly remunerative drug smuggling ring that I have the pleasure of heading.

"Unfortunately for you, I need a passport for Mr. Smathers, so that he can take the latest packet of heroin to the states. The risks are high, I suppose you might point out, but I can only say that so are the rewards."

His mouth was forming still another word, when the bottle crashed down on his head. Winters was thinking that Calossa was merely the way station, that the heroin was probably being manufactured in China or Japan, and then transported here for the final arrangements before being smuggled into America. Then he saw Gilroy, his face contorted with a mixture of drugged delirium and insane rage, catapult towards Acquila who was dropping the neck of the bottle, all that remained after the bottle had shattered on her husband's head. The knife in Gilroy's hand cut at Acquila's midriff.

Her agile body twisted to one side as the hophead, a scream of fury on his lips, chopped at her and then he mumbled, "You can't do that to Madigan . . . without him where'll I get the horse?" The knife had cut deep.

Enveloped in a feeling of continuing nightmare, Winters managed to get a grip on the man's fragile wrist and tear the hophead away from the woman.

A right jab made the drug addict collapse on the floor.

And the carnage was almost complete.

The blow that had knocked out Madigan had not forced his body to do more than relax. He sat, as though asleep, the rivulets of blood running down his face, and the shards of broken glass making a glittering collar around his thick neck. Gilroy was slumped like a broken toy next to the unconscious body of Smathers.

But Winters was blind to all that.

All he could see was the anguish on Acquila's face, and the way her fingers pressed deep into her slashed stomach as though they could weave back the ripped flesh,

"Your ship," she said through lips that were perilously close to going slack in the last relaxation that precedes death, "Man . . . with . . . passport . . . of . . ." The words were getting more and more widely separated in time, "dead man . . . in . . . inlet . . ." So this was not the first time the gang had used an innocent seaman's papers, Winters thought disconnectedly, as the dying girl said, "name . . . of . . . Black."

Pillowing her head in his lap, disregarding the horror that was now her stomach, Winters kissed her gently and said, "Thanks a million, baby, for the help you gave me . . ."

He was still sitting that way with the dead woman in his arms when the single human being in whom the authority for the preservation of peace and the upholding of law and order in Calossa, Sam Carrell, entered the bar.

The peace officer said, "C'mon, spit it out, mister."

Standing over Smathers, ready at any moment to kick the man's brains out if he showed any sign of fighting, Winters said, "It's pretty obvious. This is a gang that was smuggling heroin into the States. And that reminds me. There's a guy named Black who was killed and thrown into the inlet, and what's more, someone else is traveling on his passport, on my ship.

"The radio man," Winters said, snapping the words out, "better get him to contact my ship and have the man carrying Black's passport arrested. He must have a bundle of heroin on him, ready to take off the ship in Frisco. It'll dock there tomorrow, so we better get busy."

There was a lot more to do, but at last it was done, and Winters had found the cache of heroin in the bar, underneath the battered cash register, and what was equally damning, he found bank books in Madigan's name on a San Francisco bank and the amount that Madigan had banked was stunning.

The hut that served as a jail on Calossa was jammed when Carrell finished putting Madigan, Gilroy and Smathers behind bars.

And then it was over, and Winters had his own passport back and he had ripped out the picture of Smathers, and there was nothing left to do but wait for the next ship to dock in Calossa and that was hard, for everywhere that Winters looked, he seemed to see Acquila.

One time he would see her as she had looked without the bit of cloth wrapped around her and her eyes dancing with excitement and her breasts heaving with pleasure and she was made for love.

And then he'd see her as Madigan's wife and that wasn't so good.

But worst of all was when he saw her with her belly ripped out and he was helpless to do anything for her. That was the picture that stayed with him longest and he knew that even when Calossa had sunk down beneath the horizon and the carnage had vanished from his memory, he'd still be burdened with the picture of her as she lay dying.

# Death Lives in Brooklyn

## I

Like the sailors who spend their leaves in rowboats in Central Park, G.I.s and Marines spend a lot of time on Broadway in the shooting gallery across the street from Father Duffy's statue, between Forty-seventh and Forty-eighth Streets. The front of the shooting gallery contains a myriad of nickel and dime machines all equally confusing in their complexity. For your coin you can make a ball roll around an inclined plane and get, as a reward, a score that ranges up into the millions. That's your only reward.

Besides the pinball machines, the peep shows, the automatic cameras which take your picture, develop it and return it, all inside of one hundred and twenty seconds, there is also a counter selling what passes for food. This ranges from greasy hot dogs to tiny sections of pizza and watered-down orange and pineapple drinks.

The man who stood at the food counter wolfing down hot dogs wore an Eisenhower jacket which was skimpy protection against the winter wind that raced down the broad thoroughfare outside. His worn slacks were greasy and dirty, his wornout shoes had almost given up their task. He found that as the doughy rolls and macerated meat hit the gaping hole in his belly, he was suddenly, for the first time in a long time, interested in women.

The covey of office girls who were giggling as they saw their simpering faces reproduced by the automatic cameras, were all too interesting and much too unobtainable.

The smell of their cheap perfumes got in the way of his enjoyment of the food he was eating. He put down the last half of his sixth hot dog, finding that his sexual appetite was getting in the way of his stomach's desires. Besides, it wasn't much of a Christmas Eve dinner, he decided.

One of the girls had taken off her heavy coat and had taken a picture of herself in a low-cut blouse. He could hear her friends teasing her, asking her if she was going to give the photo to her boyfriend.

Friendless himself, as he had never been before, he found a wave of resentment rising up in him, against the girl, her boyfriend, and the faceless mob that ranged down the street outside the store, the people in the store, the men at the shooting gallery spending their money on bullets to hit iron targets, when he had remaining to him exactly twenty-seven cents.

His hand in his worn pocket, he wondered what to do next. Desperation had carried him, from a little town to New York, had kept him on freight trains, bumming his way on roads or hitchhiking.

The silver of the quarter he was feeling was no more reassuring than the two copper pennies. A cent had no value. None at all. Sneering at himself, and at the fake bravado of what he was doing, he edged past the girls, his frayed nerves reacting with pleasure when one of them brushed close against him and he could feel her softness.

Not wanting to step out into the icy blast that was whistling crazily down Broadway, he paused at the entrance of the store and dropped one of his two pennies into an automatic fortune telling machine. Inside a glass walled cabinet a wax replica of an old gypsy crone sat in dusty immobility. Behind him, he heard one of the girls pointing out to the others what he was doing. Their titters drove him out into the night.

He crumpled up the little bit of cardboard that the gypsy had ejected into a slot. Its message was a little too ironic for him. It said, "Continue as you have been and your life will be happy, contented, and long."

Uptown from where he was standing he could see the weather device on top of an insurance building. Its white lights flickered downwards, meaning a drop in the temperature, probably followed by snow.

Groaning to himself, he thought, that's all I need. A clock in front of a jewelry store next to the Palace theatre told him that it was half past eleven.

He decided he had better leave Broadway for the sight of the bejeweled and befurred women with their well-dressed, contented looking escorts was more than he could bear.

There is only one place in the length of Broadway where a down-and-outer can feel comfortable and this is a street so decayed that it has long since given up all pretense. The crummy hotels, as out of reach to him as though they charged eighteen dollars a day instead of three, bore no reproach to anyone dressed the way he was.

Pausing in front of a barroom that catered to servicemen, he smelled the warmth that came from it and was grateful. The pounding sound of a Dixieland band smothered the voices of the men and girls at the bar.

An idling patrolman came closer to the man in the worn clothes, his eyes signaling that bums were not welcome on his beat. Anxious to forestall any questioning, the lonely man entered the bar.

Before he could edge toward the men's room and so avoid the cop's attention, the bartender behind the long mahogany bar asked, "What'll it be, chum?"

"A beer."

That left him a dime, and a penny.

But it had bought him a haven for as long as he could make the drink last. It was warm in the bar, and it was good to be near people, even if the people were all either servicemen or the vultures who cluster near men on leave.

Looking at the females, he wondered how the soldiers and sailors could find them attractive. Most of them were girls in their teens, overdressed, with a ravenous hunger on their unformed faces. But some of them were older, so much older as to seem like perverted mothers of the younger girls.

The high keening of the clarinetist on the raised podium at the rear of the bar cut through the gabble of voices. The heavy thump of the bass drum made an undertone to the girls' shrill tones. Then the clarinetist and the trombonist went into a conversation and the lonely man was able to forget himself for a moment as the brass and the wooden instruments talked together.

The band was playing *When the Saints Come Marching In*, and the lonely man was wryly amused at such a song performed in such a place.

That was when it happened.

He had almost come to the bottom of the glass of beer which would have to be the signal for him to leave the bar. He had been busy looking at himself in the dim reflection of the dirty mirror behind the bar, wondering where the young man he had once been had gone, wondering how a mere thirty-five years could have aged him so, could have etched such deep lines in his face, wondering if anyone would recognize him as a lawyer called Max Farrell, when a squabble broke out.

At first he paid no attention to the two men whose voices were getting louder and louder, figuring that it was just a bar brawl. When he noticed the way the bartender's face got set, and frightened, he decided that anything that could scare a bartender in a joint like this was worth his getting out of the way of. Then one of the two men who were arguing dropped his hand into an outside jacket pocket. A young soldier standing right next to the lonely man said, with relish, "This oughta be good."

Then the squat man's hand came out of his pocket and the gun quieted everything and everyone but the band. They played louder, or perhaps that was just by contrast with the sudden hush that held everyone.

The other leaner man who had started the argument said, "Put that damn thing back in your pocket; it won't solve anything."

"Maybe not, but I like it this way." The gun was steady. Its muzzle was no more than two feet away from the belly of the man it was menacing.

The man with the gun said, "Walk on out."

The other shrugged his shoulders and said, "The boss is gonna like a grandstand play like this. He sure is."

"You let *me* worry about that. Go on, straight out."

No one else in the long narrow room moved as the two men walked towards the door.

The man in front, Farrell noticed, was slowing his pace, almost imperceptibly, forcing the man with the gun in his hand to come close behind him.

They were almost level with Farrell when the man in the lead made his play.

The bartender ducked down behind the protection of the wooden barricade as the first man suddenly stopped stock still, and reached backward over his shoulder. His desperate fingers grabbed a section of the other man's coat lapel, and instantly he fell forward, dragging the other man too close to shoot, and sending him flying over his shoulders toward the front door.

The unarmed man leaped flatly from his knees toward the other man who was sprawled full length on the filthy floor, his startled, angry face grinding into cigarette butts, his hand still retaining its firm grip on his gun.

**II**

There was a rolling tussle in which the bystanders could not make out what was happening. This was punctuated by the sound of a shot, the entrance of a cop, a drawn gun in front of him, a blast of cold air from outside the bar, and the united shrieks of the women closest to the shooting.

The man with the gun turned it toward the policeman and said, "Drop it, flatfoot, I don't want no more trouble."

While the gunman's attention was on trying to control the uniformed officer, the other, the man who had been shot, rolled closer to Farrell, his face tormented, his hands digging into his outraged stomach where the bullet had lodged.

He was trying to say something, and Farrell leaned over to hear what it was.

Between clenched teeth the wounded man said, "Toilet." Farrell waited. The man said, "Find it." Then a gasp tore itself out of his lips and for a moment he could not regain control of himself. Finally he said, "Take it to . . . DA . . . not cops . . . they're iced."

Farrell straightened up, saw that the whisper had not carried even to the GI next to him, all of whose attention was focused on the policeman who was dropping his gun. The man on the floor said, "That's smart. Real smart." He got to his feet, the gun in his hand moving in a flat arc that threatened anyone who moved. He staggered, back toward the door and was gone.

Instantly the cop left in pursuit.

The bartender picked up the phone to call for an ambulance, and Farrell found his feet leading him to the men's room. Out on the street, the gunman looked through the window momentarily.

It was just curiosity he told himself as he forced his way past the girls whose white faces needed a new supply of make-up, past the middle-aged prostitutes who were sneering at the scared kids, past the bandstand where the musicians had given up all pretense and were standing, holding their instruments slackly, waiting for what was to come next.

Inside the stench-filled little room, Farrell wondered where to look. The wounded man must have foreseen trouble and stashed whatever it was he had been talking about, here inside these scribbled-on four walls.

Farrell's eyes passed unseeingly over the obscenities that were scrawled on the blistered, once white-washed walls and wondered where he'd hide something under the same circumstances.

There was only one place, he decided, and entering one of the booths he stood on the toilet bowl and forced his unwilling hand into the box of the water closet. Nothing.

But the fourth water closet he tried had some object floating in it.

Removing it, Farrell let water drip from the envelope he had found.

Footsteps made him freeze where he was. Stuffing the sopping envelope into his back pocket, he dropped to the floor. Then he waited, holding his breath. But it was only another man.

Leaving the men's room, Farrell decided that he did not want to be held as a material witness, not, he figured, as long as he did not know what was in the envelope, anyway.

By that time other policemen had been summoned and were busy at the front of the bar. The wounded man was unconscious, Farrell could see, and wondered if the immobility meant death.

The bar wandered off at an L shape and Farrell managed to make himself as inconspicuous as possible, as he edged back and to the right, following the short arm of the L. The kitchen was back here, and where there was a kitchen, he reasoned, there must be windows.

He was right, and the kitchen was empty, either because hunger was not one of the appetites that this place catered to, or because the cook was up front, taking part in what was going on.

Passing two young GI's who had passed out, and who were sitting at a table with their heads cradled in their arms, Farrell paused a moment when he saw some silver scattered on the table. It was a tip that the avaricious hand of some waiter had missed. Scooping up a quarter and a dime, reasoning that his need was greater than the waiter's, Farrell hurried on.

The kitchen stank of stale grease, and his entrance frightened a horde of cockroaches which scurried away as he walked through the small room.

The window at the back of the room was crowded with cans and boxes, but Farrell pushed them to one side and hunkered his way out through the small rectangle.

He landed in an alleyway, and for a moment his sense of direction deserted him and he could not tell where he was. But then the neighing of a horse told him he was somewhere near the alley behind the Palace theatre. The horse, a trained one, was part of an act, and was stabled in the alley behind the theatre.

Patting the friendly creature on the nose, Farrell scooted down the long narrow exit toward the street where a single fifteen-watt bulb showed that the caretaker and doorman had left his post to investigate the hubbub next door.

Pausing at the exit from the alley, Farrell looked to his right. The ambulance was at the curb and from the expression on the attendants' faces he could tell that they were furious at being called out, only to find a DOA.

It is the job of the morgue wagon to pick up corpses and ambulance men resent it when they are called out in vain.

Farrell thought whatever he had in his pocket had caused a murder, unless the fight had been about something else. But that seemed unlikely.

A sudden thought overwhelmed him. He was sure no one of the bar patrons had seen the dying man whisper to him, but what guarantee did he have that the gunman had not seen the conversation take place? His knees got a little wobbly and he had to lean against a signboard, while he waited for strength to come back to him.

All attention, he thought and hoped, was on the scene in front of the bar, but how could he be sure that unseen eyes were not watching him? He decided that come what might he had better find out what the envelope contained, and find out fast.

Nearer the corner, back toward where he had come from earlier, back on Broadway, the animated signs, the flickering lights, the false air of gaiety and frivolity maintained itself. Suddenly he felt that he wanted to get out of the semi-darkness that he was in, out into the light, nearer to people.

The crowd behind him, around the scene of the shooting, was getting bigger all the time, as crowds do in New York at any hour of the night and day, whenever and wherever there is a scene of violence.

The gathering crowd made it safer, if not easier, to make his way towards Broadway.

Across the street the guns in the shooting gallery cracked on, imitating the reality of what had just happened.

Where could he go to open the envelope? Where *could* he, with no money, or almost no money, be momentarily unobserved?

The shooting gallery was the answer.

Hurrying across the wide thoroughfare he entered the store, and darted into one of the Photomaton stalls. No one could tell that he was not taking his picture, and in here, with the curtain drawn, he would be completely alone.

In front of him, staring at him bleakly, was the eye of the camera. Above it, the too bright bulb needed for the taking of photographs glared down at him.

He had to be careful in opening the wet envelope, for the water made it and its contents fragile.

He stared at the document that had been in the envelope.

It meant less than nothing to him.

It was an affidavit by two men of whom he had never heard, certifying that one Anthony Augustino had entered the United States of America illegally in the year 1921.

Why anyone should have been shot over this piece of paper he held in his hands was beyond him. He racked his memory trying to think if he had ever even heard of Augustino, but he knew he never had.

And a document relating to something that had happened so long ago, more than thirty years ago, why, he wondered should this suddenly cause murder?

It was beyond him, and he had patted the paper almost dry against his shirt when the thought occurred to him to hold it against the white-hot bulb in front of him. It dried rapidly, without blurring the ink too much.

He knew he couldn't stay in the booth much longer, and on a sudden impulse, he rose, stepped outside the booth, dropped the quarter he had stolen from the table in the barroom into the mechanism of the automatic camera, and re-entered the booth.

The camera, he decided, must be focused approximately where his head was. Holding the affidavit in front of his face, as much in one plane as he could, he waited until he heard the camera click.

Then he stepped outside the booth and waited.

### III

It took only one hundred and twenty seconds, but the time dragged interminably. Suddenly, standing as he was in the blue neon lights that washed down in the shooting gallery, he felt unpleasantly like one of the iron ducks who scooted along on the surface of the water in the tank, waiting to be shot.

The next moment the machine clicked, and he saw three frames drop out into the slot. Two of them were of his face—he hadn't even realized that he had wasted the two shots—the third was of the document he had held in front of him.

Reduced to an inch by an inch and a half, the lettering was indecipherable.

Ducking out of the too brightly lighted store, he hurried down the block. He had the real affidavit shoved down his shirt front, held in place by his pants belt, his lean belly aware of the still slightly moist envelope as the wind cut into him and made the moisture feel like ice. He carried the little picture in his hand. It too was a trifle damp, and he waited till it dried, and then pausing and putting one foot up on a fire hydrant, he pretended to tie his shoelace and shoved the tiny picture into his sock.

Then, still constantly on the alert, he walked downtown, away from the biggest, most garish of the lights, toward Times Square.

It was enough after midnight so that the after-theatre crowds were thinning out. The hordes of people were vanishing into the maw of the subway which was taking the now sated pleasure seekers back to their homes in the Bronx, Long Island and the other boroughs from which they dart on occasion in search of a big night.

He paused at Forty-second Street, and still keeping his eyes moving constantly, trying to determine if he was under surveillance or not, he walked west, toward Eighth Avenue. Having passed the cheap movie houses that grind interminably for twenty hours a day, and the stores which have signs in the windows advertising "Bankruptcy Sales", the flea bag hotels, the bookstores, and the cafeterias, he had almost reached the avenue toward which he was walking when a car slowed down near him, at the curb.

Intuitively he knew that this was it.

The car's driver had waited till Farrell had passed the biggest accumulation of pedestrians, and now, with no one else nearer than fifty feet, the door of the car opened, and a man leaped out of it onto the street.

Farrell knew better than to run. The man's hand was in his pocket and the expression on his face showed that he would not hesitate to use the gun he had concealed there.

The gunman's face was set, and his scar thin lips barely moved as he said, "Get in the car, quick."

Slowly, praying that a policeman might pop up out of nowhere, that some interruption might save him, Farrell walked toward the curb.

There was no interruption and as soon as Farrell was close enough, the gunman pushed a heavy hand in the small of his back and pushed. Farrell landed in the back of the car on all fours. Before he could try to get up, try to sit in the seat, the gunman was behind him. A chop of his hand on the back of Farrell's neck made Farrell black out.

When the dark curtain lifted and consciousness returned, Farrell was being eased out of the car. A man stood on each side of him, holding him upright by main force. Allowing his head to loll, Farrell decided not to let the men know that his mind was functioning, at least, not for a while.

But when they half dragged, half carried him across the pavement, he decided it would be easier to do it under his own power. He said, "Lemme go. I'm able to walk."

They did not let go, but their hands no longer gouged into his arms. The gunman said, "One peep, and it'll be the last outta you, buster."

He didn't feel much like peeping. Neck aching, his brains feeling scrambled, his body sore from the way it had lain crumpled in the rear of the car, he was not feeling in the mood for any kind of effort.

His captors forced him across the street and into the lobby of an expensive looking apartment house. A self-service elevator waited for them. Pushing him into it, the gunman said, "Press the ten button, Hippo."

The man who had driven the car did as he was told.

Farrell felt his stomach lurch as the elevator rose. The man called Hippo had almost no intelligence showing on his beetle-browed face; not even low animal cunning was revealed in his little piggy eyes. The gunman was on a little higher level, but he was no beauty. Scar tissue around his eyes showed that he had taken a lot of punches around the head at some time or other.

At the tenth floor Farrell was pushed out of the car. The elevator opened directly into a foyer. That must mean, he thought hazily, that the apartment occupied a whole floor. Whoever owned the apartment must have plenty of loot.

Soft thick carpeting caressed his worn shoes as he was half pushed, half carried through the foyer into a living room that had never had a single change made in its decor from the day a decorator had been turned loose on it. It had all the charm of a store window and looked just as unlived in. Modern furniture, beautiful and cold, in flawless taste, matched with perfect harmony the soft beige of the rug and the apple green of the walls.

The man who sat behind an object that was half desk, half bookcase, at first seemed to be in harmony with the surroundings. His tailoring was expensive. No padding marred the set of his jacket on his shoulders. A soft, button-down collar and a narrow tie made him look like any Madison Avenue advertising executive. Even his face was not too much at variance with the picture he presented to the world. Not until you looked at his eyes did you realize, Farrell thought, that here was a real bad one.

They weren't steel gray, and they weren't ice cold blue. They were brown, and they should have been warm, but they weren't. They were flat and reptilian. His swarthy complexion might have been the result of sun lamps but it wasn't.

The gunman said, "Here's the slob, boss."

"I deduced that all by myself, Champ." His tone was not cultured but it wasn't rough either. Farrell got the feeling that the man had taken elocution lessons in order to rid himself of some accent which was held in check, just barely audible.

Farrell said, "What's this all about?"

No one paid any attention to him. The gunman called Champ said,

"Right after Donny rubbed out the DA's man, this muzzler went into the men's room. Donny said he thought it meant somethin'."

"I'm sure I would rather trust Donny's opinion than yours. If he thinks the dying man communicated with this gentleman, then I am sure Donny is right."

Hippo interrupted timorously and said, "He wasn't never outta sight, boss. If he picked anything up, he's still got it. Outside of goin' into a penny arcade, that's all he did before we put the arm on him."

"I see. Thank you, Hippo." The flat brown eyes finally came to rest on Farrell. He looked for a long time before he said, "You look a little down on your luck, old-timer. Would a hundred dollars repay you for the inconvenience to which you have been put?"

A hundred dollars would make a big difference, Farrell thought tiredly. But he had the feeling that he would not have the hundred for very long.

Aloud he said, "Sure, I guess I could use some money, but I still don't know why I've been muscled around this way."

The man behind the desk leaned forward a trifle, his lean body taut as he said, "I assure you, that if we find no sign of a certain document on you, that I shall apologize, repay you for your trouble and release you. However, I feel that this is not the case. I feel that you have on you something which I want."

He gestured and Hippo and Champ closed in on Farrell. Deciding that a beating would not help anything, Farrell shrugged, reached into his shirt front and took out the envelope he had found in the water closet.

"I guess there's no point in playing hide-and-seek. Here's what I found. I haven't even had time to look at it. Your boys got me first."

Was there any chance they'd believe him? Farrell doubted it, but made the effort in any event. "I'm completely puzzled as to what this is all about. I don't know you, or any of these men. I never saw the man who got shot before in my life." That last part at least was true. For Farrell had recognized the "boss." Johnny O'Brien was the name he was known by.

**IV**

O'Brien, Farrell knew, was as big a man in the rackets as his predecessor, Lucky Luciano, had been before Lucky's exile. O'Brien's power extended all the way from his control of bookmaking, through vice and drugs. His hands controlled so many politicians that but for a few arrests in his youth, he had not seen the inside of a jail in a decade.

Farrell was entangled in something that was much too big for comfort. His hands were suddenly sweaty and he rubbed them on his worn pants.

O'Brien ripped the affidavit from the envelope and flicking a cigarette lighter set fire to the paper. He said nothing while he watched it burn. Once it was reduced to ashes, he punctiliously broke the ashes into many little dots.

Only then did he speak. "It is unfortunate that you decided to lie to me, old-timer." Then his head turned to Hippo and the man called Champ. His tone changed completely and Farrell could hear the accent that the pseudo-gentility had been covering. O'Brien snapped, "Sack him."

Farrell looked down at his hands and watched them as they shook with fear. They seemed independent of him, or of any control he had over them.

When he had tried to find refuge in alcohol after the unexpected death of his wife, he had thought dimly, that soon, sometime in the future, he would recover a little, begin to take an interest in living. But he hadn't; he had drunk his way through every cent he had ever saved, and when he went on the bum he had headed for New York. The desperation born of loneliness had prodded him without his knowing that New York can be the loneliest place in the world.

Only now, when his life could be measured in minutes, did he feel an upsurge, a desire to live no matter what the cost. Now with death at his back he knew that he belonged to life.

But it was a little late for that—and as the two hoods began to push him towards the door, he tried to force his weary brain into action, tried to think of some scheme, no matter how desperate, that would give him a fighting chance for survival.

Once O'Brien had made his decision, his attention returned to some papers on the desk. It was only when Farrell was being forced toward the foyer that a thought seemed to occur to O'Brien.

The man said, and his voice was back under control, "Hippo, why do you suppose this gentleman stopped off at a penny arcade?"

The question seemed to stun Hippo's not very agile wits. He said, "I . . . I dunno. Maybe to take a gander at the pitchers?"

"If you mean the peep show pictures, I doubt very much if a man in his position would have been in the mood for that sort of trifling. I doubt it very much."

Farrell found O'Brien was staring at him, The man had not risen to the aristocracy of mobdom because he was stupid. That was very clear.

"Strip him." O'Brien said, suddenly and decisively.

It didn't take long. Farrell's jacket, trousers, worn shirt and underwear came off quickly. They had left him his shoes. Farrell found that standing stark naked when others around you are dressed, was one of the most humiliating things he had ever endured. His strength seemed to fade as he stood there, facing the men whose fingers were going over each of his garments.

"Nothing, boss," Hippo said.

"His shoes and socks, imbecile!"

Pretending to be anxious to help, Farrell squatted down and took off his shoes and pushed them toward Hippo; next, he slipped off his worn socks, and in stripping one off, managed to get the tiny picture into his fingers. Champ was not too anxious to look at the filthy socks that were held out for his inspection.

But under his superior's baleful glare, he forced himself to examine them carefully.

Farrell stayed squatting, his fingers curled a trifle around the little picture.

O'Brien said harshly, "Stand up straight."

Doing as he was told, Farrell stood in his pelt and tried not to let his anxiety show in his face. Looking past O'Brien, out the window behind the man's head he could see soft, silent, secret snow patting against the glass. In some disconnected part of his mind, a section that was not torn by fear, he thought so the weather gadget was right when it predicted snow. To think that earlier that evening he had been afraid that bad weather was the worst of his problems.

"So I was wrong," O'Brien said.

His two men looked their puzzlement at him. He answered their unspoken question by saying, "I thought that perhaps he might have taken a photograph of the affidavit. It would have been smart."

Hippo said slowly, "If it's a little picture a guy could maybe hide it in his mouth."

"That's right," O'Brien assented. "Go ahead and take a look."

Champ grabbed Farrell's head and held it immobile while Hippo ripped open his lips. He felt the corner of his mouth rip.

The pain made his hand jerk convulsively. It happened to be the hand that held the palmed photograph.

The movement, completely by accident, brought his hand close to Hippo's outer jacket pocket.

While Hippo pressed his thumbs into the hinges of Farrell's jaws, making his mouth gape wide, Farrell pressed closer to the man and dropped the little photograph into his pocket.

Hippo said, "Nothing in his mouth, boss."

"Finish it up. Make sure." O'Brien directed.

When the two men had finished, Farrell lay on the floor swearing weakly.

O'Brien said, "I feel better now. Get him dressed and sack him."

"Okay, boss."

Hippo kicked Farrell in the rib cage and said, "Come on, let's go, sucker."

When he was able to breathe again, Farrell did as he was told. Blood was streaming down his chin and he wiped it on his shirt as he got into it.

O'Brien did not even look up as Hippo and Champ pushed Farrell out of the room into the foyer.

Farrell swayed dizzily as they waited for elevator to rise.

"Where'll we dump the bum?" Hippo asked.

"Brooklyn, where else?" Champ was elaborately disinterested.

The minutes of life, Farrell thought tiredly, were spanned by the length of time it would take to drive him to Brooklyn.

Downstairs they paused in the doorway for a moment. Farrell watched the snow, the white blanket that was beginning to hide the dirt of New York and work the winter miracle of making the city look new, and even more exciting.

But there was no time for sightseeing. His tiny hold on life depended on his being able to speak to Hippo without Champ overhearing him. How that could be worked he had no idea. But it had to be done before Hippo had occasion to put his hand in the pocket where the picture was. If his cigarettes were in that pocket he might discover it any moment.

The three men walked the ten feet that separated them from the curb where the car was parked. There was, Farrell realized, no blood lust in these men, no anger, no anything in particular. They happened to be men whose trade was murder and he was sure that they were good craftsmen or they would not have been so close to the top, to O'Brien.

Champ said as they neared the car, "In this weather we won't need no crash car."

"Nah." Hippo was contemptuous. "This kinda night them cops'll be busy hidin' out, drinkin' coffee and restin' their flat feet."

"Come on, let's get this over. I'm tired."

A businessman whose day had been too long, a worker who wanted to do the job at hand and get it over with, a craftsman whose craft demanded he work odd hours, but who still needed sleep and food. It was hard, Farrell found, to believe in the reality of the menace that these men represented.

Hippo remained at his side as Champ walked out into the street, opened the car door and entered the comparative warmth of the automobile.

Hippo yelled, "Open up, ya think I wanna freeze out here?"

A split second was all he had, Farrell realized. "Hippo, you want a lot of dough?"

The man's big, stupid face turned slowly, facing into the cutting snow. "Dough? Me? Wha' for?"

"Didn't you see how anxious your boss was to get hold of that affidavit? Imagine what he'd pay for a picture of it!"

Then the car door opened and Hippo pushed him into the back. Too soon for the man's slow wits to have had a chance to respond? Too soon to save his life? That was the big question.

**V**

Even New York becomes quiet when snow descends, and the occasional car horn that honked sounded lonely and lost. They drove through the almost deserted streets, and it took a while for Farrell to get his bearings. The heat inside the car made fog cover the windows, and it was through the gray, dimmed glass that he finally saw the superstructure of the old, tired Brooklyn Bridge rise up out of the night. Its iron framework looked spidery with the snow and ice glinting on it. It looked as if it might collapse at any moment.

Hippo sat very close to him in the back seat, his left hand in his overcoat pocket, the iron of the gun gouging into Farrell's side. In the front seat Champ drove slowly and carefully, taking no chances on being stopped by a traffic cop.

The car drove across the slippery, slick bridge and Farrell could see the city behind him as it rose like a painted backdrop out of the flatness of the East River.

How many times, he wondered, had these two men, and others like them, driven on midnight errands with death as the payoff?

Why hadn't Hippo responded? It could not be that he was incorruptible, because that is a virtue not often found in the mobs. Perhaps, Farrell thought, he was due to die because the man's moronic mind had not seen the possibility that had been extended to him.

Hippo hadn't. That was only too clear.

The car was hastening away from the bridge, down into the

tenement section that hides its shame in the shadows of the richest city in the world. All around them, old law tenements, crowded and filthy, looked down on refuse laden streets.

At any other time, without the snow, the streets would have been crowded with people for whom there is no waking room in the stinking hovels where they eat and sleep. But now the cold had cleared the streets and only an occasional gaunt alley cat minced by on careful feet as the slow-moving car headed toward a vacant lot.

The car stopped.

Champ turned around and said, "Hippo go take a gander. Be sure nobody's around." On the corner near them a broken street lamp made the darkness heavy.

Hippo left the car and as he did so, Champ drew a gun, and leaning it on the back of the seat said, "Just don't move."

"Can I have a cigarette?"

Looking out the windows, making sure that there was no danger of being seen Champ slowly nodded. "Yeah, go ahead."

Pulling the smoke down in his lungs, Farrell took his last chance. He said, "Wouldn' it put you in good with the boss to know Hippo double-crossed him tonight?"

Dead silence.

Outside could be heard Hippo's heavy-footed return to the car. Inside, Farrell could smell the rancid stink of his own fear. It was heavy, almost palpable. It rose from him in waves.

"What do you mean?" Champ asked, his face saying nothing.

"Look in Hippo's jacket pocket. He found the picture on me and stashed it when you and the boss weren't looking."

Opening the car door, Hippo said, "We use wire. We don't have to ditch our guns. Okay, Champ?"

Death by strangulation. A wire fastened to his ankles and wrists, a gag in his mouth, the wire arranged so that the slightest move on his part tightened the wire around his neck. Stuffed in a sack, thrown in a deserted, vacant lot, to be found the next day . . . Farrell's teeth almost met through his bottom lip. He'd force their hand before he'd stand still for that. He'd make them shoot him. A bullet anywhere could not be as bad as the wire.

Hippo crowded into the front seat and repeated, "We use wire, huh?"

"Lemme see your jacket pocket, Hippo," Champ said flatly.

"You flipped?"

"I said lemme see your pocket, Hippo." The gun still rested on the top of the seat.

Champ held it so that swiveling it a matter of inches from where it was pointed at Farrell's head, he could cover Hippo.

Brutish puzzlement on his unformed features, Hippo opened his overcoat and held the top of his jacket pocket open. Champ reached across Hippo's heavy body and his hand darted into the pocket.

It came out holding the tiny piece of dynamite.

"Where'd that come from?" Hippo asked.

The sight on the muzzle of the gun ripped a zigzag line down Hippo's forehead. Champ said, "Nice. Very nice."

Hippo said, "What the hell you think you're doin'?"

This time the gun muzzle caught him on the jaw and the dull crack of it was loud in the silence of the car.

The man's body slumped forward and as Champ pulled back to avoid it, Farrell threw himself forward. His arm looped out and around Champ's neck. His other hand snatched at the gun. Pulling back as hard as he could, he cut off all air from Champ's straining lungs. His other hand wrestled with the gun that Champ was trying to bring up toward him.

One thrashing hand seemed to come out of nowhere, and in the tension of the struggle, it took a moment for Farrell to realize that this was Champ's other hand, the one that didn't hold the gun.

It was clenched into a fist at first, but as Farrell pulled his garroting arm tighter and tighter, the fist opened and the little picture that Champ had been holding onto, even in the course of a fight for his life, slipped from his fingers and a vagrant draft carried it out of the open window to the left of the steering wheel.

Farrell had to force himself to resist the desire to let go of the Champ and grab for the picture. But he dared not relax for an instant. The gun was creeping higher now, almost turned directly at his face.

The little bit of paper slipped and drifted, flying farther and farther away from the car, and the silent struggle that was going on. The sound of the shot might have been a car backfiring. The snow muffled it, depriving it of all menace.

The bullet went out the back window splintering it, and then was lost in the night.

Inside the car, Farrell's face stung from the powder burn, but even the flash of the explosion was not enough to make him let go. The shot had just missed his forehead.

Champ's eyes were bulging now. It had taken his last bit of strength to pull the trigger. Farrell had no trouble in sinking his teeth into the man's wrist which served to keep the gun in the hand pointing past him.

Locked like lovers in an embrace that seemed to go on forever, Farrell prayed that Champ would pass out before Hippo came to.

There was a sudden relaxing of Champ's muscles and before Farrell could wonder if the man was playing possum, he let go his strangle hold. Champ's head fell forward and crashed into the wheel right in front of him.

Wresting the gun from the now flaccid hand, Farrell spat bits of hair and skin out of his mouth and raising the gun crashed it down on Champ's head and then on Hippo's.

Only then did he open the car door, and with sudden weakness flooding through him, he retched.

By then, the little photograph was long gone.

Standing near the car, Farrell looked around him. Enough snow had fallen since the picture drifted out the window so that the little bit of paper might have been right at his feet and he would never have been able to see it through the mantle of snow.

Sighing a little, he walked around the car and pushed Champ further over so that his unconscious body lurched into Hippo's. Then Farrell entered the car, turned the key, and put the car in gear.

All he wanted to do was drive to the nearest police station and deposit his bundles there, but he could not forget the dying man's whisper that . . . the police are iced....

Driving across a snow-covered bridge with two limp bodies next to you, Farrell found, is not the easiest thing in the world. But he made it and when the car drove off the Manhattan end of the bridge, he parked it near an all-night coffee pot. Through the blurred glass he could see a telephone booth, and that was the goal to which he was forcing his exhausted body.

He found on reaching into his pocket that he had three coins. A quarter, a dime, and a penny. Using the dime, he called information and snorted when she said, as she gave him the District Attorney's office number, "Please write this down so you won't have to call information again."

Memorizing the number he waited till his coin was returned. The steam on the windows of the coffee pot prevented him from seeing how his passengers in the car outside were faring, but he was so exhausted that he could not even worry about them.

Fear was gone, and sorrow too. Maybe, he thought, you can't make room for too many strong emotions at one time. Fear of dying had somehow washed away the agony of his wife's death.

And now that he was not in imminent danger of being murdered he found that he could be almost casual about himself. A man's voice interrupted his thoughts. "D A's office, Lonergan speaking."

"One of your men was murdered tonight."

The phone was silent.

"I saw him shot down in a bar on Forty-seventh Street."

"Yes. Will you come down to our office, please? We need witnesses."

"I think I know why he was killed."

Again silence. This joker wasn't putting out a thing. Farrell was a little irritated. He snapped, "Who is Anthony Augustino?"

That did it. The man on the other end of the phone said, excitedly, "He's the racket leader, O'Brien. We've tried to deport him for ten years. Why?"

"Then you better get up to the shooting gallery on Forty-seventh Street and Broadway and impound the first Photomaton machine you come to as you enter the place. You know the ones that give you three pictures for a quarter?"

"Yes, yes, but why?"

"I don't know when they empty the machines and get rid of the negatives. But I took a picture tonight of all you'll ever need to get rid of O'Brien."

"Who are you? Where are you?"

"No time for that, I have some of O'Brien's pigeons in a car outside a coffee pot down near Brooklyn Bridge." Farrell paused then said, "As a matter of fact, if you don't want to deport O'Brien, I can make out a good case of attempted murder on myself and I think I can tie the killing of your man right straight to O'Brien."

"What a Christmas present this'll be for the DA!" The man chuckled, then said, "Stay right there, give me the address and I'll be there before you know it."

Giving the man the information, Farrell realized that he could use some steaming coffee. Ordering a cup, he drained it at a gulp, paid a nickel for it, then went back out into the snow, his hand on Champ's gun to wait for help.

No sense in taking a chance on the two men reviving. No sense at all.

Standing there in the quiet of the street, the snow falling gently on his head and shoulders, he smiled a wry, tight grin, and reaching into his pocket, took out the last money he had in the world. It was exactly six cents—a nickel and a penny. He juggled it in his hand for a moment and then one by one he tossed the coins down the street, watching them skitter along the pavement.

Flat broke, he might be, but the mechanical fortune teller had been right. "Continue as you have been and your life will be happy, contented, and long."

If he couldn't make some dough and a new start out of what had happened to him tonight, he deserved to end up in the gutter. A man in his position, who had once been a lawyer, should be able to do real well on the DA's staff in a city like New York.

He didn't know how contented or happy he'd be because that was in the lap of the gods. But he wanted to live again and that suddenly was very important.

Through the fleecy snow he could see an official-looking car racing toward him.

He waved to it to let the driver know where he was.

The door of the car opened and an assistant district attorney stepped out of the car. He said, "You're a real skinny Santa Claus, but the DA will fatten you up."

Then they got to work.

# The Devil Was Sick

It had been eons since a really violent patient had been forcibly carried across the threshold of the Sane Asylum. So much time had passed since the brave motto was first cast in endlessly enduring crysto-metal and placed at the entrance door that passersby no longer paused to read the words. A VILLAIN IS JUST A SICK HERO.... Once a brave challenge to the unknown, passing time had changed them to a cliché. The motto had been proved true and therefore it was no longer worth consideration. But the words stayed on—until the day that Acleptos took chisel in hand and changed two of them.

It began because the problem of finding a new subject for a thesis had become harder to solve than getting a degree. Acleptos, by dint of a great deal of research, had found three subjects which he hoped the Machine would accept as being original. He gulped a little as he presented his list to the all-seeing eye of the calculator. The list read: "Activated sludge and what the ancients did about it." "The downfall of democracy and why it came about." "Devils and demons."

The Machine barely paused before it said, "In 4357 Jac Bard wrote the definitive work on activated sludge. Two hundred years later the last unknown component in regard to the downfall of democracy was analyzed to the utmost by the historian Hermios." There was a tiny wait. Acleptos held his breath. If his last subject had been collected, annotated and written about in its entirety it might mean twenty years' work finding more possible subjects. The Machine said, "There are two aspects of devils and demons that have not been presented to me so far. These are, whether they were real or hallucinatory, and if real, what they were. If hallucinatory, how brought about."

New life and hope surged through Acleptos. He braced his narrow shoulders and walked away from the Machine. At last . . . after so many years, he now had a chance. Of course, the thought brought him up short, there was still a chance that he might not be able to throw any new light on the problem of the reality of devils and demons. But that at least was something he could work on. The years spent at the reels, the work he had done going through almost all provinces of human knowledge had at last paid off.

A decade ago, the last time he had presented a list to the Machine, he had been so sure that he had found a subject when he had discovered references in some old reels to something or someone who was referred to as "God." It had been the capitalization of the "g" that had caught his eye in the first place. But the Machine had given him an endless number of theses on the subject, including one written about a thousand years prior, that had proved conclusively the non-existence of such a being. This thesis, the Machine felt, had ended all future speculations on the subject.

Out of curiosity Acleptos had checked the reference and was in complete accord, as he always was, with the Machine's summation.

It had been a stroke of genius thinking of the antithesis to God. Acleptos grinned to himself. There was no holding him back now. He would do his research, get his degree and then . . . then there would be no holding him back. He would be able to quit the Earth and go on to his next step. He threw his head back and looked at the sky. To the stars, that was the way it went. You were earthbound till you had done some original piece of research, but with that finished you were allowed to migrate anywhere you wanted to go.

There was a planet out back of Alpha Centauri that she had chosen. And she had promised that no matter how long the time, she would wait till he came. He didn't think he had ever been so depressed in his long life as he had been on the day that the Machine had passed on her thesis. For a long while it had seemed as if he had lost her completely. But now the years no longer seemed endless. His search had been fruitful.

Whistling, he entered the reel room and got to work. Pressing the button that was lettered d-e-m to d-e-v he waited until the intricate relay system had performed its function. With a low clatter the needed reels popped out of the pneumatic tube.

Three weeks later he felt that he had as much knowledge on the subject of demons, devils and the long-legged-beasties-that-go-bump-in-the-night as any human had ever had. He shook his head. To think that man had ever been so low on the scale as to believe such things. Incredible. But then, it was long ago.

He had been forced to work the translating machine overtime. Latin had been the language of much of the lore. To think that after all his years of studying he had never even heard of demons before! What garbage! He was indignant to think that there had ever been a time when *homo sapiens* had believed such trash.

He shrugged. Time to get to work on the basic problem. His closest friend, Ttom, walked into the research Laboratory. He had been so busy he had not even checked with Ttom. He hadn't even told him of his success in finding a subject!

"What in...." Ttom looked around the spotless green room. On the crystal table a stuffed alligator eyed him unblinkingly. Resting against the horny hide were oddly shaped vessels; surrounding the saurian were boxes and trays of powders. On the wall a weather machine was saying: "The moon will be full tonight and . . ." Acleptos switched it off.

"You've come just in time to watch!" he said jubilantly.

"Watch what?" Ttom's round face puckered up like a fat baby's. He said, "You've done it! You've found a subject! Acleptos! I'm so glad!"

"Thanks," Acleptos said, "and you?"

"Still nothing." But Ttom was too happy for his friend to remain dejected. He asked, "What in the universe did you stumble on?"

"Devils and demons," Acleptos said and went back to mixing some of the powders on the table.

"What are they?"

"A primitive superstition. My job is to find out if they were real, or if they were just another name for bad, or sick people."

"How are you going to do it? What are all those odds and ends?" Ttom asked.

"I'm just going to follow the formula in some old manuscripts and see what happens. It's deadly dull, really, but it's a subject!"

He had worked hard getting all the bizarre things together that the manuscripts called for, but he looked at the table—he now had everything he needed. Tonight, at midnight, with the moon full.... Aloud he said, "A lot of elements go into the 'conjuration of demons'. If you want to wait around and watch you may find it interesting."

"Sure. I have nothing to do. I thought I had a lead but as usual someone else had beaten me to it. Acleptos," Ttom asked, "what's going to happen when there are no more fields of human knowledge, when there are no new subjects to explore, when no more theses may be written?"

"I wondered about that, often, until I discovered demons.... But I think it's a long way off in the future and the Machine will take care of that eventuality when it arises, I'm sure."

"I'm beginning to think the time is now. Really, Acleptos, you're the first one who's found a subject in five years!" Ttom tried to keep any note of bitterness out of his voice.

"I know what the Machine would say, Ttom." Acleptos mixed some red liquid into a tube and added some violet powder to it. "The Machine would say that if I found a subject, so can you."

Ttom groaned. "I guess you're right. However, let's forget about me. What happens now?"

"Nothing until midnight. Then, when the moon is full, I will chant certain words, light those black fatty things . . . they're called candles, and then I wait for a devil or a demon to appear." They both laughed.

At midnight, with smiles still pulling at the corners of their mouths, Ttom sat outside the peculiar thing that Acleptos had drawn on the floor. It was called a pentacle. Acleptos had placed a black candle in each of its angles. He had burned foul-smelling chemicals and he was now chanting in some gibberish.

It was amusing at first, but as time dragged on both men became impatient. Nothing happened. Acleptos stopped chanting and said, "Well, I know the answer to the Machine's first question. Demons are hallucinatory and not real."

That was when it happened.

There was a smell in the room much worse than the chemicals. Then a sort of grey luminescence coalesced near the diagram on the floor.

Acleptos yelled, "Ttom, I forgot. The old books say that you have to be inside the pentacle to be protected from . . . whatever this is!"

Leaping to his feet, Ttom jumped for the line nearest him. Just before he got there the thing had become solid. It raised its folded lids and when its eyes hit him there was such concentrated malevolence in them that Ttom felt something he had never experienced before. It was only because of his reading that he knew that the sensation was something called fear.

The thing said, "Finally."

Even its voice grated on the nerves. Acleptos was stunned. He had performed the experiment because that was the way one found out things, but that it should be successful was beyond his wildest imaginings.

The thing rubbed its odd fingers which had far too many joints for comfort and said, "All these thousands of years. Waiting . . . Waiting in the greyness for a call that never came. At first I thought that He had won—but if that had been the case I would not have been."

It shrugged its scaly shoulders and opened its red eyes more fully. They were fascinating. The pupils alternately waxed and waned like little crimson moons. It looked from Acleptos to Ttom and said, "So nothing has changed. The adept and the sacrifice, just the way it used to be." Its chuckle was unseemly.

"And what reward," the thing looked at Acleptos, "do you want in exchange for this present?"

Ttom had never been called a present before and he found that he did not care for it particularly.

It did not wait for Acleptos to answer. Instead it rubbed its too-long fingers together. The grating sound was the only one in the room. It eyed Acleptos and said, "I see. Nothing *has* changed. A woman. Very well, here she is."

It made an odd series of gestures in the air and—before Acleptos could clear his throat to say no—she was there. She looked frightened. Her hair was as lovely as he remembered it. So was her body. She was naked, as he would have predicted since the planet she had chosen was a warm one. There was no shame in her pose, just fear.

"Send her back! How dare you drag her across interstellar space! You fool! You might have killed her!" He had no fear of the thing now. His only fear was for his beloved. She vanished as she had appeared.

The thing grumbled. "I didn't see that you loved her. I thought it was just sex you wanted." It turned its eyes back towards Acleptos. "Gold? They always want gold...." It began to make the stereotyped gestures again.

Acleptos realized that he had lost control of the situation which was ridiculous. He cleared his throat and said, "Enough!"

The thing paused in its occupation, and if it had been able to show any expression at all it would have been surprise. It said, "Now what? How can I get gold for you if you keep interrupting?"

Acleptos was angry. Anger, like the fear that had preceded it, was a new emotion. He said, "Stand perfectly still. I am the master and you the slave." That was in the directions he had read. He didn't quite know what a master or a slave was, but the book had seemed to specify those words.

The thing held its misshapen head still as its eyes wandered over Ttom's body hungrily.

Controlling his new-found emotion Acleptos said, "You don't seem to understand. I don't want any gold, whatever that is."

Ttom said, "I remember that word from my reading. The ancients used to change it into lead or some valuable metal like that."

Acleptos went on, "And I didn't want her dragged back from Alpha Centauri!"

"Power!" the thing said and this time it almost seemed to grin. "That never fails. If they're too old for sex and too rich for gold, they always want power." Its hands began to move again.

"STOP!" Acleptos yelled, for the first time in his life.

The thing froze.

Acleptos said, "Don't do that again, it makes me . . . uneasy! I don't want power and don't tell me what it is because I'm not interested. Now just stand there and answer some questions."

The thing seemed to shrink a little. It said almost querulously, "But . . . what did you summon me for? If you don't want anything from me, I can't take anything from you...." It rolled its eyes at Ttom.

"I just want some information. How long do you crea . . . devils live?"

"Live? Forever, of course."

"And what is your function?"

"To tempt man from the path of righteousness."

The words came out clearly enough but Acleptos just couldn't understand what they meant. However, it was all being recorded so he would be able to go back over it all and make sense of it later.

"Why would you want to do that?" Acleptos asked.

The demon peered at him as though doubting his sanity. It said, "In order that man have free will. He must be able to choose between good and evil."

"What are they? Those words, good and evil?"

The demon sat down on its heels, disregarding the spurs that sank into its own buttocks. It said, "All those years . . . sitting in the greyness and to be summoned for this." It shook its head. Suddenly it seemed to come to some kind of decision. Springing to its feet it made a dash for Ttom.

Simultaneously Acleptos raised the force gun he had kept by his side. He pressed the button. The creature froze and then fell face forward on the floor.

Ttom gulped. He said, "I thought you were never going to use that. I'll call the Sane Asylum and have them send for this poor, sick creature right away."

Nodding, Acleptos said, "This has turned out to be much more interesting than I would have predicted." He busied himself with his thoughts till the ambu-bus arrived. It was the first hurry call the Asylum had had in a century but the machines functioned perfectly.

Ttom and Acleptos watched the robots pick up the thing and cradle it in their metal arms. They went along as the androids placed it in the ambu-bus and flew towards the Asylum.

Halfway there Acleptos spoke for the first time. He said, "Do you see the terrible irony implicit in all this?"

"What do you mean?" Ttom still stared at the thing which lay stretched out as though in death.

"These devils, do you realize what they are?" The words spilled out of Acleptos. "They're just other-dimensional beings. Somehow, sometime, a human back in medieval times stumbled on the mathematics of causing them to cross dimensions. Not knowing what he was doing, shrouded in superstition, he thought that the mumbo jumbo was what called them up. He didn't realize that the diagram and the heat of the candles and words of the chant all combined to make a key to open the lock of that other dimension."

"It sounds reasonable but where is there any irony in that?"

Acleptos sounded ready to weep. He said, "Don't you see? Here was humanity struggling through the centuries when all the time they had darker brothers right near them who were immortal who could conquer space by merely setting their hands in the right pattern.... But man, blinded by his superstitious beliefs, was unable to learn from these 'devils'. The worst irony is, however, that the 'devils' couldn't help man because they are idiots...."

Ttom nodded. "An almost imbecile race with incredible powers living right next door to us and we never knew it. The Machine is right, there is much more for us to learn. I was wrong in thinking that all things are known."

Either the force gun wasn't set heavily enough or the "devil" had amazing recuperative powers, Acleptos thought, for as they got out of the ambu-bus the creature unfroze. It screamed as the robots tried to carry it across the threshold of the Sane Asylum.

It struggled so that even the metal muscles that animated the robots were strained. Acleptos saw its hands suddenly begin to move in that pattern.

He yelled to the robots who were restraining it, "Hold its hands!"

The metallic hands folded over the madly writhing too-many jointed fingers and the thing stopped its struggling. Ahead, a door opened and one of the doctors walked towards them.

He said, "What in the world is that?" As Acleptos explained, Ttom ran his fingers over the words of the motto on the door. He saw the words, his fingers felt them, but he had seen them too often. They didn't register on his mind.

When Acleptos finished, the doctor said, "I see. Well, we'll have it straightened out in no time. It will be quite a challenge trying to bring an other-dimensional creature to its senses!"

Acleptos asked, "Do you think it is sick or just stupid?"

The doctor smiled. "Sick, I'm sure. No well being would behave the way you have described its actions. Would you like to watch?"

"Of course. I am more than interested." Acleptos linked his arm in

Ttom's. "Imagine," he said, "if we can cure this one, it will mean communication with a whole race of the creatures. Isn't it wonderful?"

"Acleptos," Ttom sounded worried, "there's one thing we haven't considered. In all my reading, in all the data we have on the whole universe and all its creatures, I have never before heard of any that are immortal. Had you thought of that?"

"Yes, but it's just another proof of how right the Machine is in its assertion that we don't know everything. This is the most exciting thing that has ever happened to me! I can't wait till I tell her about it. Imagine how surprised she'll be to find that it was not a dream, that she was really here, warped through space and time by a sick creature who has lived, forever...."

In the operating room there were no scalpels, no sponges, no clamps. The robots had a firm grip on the thing as they stretched it out on the table. They never relaxed their hold on its hands.

The doctor picked up an instrument with an "S" shaped lens protruding from the front of it. A pulsating light came from it. The doctor bathed the thing in the light. He said, "This will only take a moment. That is, if it's going to work. If not, there are other alternatives."

The doctor's voice suddenly failed him. Acleptos backed away from the table. Ttom gasped. Only the robots were unimpressed.

For the thing was changing. Wherever the lambent light touched the creature, its scales fell away.

The doctor gasped to the robots, "Release your hold."

As they did so the creature arose in glory. A golden light played around its suddenly soft, sweet face. It stepped away from them towards the window. Standing on the windowsill, a smile played around its lips like a valedictory. It poised there for a moment and then spread its huge white wings.

It said, "*Pax vobiscum.*" The wings swirled and it was gone, wrapped in serenity.

That is why Acleptos changed the words of the motto in front of the Sane Asylum. They now read: A DEVIL IS JUST A SICK ANGEL.

Of course, the Machine has stopped. For its basis and its strength was infallibility. And it was wrong about the thesis concerning the existence of God with a capital G.

# The Last Magician

He was the last one. I guess there's always something interesting about the last anything. The last dinosaur, the last auto, the last gas-powered plane, yes, he fits right into that museum of last things. He was the last magician.

He was good, too. I've seen the old celluloids of the great ones of the past, Houdini, Blackstone and Thurston, and he was like all of them rolled into one and more, much more. They functioned in a time when people still had a hankering to believe that there was such a thing as magic but he burst forth in our time like a nova. He revived interest in his hanky-panky art and he scared the hell out of people. He may have been a charlatan and paranoid and all the other things they called him but he sure walloped the bejesus out of an audience and that's something very few performers do these days.

I never knew why he chose the place he did for his debut except that it was good publicity-wise and that was something that he knew all about. He could sure pick his shots when it came to attracting public attention.

You know what vaudeville has become in our time, an intellectual's plaything, a cult for the avant-garde. These vaudemanés sit and talk about tap dancers that were great hundreds of years ago and discuss crosstalk comics, whatever they were, and in general sit and drool about their dear, dear, dying art form.

I don't know much about art forms and I have a sneaking feeling that anything that can't support itself by public interest doesn't amount to much. Certainly vaudeville would be nonexistent if it wasn't subsidized by these cultists. But I made my living cooking up props for these phony shows and that was good enough for me. Until I joined Duneen as a prop man I had always worked with my hands and you know that means I'm good because you have to be better than a machine to get a license to work with your hands today.

But I was telling you about Duneen. He walked out on the little stage where we put on our "vaudevilles," completely unannounced. His appearance sure made everyone sit up and take notice. Heaven knows where he got his outfit because it was a real costume piece.

Black cape swirling around his tall, lean frame; a curious kind of butterfly-shaped thing at his neck that was surrounded with a high white band, a completely nonfunctional jacket that was cut away in the front and dropped down like tails in the rear and a shirt that looked as if it was made of some stiff plastic. It would have looked funny on anyone else but it didn't on him.

I suppose the hair he had on his lip and chin was fake because all males have their face hair extirpated at puberty now, but I never saw him without it. He called the hair a mustache and goatee and it did strange things to his hollow cheeked face.

He walked out to the center of the stage and bowed obsequiously to the handful of avant-gardists that made up the audience. But somehow, even the bow, even the mock humility was an insult. It was as though he was just pretending to be humble because he knew he was superior. He could get under your skin like that in a million ways but I didn't learn that till later.

I could hear a little rustle in the audience as they looked through their programs trying to figure out who Duneen was. They didn't have much time for that though, because as he bowed he swept off his cape and gracefully showed both sides of it.

His curious lip-tilted grimace that was halfway between a smile and a sneer appeared as he draped the cape over his arm. Suddenly there was a form under it. When he whipped the cloth away a Martian girl, naked, stood shyly revealed. Duneen looked at the audience out of the corners of his eyes as though trying to gauge the effect and then plucked a wand out of the air. This is a long black stick with white tips. It is an adjunct that old time magicians always used.

Gesturing at the girl with the "wand" he then snapped his fingers. Suddenly a brassiere appeared clothing her breasts. Another snap of those long, thin fingers and her legs and thighs were covered. Then he gestured around her with the "wand" and she was fully dressed. The cloth seemed to come from nowhere, seemed to be produced at the tip of the "wand."

From then on she assisted him as you have seen her do on TV. The only reason I'm telling you about this first opening is that they never let him repeat it on the air. The Martian ambassador complained and there was some kind of a stink; I don't know what it was all about, but Duneen never started his show that way again.

You remember the rest of his act, of course; the sawing of the Martian girl in half with a G-ray and her restoration after which you would have sworn she was dead. The way he would cause her to vanish from a hermetically sealed rocket blast tube and the way he produced her from a previously shown empty Liane lizard shell. All these things became household words and that was just the trouble.

Just because he was the last of the magicians, just because he had such a terrific effect on show business, he had to keep topping himself. He had to keep inventing newer and more amazing tricks and it almost drove him crazy.

Then there was the other reason which had been true since the beginning of TV. TV is a bottomless maw into which entertainment is shoveled only to vanish like one of Duneen's tricks. Centuries ago, when the TV audience was just made up of millions of people, you could repeat yourself once in a while, I suppose, and figure that not everyone had caught you the first time. But now, when the audience is up in the hundreds of millions, the problem has become so bad that lots of performers crack under the strain.

The old-time magicians used to meet their audiences bit by bit through the years and if there was any overlapping it didn't matter very much. But now, today, you meet all the people in the world with one performance.

I've read in the old magic text books that magicians could, and did, do the same tricks over and over for the length of their professional careers. Imagine that!

But Duneen, of course, could never repeat himself; even once. He had to keep inventing more and more exciting variations on his basic tricks.

That was where I came in, me and my capable hands. I guess maybe I wouldn't have helped him if it hadn't been for Aydah, his Martian girl assistant—but I felt sorry for her. He was nasty to her most of the time, but he was at his worst when he was wracking his brain trying to cook up a new pseudo-miracle.

I heard her crying one day. Heard it right through even the thick walls of the dressing room at the TV studio. You could say it was none of my business but I busted in anyway and said, "Can I help, Aydah?"

You wouldn't think a girl seven feet tall and so thin that her veins stood out like cords could look wistful and appealing, but she did. Her bright red eyes were glistening with tears which she certainly could ill afford to waste, considering how dehydrated Martians are.

She said, "What can you do? What can anyone do?" Luckily she was sitting down, sort of scrunched over because I put her head on my shoulder and patted the long, thin white hair, which I certainly would not have been able to do without a ladder if she'd been standing, and said, "Tell me about it."

"Mr. Barrow," she gulped, "I guess I sort of love him or I wouldn't stay on—but how can I love and hate someone at the same time?"

I patted her head and was silently sorry for her.

She asked, "Don't you know? I've read all the Earth books I could find, all that have anything to do with love and I can't find any answer." She sobbed, "They don't explain it at all. Can't you tell me?"

That was a poser all right. I'm past the age where sex or love or any of that sort of nonsense means very much to me, but I have a good memory....

"Whatever possessed you to fall for an Earthman, Aydah?" It was a stupid question but I was just making conversation.

She lowered her head and rested it on my chest. I kept patting it sort of ineffectually while she talked. "I don't really know. He came along when I was the right age and mother had always kept me away from Martian boys. She kept saying I wasn't old enough.... she didn't see any danger in an Earthman, I guess. But Duneen isn't fat like you, Mr. Barrow, or like most Earth people. He's almost as thin and handsome as a Martian. And he can talk so beautifully . . . when he wants to." She was off in racking sobs again.

That was when Duneen stalked in. He was in high, low and medium dudgeon. He said, "Why you—Martian guttersnipe! I take you in and this is the way you behave the first time my back is turned. Carrying on with an old man! Why you . . ."

He looked all set to beat her up so I intervened. "Look, Duneen, you know that I've come up with some good ideas for your show."

He nodded. At least I had his attention. I went on quickly, "I think I have a brand-new idea for an escape."

Jealousy faded before his interest in a new trick. He asked, "What's the gag?"

"You've escaped from every kind of gadget that anyone could think up. You've challenged people to think of restraints that will hold you for more than five minutes, right?"

"Of course," Duneen said impatiently. "I've escaped from things that would have killed that old-timer, Houdini!" He grunted. "That old faker! I get mad every time I read about him!"

He did too. He seemed to be furious because he had come too late in time to match wits with the great magicians of the earlier days. He felt, and I guess he was right, that he could have topped any of them.

"What is it?" he asked impatiently, turning back to face Aydah.

I said quickly, "How about escaping from a Klein bottle?"

"What? What's that?"

I sighed. Sometimes his stupidity about anything outside of his own field appalled me. I made it as simple as I could. "Look," I said, picking up a narrow strip of paper, "you know what a Möbius strip is?"

He looked unsure so I glued one end of the strip to the other end making the half twist in the paper that has to be made in order for the topological principle to work. Using a pencil I showed him how a line could be drawn on both sides of the paper despite the fact that I didn't lift the pencil from the paper. I said, "See? It's a one-sided figure!"

He grunted. "Oh that!" He picked up a pair of scissors and cut around the loop of paper. It formed into two interlocked circles, of course. He said, "This is the Afghan bands. Why didn't you say so?"

"Maybe that's what magicians used to call it," I said, "but it's a Möbius strip and it will help . . ."

He was scowling now, all thought of Aydah gone from his mind. He asked, "What's all this got to do with me? I can't escape from a strip of paper. That's ridiculous!"

"No, of course not. But if you think of this strip of paper as a two-dimensional object that has strange properties because of the twist in it, which is in the third dimension, it will help you to think about the Klein bottle."

He raised his eyebrows.

"Look," I said, "a Klein bottle is a fourth dimensional equivalent of the Möbius strip. Picture a bottle made out of a hard rubbery substance. Now bend the neck of the bottle down and around, and push the mouth of the bottle through the side of the bottle without breaking the surface of the bottle."

He really wasn't too stupid. He said, "That's the point at which it goes through the fourth dimension, eh?"

"Yes, now suppose I made up a bottle like that big enough for you to get into . . ."

"So what's so good about escaping from a bottle? That has no drama, no excitement!"

"You don't get it! According to topological laws which were proved the first time they made a real Klein bottle 50 years ago, a fly walking on the surface of the bottle is on the inside-outside of the bottle and can never get in or out of the bottle. Any school boy knows that!"

He whistled through his teeth. "I think you have something there. Not that the basic idea is much good, but I'll build on it. I'll make this the most sensational escape that has ever been done. Houdini!

Phooey!" A sudden thought stopped him. "What's the gaff?"

I said, "Huh?" But I knew what he meant. He always irritated me, using show business terms that had been obsolete for many years, although I've noticed lately that he has me doing it too.

"What's the gaff," he repeated, "how do I escape the fate of the fly?"

"You're not thinking, Duneen. If you ever climbed into a real Klein bottle that would be the end of you. You'd be alive-dead. Halfway between here and the fourth dimensional world you'd be stranded!"

"So?" he asked.

"So we have to rig up a substitute bottle. A fake."

"Okay, it's a deal. You get to work on it." He turned his attention back to Aydah. He said, "Now you, listen to me!" She cowered away from him.

She had to listen to him. I didn't. I left but I was mad. Bullying Aydah was about on a par with kicking a sick puppy. If I could, I would have taken a punch at him, not that it would have done any good.

He could sneer all he wanted to at Houdini and the other old-timers but he had learned their lessons well. His publicity on the Klein bottle escape was a masterpiece. By the time I had constructed the two bottles, the real and the fake one, he had everyone talking about Klein bottles and how foolhardy he was, how he was defying the most dreadful fate a man had ever faced. He planted pieces in the news about topology. He had planes drop hundreds of thousands of Möbius strips and each strip had DUNEEN DEFIES DEATH! lettered on it along with instructions about the strip. He bombarded the press services with handouts. He challenged Miklav and Ronner, the two top topologists of the day, to figure out how he would escape. He bet them 10,000 credits that he would escape in five minutes, with a proviso that he would pay a thousand credits a minute to their favorite charity for every minute over five that he was stuck in the bottle.

The harder he worked the worse he treated Aydah. I had to keep out of the way or I would have hung a punch on his long, aquiline nose.

It seemed as if every time I turned around I'd find her hiding in some corner, crying. The loss of water through her tears began to tell on her. I finally had to call in a doctor and have some saline solution injected intravenously or she would have just faded away. It was when she was stretched out getting the intravenous that I first noticed that her ordinarily concave stomach was getting a little convex.

I guess that was when I began to get really mad at Duneen. Mad enough to do something about the whole bloody mess . . .

But she never really complained, not out loud anyway. That one outburst to me was all. She would just mope around and look at Duneen hopefully, and then her eyes would fill up with tears and off she'd go for another quiet cry.

I tell you it got me down. But there was nothing I could do, not even when I found out what was back of it all. I spotted Duneen one night with another girl, an Earth girl, but I couldn't see where it would do any good to tell Aydah that. So I just kept busy on my props, getting everything ready and keeping my fingers crossed.

If you were anywhere within eyesight of a TV set that night you saw what happened, at least from out front. But I know what happened backstage and that's what I wanted to tell you about.

Everything went off like clockwork and you can believe me when I say that he was magnificent. With all his faults, with all his pettiness, despite his charlatanry, or maybe because of it, he was great. The last of the magicians and the greatest!

Naturally, he didn't open with the escape. That was to be his climax. He prefaced it with little run-of-the-mill items like an endless production of Martian geezers, those cute little six-legged creatures with the red eyes and white hair. They always reminded me of Aydah and that night I was more aware of the resemblance as he kept reaching into his tall hat and producing the little things as though the supply was endless. Then it was pure poetry when he plucked obsolete coins of every denomination out of the air and sent them clattering into a metal bowl. You know: parlor tricks, simple little things, but he did them with such an air!

Backstage the technicians kept a wary eye on the real Klein bottle which I had ready. I could see that they wanted no part of it or of the fate of the man who was supposed to escape from it.

When Duneen was sure that he had milked every bit of suspense out of his act he stopped and held up his hands in that corny, theatrical gesture of his and said, "Ladies and gentlemen, next—I present the challenge escape of all time! I shall enter a Klein bottle...."

He gestured at it as it was wheeled on stage. There was no sound as the stage hands placed a three-fold screen around the bottle. Duneen went on, "I will escape from that bottle in five minutes or . . ." He was a good enough showman not to finish the sentence.

He had Miklav and Donner come on stage and examine the bottle. They seemed oddly out of place, these men of science, these topologists, as they examined the bottle.

Duneen said, "Gentlemen, do you agree that the bottle is a true Klein bottle?" They nodded.

Duneen went off stage. He was sure enough of himself to leave the stage empty while he changed into trunks. His excuse was to show that he had no gadgets on his person to aid him. He always performed his escapes that way. But I never thought that this was the real reason he stripped. I think he liked to hear the shocked gasp when people saw his skeletally thin frame. Of all earthmen I've ever seen, he came closest to looking like a Martian. Seeing him that way I could understand a little better why Aydah had fallen in love with him.

I was off stage, left. I had nothing to do but keep an eye on things. Nothing much could go wrong because I had decided that the best way to switch the real and the fake Klein bottles would, after all, be the simplest way. I had made two trapdoors in the stage. I don't suppose anyone has used traps for tricks for centuries. That's why I was sure the hoary old gag would fool the audience. Duneen agreed with me and he was never wrong about what would fool people.

The arrangement was merely this. The real Klein bottle was on stage and would stay there until the experts had examined it and pronounced it to be indubitably what it was, a fourth dimensional bottle. Once they had pronounced it legitimate, Duneen would conceal it behind a threefold screen; pressure on a button would activate the trapdoors. The real bottle would sink out of sight. A fake Klein bottle, which looked real enough but did not have the properties of the topological figure, would rise up to replace the genuine one.

As you can see, the mechanics of the trick were a cinch. But, according to Duneen, that was the real secret of good magic. Complexity, he maintained, is no good. People can dope it out. You must use a simple device, so simple that your audience discards it as a possibility just because of its simplicity.

Duneen stood next to me in the wings, breathing deeply, bracing himself for his appearance on stage. The button that made the trapdoors work was near us, on the wall. He pressed the button. Aydah ran over to join us as, outside, on stage, the announcer was saying, "And now—we have the honor and privilege of presenting . . ." There was a long drum roll and then, "Duneen!"

That was the cue. He stalked out on stage. Aydah was next to me. We both watched him. Duneen was bowing to the audience. He blew a kiss to a girl who was sitting down front. She was the earth girl I had seen him with. I was near enough to Aydah to feel her thin body stiffen. Then she did know about Duneen and . . .

On stage center Duneen motioned for the stagehands to remove the screen that had masked the man-sized bottle. He gestured at it. His grin was at its most sardonic as he lifted one of his spidery legs and placed it around the shoulder of the bottle. The stagehands stood ready with the screen and as he nodded to them they stepped forward with it. He lifted his other leg preparatory to mounting the bottle like a horse.

Aydah shivered and then sobbed, "I can't . . . I can't let him do it!" The screen was almost around the magician now. She reached over my shoulder and tried to press the button that would switch the bottle.

"What are you doing?" I asked.

"I . . ." Her eyes were frantic. "I can't do it! I switched the bottles before! That's the *real* Klein bottle he's . . ."

It was too late to press the button. She said hastily, "I'll go tell him to stall! Then when the screen hides him completely, you press the button and switch back the fake bottle! How could I have been so cruel!" She ran out on stage.

Darting to his side she whispered to him. Even then, with the eyes of the world on him, he almost cuffed her. I saw his hand start up, saw her back away, before he caught himself and remembered where he was. He managed to turn his grimace of hatred into a smile as he turned to face the audience.

"Ladies and gentlemen, my 'invaluable' assistant tells me that there are some reporters backstage who would like to be out here as a committee. I extend my welcome to them!"

It was a good stall. I don't think anyone knew what had really happened. The stagehands surrounded the bottle with the screen while Duneen bowed to the reporters.

Aydah ran to my side. "Press the button."

She watched me while I did so and then turned and made a motion for Duneen to proceed. The side of his face to the audience was smiling, but there was black and bitter loathing in his eyes when he turned away.

He faced the bottle again. The screen was brought forward. Mounting the bottle, his arms and legs straddled the shoulder of it. Then, as he allowed himself to slide down towards the spot where the mouth of the bottle went through the side of it, a curious thing happened.

He seemed to become rubbery. One moment he was all on the outside of the bottle, the next, a cross section of him seemed to be inside it. That was all anyone saw as the screen cut off the view.

Aydah sobbed at my side. "Let him go to her. I have no hold on him. We're not married . . . we could never marry, not with the law about miscegenation between Mars and Earth people. Let her have him."

"None," I agreed, "except for the fact that he has condemned you to death!"

Involuntarily she looked down at her little belly. Then she looked at me. "You knew?"

"Sure, I could see you were pregnant a month ago. And there's no escape from the death penalty for miscegenation." I patted her shoulder. "He should have had you aborted while there was still time."

"It's too late now," she said and turned her back. I knew that as well as she did.

On stage the reporters were eyeing their watches. The music, keyed for suspense, was getting nerve wracking as the minutes dragged by. The audience became restive. The two professors of topology looked frightened. One of them, I think it was Miklav, broke away from a friend who tried to restrain him. Miklav shouted, "What do I care about any bet! That man is in trouble!"

He shoved aside the screen and, of course, he was right. Duneen was in real bad trouble. He was half in and half out of the Klein bottle. He was on the inside-outside, never-come-right-side of the bottle. There he was, and there he is now. In the museum with all the other last things. And there he'll stay. They can't break the bottle because that would divide him. And since they can't break the bottle there he will remain, not alive and not dead— suspended midway between here and there. Wherever *there* is in the fourth dimension.

It isn't very pretty. But then neither was what he did to Aydah. I might have felt just a little pity for him, but I saw her die. She killed herself just before the authorities got around to it.

I knew she would have to die . . . That was why I had pressed the button that switched the bottles the first time, before she ever did . . . That cancelled out the later switch when she thought she was saving him . . . It made an odd sequence.

Get it? The real bottle was up there on the stage when the topologists looked at it. I switched it for the fake one so, when Duneen made his switch, it was the real one that came up! Aydah almost screwed up the works when she pulled her switch and brought the fake bottle back up on stage. It turned out okay, though. She thought the real bottle was up there and when she begged me to make the change—the real Klein bottle was ready and waiting for Duneen!

Sometimes when I go the museum of last things to look at him, I think of the old stories about evil genies and the way they were stuffed into bottles. I guess I must be getting old; lately I've taken to wondering about King Solomon. He knew so much, I wonder if he knew about Klein bottles . . .

# Wolves Don't Cry

The naked man behind the bars was sound asleep. In the cage next to him a bear rolled over on its back, and peered sleepily at the rising sun. Not far away a jackal paced springily back and forth as though essaying the impossible, trying to leave its own stench far behind.

Flies were gathered around the big bone that rested near the man's sleeping head. Little bits of decaying flesh attracted the insects and their hungry buzzing made the man stir uneasily. Accustomed to instant awakening, his eyes flickered and simultaneously his right hand darted out and smashed down at the irritating flies.

They left in a swarm, but the naked man stayed frozen in the position he had assumed. His eyes were on his hand.

He was still that way when the zoo attendant came close to the cage. The attendant, a pail of food in one hand, a pail of water in the other, said, "Hi Lobo, up and at 'em, the customers'll be here soon." Then he too froze.

Inside the naked man's head strange ideas were stirring. His paw, what had happened to it? Where was the stiff gray hair? The jet-black steel-strong nails? And what was the odd fifth thing that jutted out from his paw at right angles? He moved it experimentally. It rotated. He'd never been able to move his dew claw, and the fact that he could move this fifth extension was somehow more baffling than the other oddities that were puzzling him.

"You goddamn drunks!" the attendant raved. "Wasn't bad enough the night a flock of you came in here, and a girl bothered the bear and lost an arm for her trouble, no, that wasn't bad enough. Now you have to sleep in my cages! And where's Lobo? What have you done with him?"

The naked figure wished the two-legged would stop barking. It was enough trouble trying to figure out what had happened without the angry short barks of the two-legged who fed him interfering with his thoughts.

Then there were many more of the two-leggeds and a lot of barking, and the naked one wished they'd all go away and let him think.

Finally the cage was opened and the two-leggeds tried to make him come out of his cage. He retreated hurriedly on all fours to the back of his cage towards his den.

"Let him alone," the two-legged who fed him barked. "Let him go into Lobo's den. He'll be sorry!"

Inside the den, inside the hollowed-out rock that so cleverly approximated his home before he had been captured, he paced back and forth, finding it bafflingly uncomfortable to walk on his naked feet. His paws did not grip the ground the way they should and the rock hurt his new soft pads.

The two-legged ones were getting angry, he could smell the emotion as it poured from them, but even that was puzzling, for he had to flare his nostrils wide to get the scent, and it was blurred, not crisp and clear the way he ordinarily smelled things. Throwing back his head, he howled in frustration and anger. But the sound was wrong. It did not ululate as was its wont. Instead he found to his horror that he sounded like a cub, or a female.

What had happened to him?

Cutting one of his soft pads on a stone, he lifted his foot and licked at the blood.

His pounding heart almost stopped.

This was no wolf blood.

Then the two-legged ones came in after him and the fight was one that ordinarily he would have enjoyed, but now his heart was not in it. Dismay filled him, for the taste of his own blood had put fear in him. Fear unlike any he had ever known, even when he was trapped that time, and put in a box, and thrown onto a wheeled thing that had rocked back and forth, and smelled so badly of two-legged things.

This was a new fear, and a horrible one.

Their barking got louder when they found that he was alone in his den. Over and over they barked, not that he could understand them, "What have you done with Lobo? Where is he? Have you turned him loose?"

It was only after a long time, when the sun was riding high in the summer sky, that he was wrapped in a foul-smelling thing and put in a four-wheeled object and taken away from his den.

He would never have thought, when he was captured, that he would ever miss the new home that the two-leggeds had given him, but he found that he did, and most of all, as the four-wheeled thing rolled through the city streets, he found himself worrying about his mate in the next cage. What would she think when she found him gone, and she just about to have a litter? He knew that most males did not worry about their young, but wolves were different. No mother wolf ever had to worry, the way female bears did, about a male wolf eating his young. No indeed; wolves were different.

And being different, he found that worse than being tied up in a cloth and thrown in the back of a long, wheeled thing was the worry he felt about his mate, and her young-to-be.

But worse was to come: when he was carried out of the moving thing, the two-legged ones carried him into a big building and the smells that surged in on his outraged nostrils literally made him cringe. There was sickness, and stenches worse than he had ever smelled, and above and beyond all other smells the odor of death was heavy in the long white corridors through which he was carried.

Seeing around him as he did ordinarily in grays and blacks and whites, he found that the new sensations that crashed against his smarting eyeballs were not to be explained by anything he knew. Not having the words for red, and green, and yellow, for pink and orange and all the other colors in a polychromatic world, not having any idea of what they were, just served to confuse him even more miserably.

He moaned.

The smells, the discomfort, the horror of being handled, were as nothing against the hurt his eyes were enduring.

Lying on a flat hard thing he found that it helped just to stare directly upwards. At least the flat covering ten feet above him was white, and he could cope with that.

The two-legged thing sitting next to him had a gentle bark, but that didn't help much.

The two-legged said patiently over and over again, "Who are you? Have you any idea? Do you know where you are? What day is this?"

After a while the barks became soothing, and nude no longer, wrapped now in a long wet sheet that held him cocoonlike in its embrace, he found that his eyes were closing. It was all too much for him.

He slept.

The next awakening was if anything worse than the first.

First he thought that he was back in his cage in the zoo, for directly ahead of him he could see bars. Heaving a sigh of vast relief, he wondered what had made an adult wolf have such an absurd dream. He could still remember his puppyhood when sleep had been made peculiar by a life unlike the one he enjoyed when awake. The twitchings, the growls, the sleepy murmurs—he had seen his own sons and daughters go through them and they had reminded him of his youth.

But now the bars were in front of him and all was well.

Except that he must have slept in a peculiar position. He was stiff, and when he went to roll over he fell off the hard thing he had been on and crashed to the floor.

Bars or no bars, this was not his cage.

That was what made the second awakening so difficult. For, once he had fallen off the hospital bed, he found that his limbs were encumbered by a long garment that flapped around him as he rolled to all fours and began to pace fearfully back and forth inside the narrow confines of the cell that he now inhabited.

Worse yet, when the sound of his fall reached the ears of a two-legged one, he found that some more two-leggeds hurried to his side and he was forced, literally forced, into an odd garment that covered his lower limbs.

Then they made him sit on the end of his spine and it hurt cruelly, and they put a metal thing in his right paw, and wrapped the soft flesh of his paw around the metal object and holding both, they made him lift some kind of slop from a round thing on the flat surface in front of him.

That was bad, but the taste of the mush they forced into his mouth was grotesque.

Where was his meat? Where was his bone? How could he sharpen his fangs on such food as this? What were they trying to do? Make him lose his teeth?

He gagged and regurgitated the slops. That didn't do the slightest bit of good. The two-leggeds kept right on forcing the mush into his aching jaws. Finally, in despair, he kept some of it down.

Then they made him balance on his hind legs.

He'd often seen the bear in the next cage doing this trick and sneered at the big fat oaf for pandering to the two-leggeds by aping them. Now he found that it was harder than he would have thought. But finally, after the two-leggeds had worked with him for a long time, he found that he could, by much teetering, stand erect.

But he didn't like it.

His nose was too far from the floor, and with whatever it was wrong with his smelling, he found that he had trouble sniffing the ground under him. From this distance he could not track anything. Not even a rabbit. If one had run right by him, he thought, feeling terribly sorry for himself, he'd never be able to smell it, or if he did, be able to track it down, no matter how fat and juicy, for how could a wolf run on two legs?

They did many things to him in the new big zoo, and in time he found that, dislike it as much as he did, they could force him by painful expedients to do many of the tasks they set him.

That, of course, did not help him to understand why they wanted him to do such absurd things as encumber his legs with cloth that flapped and got in the way, or balance precariously on his hind legs, or any of the other absurdities they made him perform. But somehow he surmounted everything and in time even learned to bark a little the way they did. He found that he could bark *hello* and *I'm hungry* and, after months of effort, ask *why can't I go back to the zoo?*

But that didn't do much good, because all they ever barked back was *because you're a man*.

Now of many things he was unsure since that terrible morning, but of one thing he was sure: he *was* a wolf.

Other people knew it too.

He found this out on the day some outsiders were let into the place where he was being kept. He had been sitting, painful as it was, on the tip of his spine, in what he had found the two-leggeds called a chair, when some shes passed by.

His nostrils closed at the sweet smell that they had poured on themselves, but through it he could detect the real smell, the female smell, and his nostrils had flared, and he had run to the door of his cell, and his eyes had become red as he looked at them. Not so attractive as his mate, but at least they were covered with fur, not like the peeled ones that he sometimes saw dressed in stiff white crackling things.

The fur-covered ones had giggled just like ripening she-cubs, and his paws had ached to grasp them, and his jaws ached to bite into their fur-covered necks.

One of the fur-covered two-leggeds had giggled "Look at that wolf!"

So some of the two-leggeds had perception and could tell that the ones who held him in this big strange zoo were wrong, that he was not a man, but a wolf.

Inflating his now puny lungs to the utmost he had thrown back his head and roared out a challenge that in the old days, in the forest, would have sent a thrill of pleasure through every female for miles around. But instead of that blood-curdling, stomach-wrenching roar, a little barking, choking sound came from his throat. If he had still had a tail it would have curled down under his belly as he slunk away.

The first time they let him see himself in what they called a mirror he had moaned like a cub. Where was his long snout, the bristling whiskers, the flat head, the pointed ears? What was this thing that stared with dilated eyes out of the flat shiny surface? White-faced, almost hairless save for a jet-black bar of eyebrows that made a straight line across his high round forehead, small-jawed, small-toothed—he knew with a sinking sensation in the pit of his stomach that even a year-old would not hesitate to challenge him in the mating fights.

Not only challenge him but beat him, for how could he fight with those little canines, those feeble white hairless paws?

Another thing that irritated him, as it would any wolf, was that they kept moving him around. He would no sooner get used to one den and make it his own but what they'd move him to another one.

The last one that contained him had no bars.

If he had been able to read his chart he would have known that he was considered on the way to recovery, that the authorities thought him almost "cured" of his aberration. The den with no bars was one that was used for limited liberty patients. They were on a kind of parole basis. But he had no idea of what the word meant and the first time he was released on his own cognizance, allowed to make a trip out into the "real" world, he put out of his mind the curious forms of "occupational therapy" with which the authorities were deviling him.

His daytime liberty was unreal and dragged by in a way that made him almost anxious to get back home to the new den.

He had all but made up his mind to do so, when the setting sun conjured up visions which he could not resist. In the dark he could get down on all fours!

Leaving the crowded city streets behind him he hurried out into the suburbs where the spring smells were making the night air exciting.

He had looked forward so to dropping on all fours and racing through the velvet spring night that when he did so, only to find that all the months of standing upright had made him too stiff to run, he could have howled. Then too the clumsy leather things on his back paws got in the way, and he would have ripped them off, but he remembered how soft his new pads were, and he was afraid of what would happen to them.

Forcing himself upright, keeping the curve in his back that he had found helped him to stand on his hind legs, he made his way cautiously along a flat thing that stretched off into the distance.

The four-wheeler that stopped near him would ordinarily have frightened him. But even his new weak nose could sniff through the rank acrid smells of the four-wheeler and find, under the too sweet something on the two-legged female, the real smell, so that when she said, "Hop in, I'll give you a lift," he did not run away. Instead he joined the she.

Her bark was nice, at first.

Later, while he was doing to her what her scent had told him she wanted done, her bark became shrill, and it hurt even his new dull ears. That, of course, did not stop him from doing what had to be done in the spring.

The sounds that still came from her got fainter as he tried to run off on his hind legs. It was not much faster than a walk, but he had to get some of the good feeling of the air against his face, of his lungs panting; he had to run.

Regret was in him that he would not be able to get food for the she and be near her when she whelped, for that was the way of a wolf; but he knew too that he would always know her by her scent, and if possible when her time came he would be at her side.

Not even the spring running was as it should be, for without the excitement of being on all fours, without the nimbleness that had been his, he found that he stumbled too much, there was no thrill.

Besides, around him, the manifold smells told him that many of the two-leggeds were all jammed together. The odor was like a miasma and not even the all-pervading stench that came from the four-wheelers could drown it out.

Coming to a halt, he sat on his haunches, and for the first time he wondered if he were really, as he knew he was, a wolf, for a salty wetness was making itself felt at the corners of his eyes.

Wolves don't cry.

But if he were not a wolf, what then was he? What *were* all the memories that crowded his sick brain?

Tears or no, he knew that he was a wolf. And being a wolf, he must rid himself of this soft pelt, this hairlessness that made him sick at his stomach just to touch it with his too soft pads.

This was his dream, to become again as he had been. To be what was his only reality, a wolf, with a wolf's life and a wolf's loves.

That was his first venture into the reality of the world at large. His second day and night of "limited liberty" sent him hurrying back to his den. Nothing in his wolf life had prepared him for what he found in the midnight streets of the big city. For he found that bears were not the only males from whom the shes had to protect their young....

And no animal of which he had ever heard could have moaned, as he heard a man moan, "If only pain didn't hurt so much . . ." and the strangled cries, the thrashing of limbs, the violence, and the sound of a whip. He had never known that humans used whips on themselves too....

The third time out, he tried to drug himself the way the two-leggeds did by going to a big place where, on a screen, black and white shadows went through imitations of reality. He didn't go to a show that advertised it was in full glorious color, for he found the other shadows in neutral grays and blacks and whites gave a picture of life the way his wolf eyes were used to looking at it.

It was in this big place where the shadows acted that he found that perhaps he was not unique. His eyes glued to the screen, he watched as a man slowly fell to all fours, threw his head back, bayed at the moon, and then, right before everyone, turned into a wolf!

A *werewolf*, the man was called in the shadow play. And if there were werewolves, he thought, as he sat frozen in the middle of all the seated two-leggeds, then of course there must be *weremen* (would that be the word?) . . . and he was one of them....

On the screen the melodrama came to its quick, bloody, foreordained end and the werewolf died when shot by a silver bullet.... He saw the fur disappear from the skin, and the paws change into hands and feet.

All he had to do, he thought as he left the theatre, his mind full of his dream, was to find out how to become a wolf again, without dying. Meanwhile, on every trip out without fail he went to the zoo. The keepers had become used to seeing him. They no longer objected when he threw little bits of meat into the cage to his pups. At first his she had snarled when he came near the bars, but after a while, although still puzzled, and even though she flattened her ears and sniffed constantly at him, she seemed to become resigned to having him stand as near the cage as he possibly could.

His pups were coming along nicely, almost full-grown. He was sorry, in a way, that they had to come to wolfhood behind bars, for now they'd never know the thrill of the spring running, but it was good to know they were safe, and had full bellies, and a den to call their own.

It was when his cubs were almost ready to leave their mother that he found the two-leggeds had a place of books. It was called a *library*, and he had been sent there by the woman in the hospital who was teaching him and some of the other aphasics how to read and write and speak.

Remembering the shadow play about the werewolf, he forced his puzzled eyes to read all that he could find on the baffling subject of lycanthropy.

In every time, in every clime, he found that there were references to two-leggeds who had become four-leggeds, wolves, tigers, panthers ... but never a reference to an animal that had become a two-legged.

In the course of his reading he found directions whereby a two-legged could change himself. They were complicated and meaningless to him. They involved curious things like a belt made of human skin, with a certain odd number of nail heads arranged in a quaint pattern on the body of the belt. The buckle had to be made under peculiar circumstances, and there were many chants that had to be sung.

It was essential, he read in the crabbed old books, that the two-legged desirous of making the change go to a place where two roads intersected at a specific angle. Then, standing at the intersection, chanting the peculiar words, feeling the human skin belt, the two-legged was told to divest himself of all clothing, and then to relieve his bladder.

Only then, the old books said, could the change take place.

He found that his heart was beating madly when he finished the last of the old books.

For if a two-legged could become a four-legged, surely ...

After due thought, which was painful, he decided that a human skin belt would be wrong for him. The man in the fur store looked at him oddly when he asked for a length of wolf fur long and narrow, capable of being made into a belt....

But he got the fur, and he made the pattern of nail heads, and he did the things the books had described.

It was lucky, he thought as he stood in the deserted zoo, that not far from the cages he had found two roads that cut into each other in just the manner that the books said they should.

Standing where they crossed, his clothes piled on the grass nearby, the belt around his narrow waist, his fingers caressing its fur, his human throat chanting the meaningless words, he found that standing naked was a cold business, and that it was easy to void his bladder as the books had said he must.

Then it was all over.

He had done everything just as he should.

At first nothing happened, and the cold white moon looked down at him, and fear rode up and down his spine that he would be seen by one of the two-leggeds who always wore blue clothes, and he would be taken and put back into that other zoo that was not a zoo even though it had bars on the windows.

But then an aching began in his erect back, and he fell to all fours, and the agony began, and the pain blinded him to everything, to all the strange functional changes that were going on, and it was a long, long time before he dared open his eyes.

Even before he opened them, he could sense that it had happened, for crisp and clear through the night wind he could smell as he knew he should be able to smell. The odors came and they told him old stories.

Getting up on all fours, paying no attention to the clothes that now smelled foully of the two-leggeds, he began to run. His strong claws scrabbled at the cement and he hurried to the grass and it was wonderful and exciting to feel the good feel of the growing things under his pads. Throwing his long head back he closed his eyes and from deep deep inside he sang a song to the wolves' god, the moon.

His baying excited the animals in the cages so near him, and they began to roar, and scream, and those sounds were good too.

Running through the night, aimlessly, but running, feeling the ground beneath his paws was good . . . so good . . .

And then through the sounds, through all the baying and roaring and screaming from the animals, he heard his she's voice, and he forgot about freedom and the night wind and the cool white moon, and he ran back to the cage where she was.

The zoo attendants were just as baffled when they found the wolf curled up outside the cage near the feeding trough as they had been when they had found the man in the wolf's cage.

The two-legged who was his keeper recognized him and he was allowed to go back into his cage and then the ecstasy, the spring-and-fall-time ecstasy of being with his she . . .

Slowly, as he became used to his wolfhood again, he forgot about the life outside the cage, and soon it was all a matter that only arose in troubled dreams. And even then his she was there to nuzzle him and wake him if the nightmares got too bad.

Only once after the first few days did any waking memory of his two-legged life return, and that was when a two-legged she passed by his cage pushing a small four-wheeler in front of her.

Her scent was familiar.

So too was the scent of the two-legged cub.

Darting to the front of his cage, he sniffed long and hard.

And for just a moment the woman who was pushing the perambulator that contained her bastard looked deep into his yellow eyes and she knew, as he did, who and what he was.

And the very, very last thought he had about the matter was one of infinite pity for his poor cub, who some white moonlit night was going to drop down on all fours and become furred . . . and go prowling through the dark—in search of what, he would never know....

# "So Sweet as Magic..."

*"Nothing so sweet as magicke is to him,*
*Which he prefers before his chiefest bliss . . ."*
> —*Dr. Faustus*, Christopher Marlowe

**I**

The nightclub was as quiet as it ever got. That is, there was a constant flurry of low voices as gentlemen made ungenteel suggestions to the young ladies they were with; there was the steady clinking sound of ice cubes in glasses, but aside from that and the voice of the M.C. all was still.

"But now to be serious for a moment, folks." The master of ceremonies made a hideous grimace, at the word serious. "I'd like to introduce a man who'll bring you a mad mélange of mirth, mystery and magic.

*"Take it away, Bardoni!"*

Looking neither to right or left, a caricature of an old-time magician in white tie, tails, cape, and high hat, Bardoni strode across the handkerchief-sized dance floor, rapping his cane on the polished wood as he approached the microphone. A smile showed under his curled mustache; his goatee projected forward as though challenging the world. But despite his seeming coolness, Bardoni was furious. Of all the lousy intros! He'd have to bandy a few words with that M.C., that was all there was to it.

His smile became almost a sneer, as he bowed too low to the audience, doffed his hat, and said, "My name is Bardoni. I will now pause for a moment while you turn to each other and ask, 'Who's he?' I shall endeavor by the aid of my skill in legerdemain to refute, to set at nought all the laws of a well-ordered universe . . ."

When he said this, he deliberately pitched his voice low, made it orotund, so that the audience would know he was kidding. The day was long past when magic could be presented seriously. He still bore scars from the period when he had attempted that! No, the thing to do was kid it, much as he hated to.

Rapping his cane on the base of the microphone, he said, "One more whispered word out of madam, and I shall turn you into a rabbit!"

The lady, if that was the correct word, giggled nervously.

Bardoni said, "Behold, a reasonably priced miracle!"

The cane vanished from his hand and in its place he now held a foulard. Showing both sides of the foulard, he said, "And now let's have a Welsh rabbit!" Reaching into the folds of the garishly colored silk he produced a shining chromium pan. From it leaped flames that threatened to singe his goatee. Placing the fire bowl on his black velvet covered table, he doffed his topper, closed it and popped it open, thus demonstrating its emptiness and, holding it in his left hand, he wove his right fingers in a curious pattern over the hat.

Suddenly two white ears appeared. Reaching into the hat he pulled the rabbit up into view, holding it by the nape of the neck, not by the ears, as cartoonists always pictured a magician doing. Lift it by the ears, he thought irritably, do that often enough and you'd kill the little animal.

As always the women in the audience oo-ed and ah-ed when he produced the little furry white animal. Its angry red eyes surveyed the crowd and Bardoni said in an undertone, "Take it easy Sylvester, I know they're just a bunch of crumbs, and they don't appreciate us, but your work will be over in a second."

The flames in the pan he had just plucked from the fold of the silk were dying down. Just as they flickered out, he dropped the rabbit into the shining pan, and placed a cover over it.

He had the audience's attention now, and therefore did not bother to speak. Instead he showed the inside of the cover, and then dropped it into the pan where the rabbit was sitting irritably nibbling its front feet.

Instantaneously—that is, as soon as he had lowered the cover—he lifted it again, and tossed it to one side. Lifting the pan, he said, "On second thought a Welsh rabbit is a little messy . . . perhaps you'd prefer . . . kisses . . ." Thrusting his hand into the pan, he began to pluck out handfuls of candy kisses which he threw to the ladies in the audience. But for the candy, the pan was empty.

A drunken woman at the ringside said, "I want the cute little bunny . . . bring him back, you big slob!"

Swearing under his breath, he paced towards the woman, gestured in the air in front of her almost oppressively large bosom and seemed to produce a brassiere from the air. She was shocked into silence. Depositing the article of intimate underwear in her lap, he strode back to the microphone, his cape swirling out in large angry curves. Thank God, he thought, he'd figured out that angle as a heckler stopper. Drunken women had formerly been the bane of his existence. Paying no attention to the roars of laughter that followed the woman as she left her table and ran to the ladies' powder room, he showed his hand empty, back and front, and then said, "Observe if you will that at no time in the course of this present experiment, do my fingers ever leave my hand." As he spread his fingers wide, and then closed them again, he darted his hand forward into a tiny pin spot of light and produced a silver dollar into the bucket. It clanked as it hit the bottom of the container.

"The dream of mankind, come true," he said sonorously. "I pluck silver from the circumambient ether . . ." Then in an aside, he said in a tough punch-drunk prize fighter's voice, "Wha'd he say? Duh? Wha'd he say?"

While he meandered around the dance floor, with the pin spot following his hands, he produced what seemed to be an endless flow of coins. They tinkled and rattled as he dropped them from his agile fingers into the champagne bucket.

Finally, as though tiring of the sport, he stepped to the side of a bald-headed gentleman at a ringside table and said, "You've heard the expression a nose full of nickels? Watch . . ." As he held the bucket under the man's nose, a noisy silver stream of dollars poured into the container.

The man was nonplussed and was still fondling his nose in puzzled amazement as Bardoni walked back to the microphone and said, in pseudo-British tones, "You've been so bully, all of you, through this whole despicable mess, that I'd like to show my appreciation." Holding the bucket high in the air, he tossed its contents out over the audience's heads.

They ducked, expecting a shower of silver dollars. But instead of the heavy coins, confetti rained down around them.

Bowing, Bardoni said, "Most performers wait till they exit and return to give their encore. I'm no fool. I shall now present my first prepared encore."

Lifting his black cape off his shoulders, he swirled it in front of him, displaying the red silk lining. Then, whipping it in an arc, he let it fall from his hands. It parachuted outwards, and downwards; but instead of landing in a heap on the floor, it suddenly showed a form beneath it. Whipping the cape up into the air, and while the orchestra hit a sustained *Ta-daaaaa*, he revealed what the form had been.

It was a girl.

Dressed in a female version of his own costume, in a cutaway jacket, white tier white vest, and long black opera length hose, she rose to a standing position, and as the audience reacted with an oooh of surprise, Bardoni stepped backwards out of the spotlight and let his assistant go into her dance.

Much as he loathed relinquishing the center of the floor, even for a moment, he had found that people needed a break from straight magic; he had found that they soon became bludgeoned into an acceptance of what he did, and that it was to his advantage to have a change of pace.

With the spotlight on his assistant, he was able to count the house. Not too bad, for a Friday night before Lent. Not bad at all. Then he watched Judy as she went into the series of spins that was always guaranteed to garner her more applause than any of his most difficult feats of magic.

Bowing to the sound of many palms beating on each other, she stepped back with a graceful gesture and turned the spotlight back to Bardoni.

Adjusting his tie, he said, "Now for my second prepared encore, I shall endeavor to present one of the most baffling illusions ever seen by the human eye."

Two men wheeled the box out into the center of the floor, and Judy hopped into it. Her head projected out of one end, her feet the other. He closed the top on the box, bent over and said, "Don't forget the cue."

Then he said, "If I may have the assistance of the leader of this noble band . . . you know his famous slogan, of course, 'Swing and sweat with Davy Harnet.'" That got a giggle, as the bandleader joined Bardoni.

Davy asked, "What can I do for you, Bardoni?"

"As if you didn't know." Bardoni picked up one end of the two-man saw and waited while Davy got hold of the other. They then proceeded to saw the box containing Judy in half.

The saw rasped at the wood, the sharp teeth came down closer and closer to where the audience knew that the girl's stomach must be, as Bardoni said under his breath . . . "Now!"

Judy's scream, as always, electrified the audience, just for a second, and then they laughed as the saw cut deeper and deeper. The metal was through the wood now, and Bardoni shoved two metal plates down into the section where seemingly the girl's body had been cut in two.

With the metal plates in place, he then swung the box around, and as Judy's hair fanned out, and she smiled gaily at the audience, Davy tickled her feet in the other half of the box, making her wiggle them. Bardoni said, "Silence please . . . the slightest sound may be instantly fatal to the Princess Ayesha . . ."

Sure it was corny; he'd be the first to admit it; but it did help sustain the tension while he swung his half of the box back into place, ripped out the metal plates, dropped them resoundingly to the floor, and then, ripping the top off the box, had Judy pop out, all in one piece.

A deep bow, a curtsy from Judy, and, as the band leader led the applause, the audience took over, and Bardoni was able to make his exit to a good hand.

As he waited to see if there would be enough applause for a return bow, the head waiter said, "Here's a note for you, Bardoni."

A little irritated, Bardoni crumpled it in his hand, and with ear cocked, he waited, milking the applause as long as he dared. Then, grabbing Judy's hand, he stepped back into the spotlight and they took a bow together.

Holding his hand up for silence, he pretended to gasp for breath, and then said, "I was almost up to my dressing room when the sound of the applause drew me back . . . like a magnet." He took the curse off the haminess of the statement by grinning like a young Mephistopheles. Then plucking his white silk handkerchief from his breast pocket, he whipped it on itself till it was snakelike in shape. Holding it by one end in one band, he gestured at it with the other. Slowly, very slowly, the dangling end of the silk rose, formed into a knot, and then just as slowly disentangled itself.

As the silk went through its maneuver as though possessed of some kind of uncanny life of its own, he and Judy were walking off stage towards the exit.

As they got to the right side of the dance floor and there was just another foot to go, the silk suddenly fell limp again. Bardoni rolled it into a ball between his palms and then threw his hands up and outward.

The silk vanished and he took another bow, and made his exit.

This time the applause was just a mild patter.

As he and Judy went upstairs to the dressing rooms and the band picked up their cue and began to play a mambo, he said, "We've got to get a better walk off, honey. I don't care what anyone says, that's a lousy ending for the act."

She patted his shoulder and said, "I think the act went very well tonight, Bardoni. Take it easy. Don't always be trying to top yourself."

"Yeah," he said, his tone heavy, as he slumped into the rickety chair in front of his dressing room mirror and began to rip the crepe hair goatee off his chin. "Relax, take it easy . . . why, do you know that when Houdini was my age, he was making five grand a week and that was back in the twenties when a dollar was a dollar!"

"Times change," she said. "You've got to resign yourself to that. Magic just isn't the draw that it used to be."

"But it could be," Bardoni said angrily. This was an old argument and the words came without thought. He was wiping the sun-tan make-up off his face. Without the goatee and without the artificial points on his eyebrows, it could be seen that he was about thirty and but for the exaggerated widow's peak of his jet-black hair, and the bushiness of his hair at his temples, he might have been a bond salesman, or a dentist just beginning to practice. "Oh, brother, it could be. It just needs some new gimmick! After all, as long as Houdini just did magic, he was a slob working carnies, but as soon as he thought of escapes, or getting out of strait-jackets, and milk cans and prisons, then there was no holding him back. If I could only think of an angle."

His face clean, he began to take off his tailcoat. He stopped with the coat half off and half on and said, "You want to go out for late lunch with me?"

She was at the door now, and he was pleasantly aware of her trim figure, and her straight handsome legs in their long stockings. Her pretty face went blank, and she said, "Gee, I'm sorry, Bardoni, but I got a date. Y'know that cute sax player in the band? Well, he asked me out. Let me have a rain check, huh?"

"Sure, sure." Bardoni went back to changing into his street clothes. He was about to hang up his working pants when he remembered the note he'd been handed by the headwaiter.

Probably some fumble-fingered, ham-headed amateur magician who wanted to buy him a drink and then bore him stiff with some junk about how Bardoni could improve his act if he'd only listen to the priceless words of wisdom that the amateur was willing to exchange for the secret of just how that rabbit change was worked . . .

Unwrinkling the card, he eyed it.

"Count Saint Germain." Engraved too. He damn near cut his thumb, the engraving was raised so high. Count Saint Germain? What kind of fiddle-faddle was this? He was a charlatan of the seventeenth century, a faker like Cagliostro. As a matter of fact, Cagliostro had always maintained that it was the Count from whom he'd learned everything he knew.

Bardoni was interested.

If this fellow was a professional, how come he'd never heard of him?

It was a lot drunker in the joint, Bardoni saw as he reentered the room. Now that the last show was over, the audience had to drink faster unless they wanted to leave at closing time cold sober, and that Bardoni knew was the last thing they wanted.

Looking around, he spotted the headwaiter. "Where's the guy who sent me the card?"

He needn't have asked, for as soon as the Count was pointed out, Bardoni realized he would have spotted him. At twenty paces the Count looked about thirty-five, handsome, well set up, straight-backed and elegant. But as Bardoni wove his way through the narrow aisle that separated the tables, each step he took seemed to age the Count.

Count Saint Germain, he was thinking. That was the one who "cured" Louis the Fourteenth's diamond. If it hadn't had a flaw in it the stone would have been worth a quarter of a million dollars . . . and then Le Comte de Saint Germain took it, did something to it, and returned it to the Golden King with his compliments. The flaw in the diamond was gone, and the grateful king was nonplussed when Le Comte would take no reward from him.

What a bit of publicity, Bardoni thought. Those old-timers knew how to do it up brown.

By then he was only five feet from the man who had sent the card. Now the man looked about sixty. A fine network of wrinkles had become visible.

And now that Bardoni was this close, and the man who called himself Count Saint Germain was rising and bowing, Bardoni could see that the man's dress clothes were a little peculiar. He was wearing tails, but they were not cut like any Bardoni had ever seen. Tiny ruffles cascaded down the Count's shirt front, and his cuffs seemed to be ruffled too.

Two ornate rings ornamented his womanishly soft, womanishly white hands. His tie was soft and tied in a strange way. Bardoni extended his hand and said, "You wished to see me?"

"Ah, yes, indeed I did." There was a heaviness to the man's voice, a sort of constriction, as though the words came with some difficulty.

But as soft and effeminate as his hands looked, his handshake was firm and hearty. He gestured for Bardoni to be seated. There was a champagne bucket at the table, and at a word from the Count, the waiter poured some for Bardoni.

There was something peculiar about the Count's eyes, Bardoni realized, and he was trying to figure out what it was, when the Count lifted his glass in a toast.

"May you live for a thousand years," the Count said in those peculiar tones, and then paused as Bardoni picked up his glass, before going on. "And may I live forever."

Draining his glass off at a gulp, Bardoni suddenly saw what it was about the Count's eyes that he had found so distressing. The man had nictitating eyelids . . . a third eyelid, transparent, and capable of going over his eyeballs independently of his regular lids. It was quite disturbing, for as far as Bardoni knew, only birds possessed such an attribute.

"What can I do for you, sir?" Bardoni asked, as he picked up the wine bottle himself, not waiting for the waiter, and poured himself some more. He had a feeling he was going to need something to buck him up.

"Mmmm . . . I do not think you can do quite as much for me as I can do for you."

The words were stressed oddly, but Bardoni could not determine what accent the man had, if it was an accent. It sounded almost like a person who had not spoken for a long, very long time. As though the man's vocal cords were a little rusty with disuse.

"You can have no idea . . ." the Count said, and now that he was this close, Bardoni decided that the Count was older than anyone he had ever seen before. The network of wrinkles was so all-encompassing that the wrinkles had wrinkles. And yet the man was not feeble. Far from it, that handshake . . . The Count went on, ". . . no idea at all, how strange it is to come back here after a long absence."

"Back to America, to New York?" Bardoni asked.

"Ummm." The Count pressed his fingertips together and the heavy rings caught and reflected back the lights, sparkling and bright. "In a manner of speaking. No, I really meant it is strange to come back to your world."

Rich the man might be, old—incredibly old—he must be, but nutty as the proverbial fruit cake, Bardoni decided. Then, curiosity overrode his feeling of revulsion at the man's obvious insanity and Bardoni asked, "Been away long?"

"Yes, long in your terms. Roughly two centuries."

Bardoni stared at the man's long aquiline nose, his deep-set eyes with that disconcerting extra lid, the hair which must be a wig, for surely no man as old as this had ever retained a full head of hair, at the man's deep sunken cheeks, and scar-thin lips. Just what in hell was this old boy up to?

"That's quite a while to be away," Bardoni said gently as he refilled his glass. Might as well get plastered. He wasn't going to believe any of this tomorrow anyway.

Whatever was on the old bird's mind was a long time in coming to the surface. Four bottles later, Bardoni, who had drunk most of the champagne, left the club with his arm around the Count's shoulders.

Holding himself very erect, and thinking, "No sense in letting the boss see I'm loaded," he sallied forth into the night with his new bosom buddy.

"Where'll we go, old pal, old sock?" Bardoni asked.

"The night is young," the Count answered, which was a lie, since it was after four o'clock in the morning. "Why do we not repair to your rooms?"

"Good idea. A bird can't fly on one wing, and I got a bottle home."

Staggering into a cab, Bardoni attempted to talk the Count into taking the tenor in a spirited rendition of *Little Red Wing*, but the Count was obdurate, and Bardoni had to sing, alone.

The Count seemed pleased by Bardoni's hotel suite, and most pleased when Bardoni introduced him to Sylvester's lady friend, Abigail. The rabbit sat perkily in its pen, its red eyes alert, as the Count crooned to it, and petted it between its ears where all rabbits like to be scratched.

Around Bardoni's rooms were scattered the paraphernalia of a dozen acts that he had tried before working out the one he now used. In one corner was an ornately painted box with three doors on it. It was a little larger than life size and when the Count had ceased petting Abigail, he said, "That box, sir, what is it used for?"

Considering it blurrily, Bardoni said, "Oh, that . . . girl without a middle."

"Do I understand that you place your so charming assistant in that box, then seem to demonstrate that there is no middle section to her?"

"Thass righ'. Good trick. But old hat now. Used to throw knives through the middle, prove Judy had no belly."

"Charming. Charming."

Bardoni knocked a production box off a sofa and said, "Sid-down, this freedom house. Kick off your shoes, make yourself homely."

Opening a bottle, Bardoni poured his guest a short drink, and himself a man-sized gulp of bourbon.

"I think I have had enough, thank you." The Count sat back on a chair that had two mirrors set between its four legs. The reflections made the Count look as many legged as a centipede, which Bardoni found, in his present state, to be hilarious.

Polishing off the drink, Bardoni asked, "And now, what can I do for you, Count?"

The sight of the man's ancient visage, its many wrinkles working excitedly as he blocked out a story that Bardoni felt at the moment was one of the most fantastic things he had ever heard, was the last thing Bardoni remembered.

## II

The noon sun was full in Bardoni's eyes when he finally awoke. Not daring to move a muscle, he lay perfectly still. The room was swirling gently. The bed was possessed of an independent life of its own, a gentle vertiginous flow, that Bardoni feared would have drastic results.

What in the world had possessed him to get sozzled? That wasn't like him. He was, at best, a sociable drinker, but far from a lush. He couldn't remember the last time he had been fully drunk.

He had really tied one on, he decided as, risking all, he slowly lifted his balloon-sized head. Lifting his hand to his aching forehead, he saw a ring on his middle finger. Ancient, ornate, with a preposterous red stone in it. He knew he had seen the ring before, but at the moment he could not remember where, or why, or what the ring meant.

Water.

If he didn't have a drink of water, he'd die. That was one sure thing in an unsure world.

Staggering to the bathroom, he stared at his red-rimmed eyes. They reminded him that Abigail must be starving. He always fed her first thing when he got up. But first, water. Draining four glasses, he suddenly had to hold onto the basin for support. Fool! Dolt! Imbecile! Water on top of a champagne drunk! He was plastered again.

Head reeling, a silly smile plastered on his face, he made his way out of the bathroom and to Abigail. Patting her, he went to the kitchen and grabbed a handful of carrots and some lettuce. Dropping them down to her, he fell into a chair and tried to remember the events of the previous evening. As he sat in drunken thought, he found himself rotating the ring on his finger. A dry, rusty voice seemed to say in his ear the words that he vaguely remembered having heard before: "As you value your life, do not remove this ring!

Remember, no matter what the occasion, no matter what the temptation, if you remove the ring, you die!" That was pretty ridiculous, he decided, looking at the ring, but he suddenly found that he had no great desire to take it off his finger.

Putting it completely out of his mind, he brought his eyes to bear on the clock. One on the button, the time he had a weekly appointment at the magic shop to meet his confreres and bitch about conditions, discuss new tricks, variations on old ones, and in general, carry on as all magicians did when they weren't performing.

Maybe about two gallons of black coffee would do it. He did not feel up to puttering around in the kitchen, so by a great display of manly will power he managed to force his body into clothes.

Reaching for the doorknob brought the ring back to his attention again. He turned to see that Abigail was all taken care of, and just as he opened the door, he said, "You were here, you heard what went on last night, and you weren't drunk. You'd remember the whole thing. If you rabbits could only talk . . ."

Abigail said slowly, distinctly, and with much wrinkling of her tiny pink nose, "That's just silly. Rabbits can't talk."

Out on the street, in front of his apartment hotel, Bardoni found himself talking to himself. "You're drunk, you jerk, that's all. What's the matter with you? Got a hole in your head? Rabbits can't talk, just as Abigail said." But that led into a trap because she had talked and very plainly too.

The afternoon sun felt good on his addled brain. Coffee. That was of the essence. Staggering into the coffee pot on the ground floor of his hotel he sat perfectly still, deliberately trying not to think until he had had four cups of coffee. Then reaching out into the air, he absentmindedly plucked a lighted cigarette from nowhere, making an old lady at the next table do a double take, which he was completely unaware of. Puffing on the cigarette he decided that except for the evidence of the ring he wore, he would rather like to doubt the existence of a certain old gentleman with a rusty voice.

The coffee helped as it generally did, and by two o'clock he was meandering slowly along Forty-second Street, making his way to the magic shop. He paused in front of the music store that was midway in the block between Sixth Avenue and Seventh and eyed the instruments on display. A shining grand piano reflected back a slightly distorted view of his face. His eyes were still bleary looking, but aside from that he looked up to snuff, he decided.

Entering 120, he ambled to the elevator, said hello to the starter, and as the bent old man expected, he reached out and plucked a silver dollar from the starter's uniform. But his heart wasn't in it; he didn't bother to vanish it the way he usually did because he loved to see the old boy's eyes pop. Instead he did the steeplechase, which is an involved and spectacular looking maneuver, in which the coin rotates along the back of the fingers of the hand, around the palm and then again rolls across the backs of the fingers.

The starter said, "Take Mr. Bardoni right up to the twelfth floor, Jack."

The elevator operator grinned hello, and Bardoni, feeling a little better, plucked a lit cigarette from his ear, and rode up to his floor, chatting amiably with the operator about baseball, which was in bad shape for a Brooklyn rooter like the operator.

At the twelfth floor, Bardoni did not even bother to read the sign that said *Louis Tannen, Magic Supplies*. Instead he walked to his left and entered his home-away-from-home. They were all there. Jay Marshall, Rickie Dunn, Jack Miller, looking like an English professor, with his pince-nez dangling from a black ribbon, Dai Vernon off in a corner, the ever-present cigarette dangling from the side of his mouth, the omnipresent deck of playing cards held in his deft hands, his man-of-distinction look as much his trademark as ever, from his handsome face to his pewter-like gray hair that made a helmet for his well-shaped head.

With his back to the glass counter, Norman Jensen was demonstrating something that Bardoni could not see, but it must have been funny, for the group around him, from Bill Simon to Dr. Braude, all went off into a roar of guffaws.

They all turned and said hello as Bardoni bowed in the doorway.

Behind the counter, Tannen's flaming red hair beckoned Bardoni. "C'mere, I wanna show you a new one just came in from England. Darnedest thing you ever saw! An idea of Peter Warlock's!"

Pushing through the crowd, shaking hands, Bardoni made his way towards the counter. To one side of Tannen, Herpick, the trick demonstrator who looked more like Donald O'Connor than O'Connor did, was doing something that puzzled Bardoni.

He seemed about three feet taller than usual.

Must be standing on something back of the counter, Bardoni decided.

All in all it was the usual Saturday afternoon crowd in any magic store in any big city all over the country. This was where magicians and magic fans met, exchanged gossip, tricks, and tried their damnedest to fool each other, for there is no more delightful sensation to a magician than to fool a brother magician. Fooling a layman is pretty much like shooting fish in a barrel. No sport at all. But to fool a brother adept, ah, Bardoni thought, that was a real kick.

Before he could get to Tannen however, he got close enough to the counter so that he could see that Herpick was not standing on anything. Instead, his feet were firmly planted in mid-air. He was not being a show-off about it. Far from it. He was merely standing three feet off the ground as though it was perfectly normal to do so.

"What's the gaff?" Bardoni asked feeling that he was being made a sucker of. "A gooseneck behind you?"

"You kidding?" Herpick's bland face was even blander than usual. "What's new about this? I'm just levitating, like any third-class adept."

Okay, okay, Bardoni thought, so he'd been fooled, but did Herpick have to keep up the pretense?

Then he looked down into the long glass counter where ordinarily the shelves were jammed with every kind of close-up gimmick from thumb tips to finger choppers, from vanishing cigars to appearing wands, from color changing silks to decks of cards that worked themselves automatically with no need for any kind of finger-flinging skill, and what Bardoni saw in the counter, instead, made his stomach lurch and his mind flee from reality.

No shiny chromium gimmicks. No fake fingers. No silks that could be compressed up into almost no space at all.

No gadgets of any kind.

Instead the counter was filled with phials, alembics and powders in tiny containers like ornate snuff boxes. That was strange but might have been just a new display. It was the little neatly lettered cards next to the objects that made Bardoni doubt his own sanity.

Instead of saying, as the cards generally did, *Miniature Die Box, A Howl, Yours for only $2.50,* the signs read, unless his eyes were lying, *Three drops of Dragon's Blood. Best grade, donated by Oliver J. Dragon.* Another smaller card said with a certain simple dignity, *Witchbane.* Rubbing his knuckles in his red-rimmed eyes, Bardoni shook his head, tried to clear it. That little sign in front of the big glass alembic—it still read, as it had a moment ago, *Unicorn horn. Dehydrated. Ready at a moment's notice, just add three drops of virgin's blood and you're all set.*

There were knucklebones, which had a tag saying, *You've cast the rest, now cast the best,* and next to them a box perhaps thirty-six inches long. Lettered on it was, *Why spend more? Buy the conjuror's kit. We've done the work, you have the fun.*

## CONTENTS

Poisoned entrails (*Wow!*)
Swelter'd venom (*No one, but no one else has this*)
Fenny snake fillet (*try ours*)
Root of hemlock (*the bitterest*)
Gall of goat (*And what gall!*)
Eye of Newt (*A real beaut!*)
Toe of frog (*Best by test*)
Wool of bat (*Grade A*)
Tongue of dog (*Pedigreed*)
Adder's fork (*A delight*)
Blind worm's sting (*Hard to get*)
Lizzard's leg (*2, very fragile*)
Howlet's wing (*Unique*)
Scale of dragon (*Superior grade*)
Tooth of wolf (*With cavity*)

*And many more! Why waste time with substitutes when for a measly hundred and fifty dollars, you can have the best?*
*Recommended by the Great Bardoni who used this kit himself!*

That did it.

If there was one thing that Bardoni was still sure of, it was that he had never in his life recommended a kit containing any of these oddments. Nor had he ever used one. Nor could he, for he hadn't the slightest idea what conceivable use any magician could possibly have for a single one of the ingredients that he was supposed to be so enthusiastic about.

That this might be a vast practical joke seemed improbable, but magicians as a breed are fond of hoaxes ... Bardoni hoped against hope that he was being made the butt of a complicated joke. To one side, on the book-lined shelves, he saw two text books on magic which he always kept near him at home. No matter how fantastic the joke might be, he thought, taking down the two books, looking at their jackets, their titles, *Magic as a Hobby* and *Classic Secrets of Magic* no one would have, or could have, reset the type in the books just for a gag.

Opening the familiar looking books, he riffled through the pages. Although the dust wrappers were identical with those he owned, the contents, he saw, his head whirling, were completely different. Here were no illustrations on how to double lift a card, or perform the pass with a deck of cards. Instead, he saw diagrams, symbols, pentagrams and other cabalistic diagrams, which meant less than nothing to him.

It was not a joke, practical or impractical.

Slowly, his brain numbed, and feeling about as useful as a glass of calf's liver, he returned the books to the shelves. Meanwhile, behind the counter, Jimmy Herpick was now lying on his side in the air. Perhaps four feet off the ground, he lazed there as he chatted amiably with a young magician.

It was too much, Bardoni thought. Much too much. But Lou Tannen was one of his best friends, even in a nightmare like this. Going behind the counter, he grabbed the redheaded man by the elbow and pulled him into the back of the store. Even there everything was as it should be. Dick Piser was busy at work wrapping parcels, preparing them for mailing, and in Lou's office his secretary was just as busy as ever, billing and doing bookkeeping.

Lou asked, "What's up, Bardoni? You look sick or scared." His red hair flaming in the afternoon sun, Bardoni's friend seemed quite concerned.

Bardoni said, "Lou, you've known me a long time."

"Ever since you changed your name from Tommy Gardner to the Great Bardoni." The man chuckled. "But what's up?"

Nervously, Bardoni sat and turned the curious antique ring around and around on the middle finger of his right hand. "I think I've gone nuts, Lou."

"Take it easy. Tell me about it." The redheaded businessman turned to his secretary and said, "Leila, tell the boys out front to carry on. I'm not to be disturbed."

Bardoni got to his feet and looked out the office window down onto the unchanged street below. As usual in New York, the streets were black with people, the cars were jammed together nose to fender. All around Bardoni, all seemed as usual. And yet . . . and yet . . . Aloud he said, "I want to test something, Lou. Give me a deck of cards."

Reaching into a desk drawer, the redhead threw a deck to Bardoni.

Bardoni riffled them, fanned them and extended the fanned pack to have the redhead select a card at random. Once it had been selected and returned to the pack, Bardoni shuffled the pack, and said, "What card did you select, Lou?"

Puzzled, the man said, "The three of hearts. Why?"

"Watch," Bardoni said, and then proceeded to seem to demonstrate that all the cards the deck had turned into threes of hearts.

His heart sank when he saw the expression of complete befuddlement cross over his friend's face. Bardoni asked, "Any idea how I did that, Lou?"

"Good grief, no! You've stumbled on something completely new, Bardoni! When you're tired of using that, may I put it on the market?"

"Lou," Bardoni said tiredly, the little hairs on the back of his neck raising with fear of the unknown. "Yesterday or the day before if I had done that trick for you, you would have laughed at me. Yesterday any ten-year-old boy could have done the same trick. What's happened? How can Jimmy float in mid-air, and what's all that hocus-pocus with bat's blood, and newt's eyes?"

Reaching out his hand, the redhead touched Bardoni's forehead. He said, "You don't seem to be feverish. Look, Tommy, what's wrong with you? How would our magic work if we did not use magical ingredients? As for Jimmy's floating in mid-air, you learned that when you were in your teens. You stopped doing it in your act, because it got kicked around so. You said only amateurs were using it now." Then the redhead pointed to the pack of cards and said, "But that card trick, what's the magic formula? Can you tell me? I'd love to sell it."

Shaking his head to try and chase away the cobwebs that seemed to be gathering there, Bardoni tried a wild stab in the dark. He asked, "Lou, do you know a man named the Count Saint Germain?"

Instantly his redheaded friend leaped to his feet, ran to the office door and slammed it shut. Then, his forefinger pressed to his lips, he came close to Bardoni and whispered, "Shhh . . . don't you know the police are investigating his disappearance?"

Bardoni put his hands to his aching head and tried to think. Lou Tannen pointed an excited finger at the ring on Bardoni's hand and said, "Tommy! Where did you get that ring?"

"Saint Germain gave it to me!" Bardoni lowered his hands and looked at the ring.

"Get rid of it, throw it away, take it off this instant! The police think that he met with foul play. I've seen him wearing that ring and if I remember it, then so will a lot of other people!"

Responding instinctively to the urgency of his friend's voice, Bardoni put his left fingers around the ring and began to pull it off his finger. Instantly he seemed to hear, deep inside his brain, that rusty voice saying, "If you remove the ring, you die . . ."

Jamming his hands into his pockets, Bardoni said, "I can't take it off Lou. I can't!"

Through the office door came an official voice, ponderous and heavy.

"Open this door. Open up in the name of the law!"

Tannen said, "The cops! I suppose it was inevitable that they check on the Count Saint Germain in all the magic shops!"

"What'll I do?" In a panicky state that deprived him of all intelligence, Bardoni looked wildly around him. The Count gone, the police after his "killer" and he, Bardoni, stuck with a ring that had belonged to the Count, and that he could not remove from his finger . . . What could he conceivably do?

Tannen looked from the door, which was vibrating under the pounding that it was getting, to Bardoni. "Quick, the fire stairs."

Pushing Bardoni towards a back door, Tannen said, "If you're really as confused as you say, go to the Coven, ask the wizard there what you can do. He may recommend a psychiatrist, or perhaps you are under a spell. In either case, the wizard will be able to tell you what to do!"

By that time, Tannen had almost bodily pushed Bardoni out the door. Aloud he yelled, "I'm coming, you don't have to knock my door down."

Bardoni asked hurriedly, "But where? How'll I find the Coven?"

"You are in a bad way!" Quick concern showed on Tannen's face. "If you've forgotten that, what else must you have forgotten? But . . . no time for that. Hurry. The Coven is at Seventieth Street and West End Avenue . . . the number is . . ." and he whispered the address as Bardoni slipped out the door and began to run down the stairs.

Behind him Bardoni could hear his friend locking the fire door.

Then that was all he could hear.

Hoping against hope that his friend would be able to stall the cops a little while, Bardoni ran down the stairs faster than he had ever run in his whole life.

### III

Gasping for breath, Bardoni lurked just inside the door down on the street level. If the cops had staked out the area he was a dead duck. But a hurried look showed no sign of the men in blue. It must just have been a check-up that the police were on; they had no evidence in particular; their thinking, Bardoni thought, must simply be that if a magician disappeared, it was a good idea to check up on other magicians.

Hailing a cab, he threw himself into it, and while the car drove at a snail's pace through the Broadway traffic, he looked around for any other signs of Insanity that might be a clue as to what was wrong with him. But every shop was where he remembered it being, every theatre was where it should be, and they were all showing movies that he remembered being on display. This was the world as he knew it. All except for the little area of magic and magicians.

Or in some tiny spot in his brain, Bardoni realized, where something seemed to have snapped.

The cab finally got to Eleventh Avenue and then it made a little better time. Sailing up the avenue he saw that it changed to West End Avenue just as it should, at Fifty-seventh Street. In the Hudson River he could see the normal amount of pleasure boats, tugs, and scows . . . It was a completely ordinary Saturday afternoon to all intents and purposes.

It wasn't until the cab drove into Seventieth Street that Bardoni realized that the address should have rung a bell. He knew the house he was going to; he'd been there often. Every Friday night most of the magicians in town dropped in and visited with the man who lived there. Bardoni had been there often. The man published a trade paper for magicians called the *Phoenix*.

Paying the cab, he went slowly up the four brown stone steps. On the mailbox in the hall, he saw, as usual, the man's name on the letterbox, and under it, as always, a neatly lettered sign that read, *The Phoenix*. But . . . under that, equally neatly lettered was something that Bardoni knew he had never seen before: *Covens every Friday night.*

Ringing the bell, he waited.

The man who answered, he knew should be about five feet nine inches tall, heavy set, wearing tortoise shell rimmed glasses, and a drooping mustache that was oddly at variance with his short, crew cropped hair.

Bardoni heard the shrill yapping of the man's French poodle, just as he had every Friday night in the past when he had come to visit, to gossip, and swap tricks . . .

The door opened and, also as usual, the man he had come to see was dressed in a T-shirt and a pair of wildly patterned shorts. Nothing had changed. The man said, "Bardoni! Long time no see. Welcome may you be."

Bowing satirically, the man ushered Bardoni into a cluttered room where two desks were piled high with manuscripts, and the walls were lined with books.

Bardoni dropped his body wearily into one of the two sagging overstuffed chairs that room boasted and said, "You've got to help me."

"Sure," the man said, the epicanthic fold over his eyes making them look Oriental, and reminding Bardoni a little unpleasantly of the nictitating eyelids that the Count Saint Germain possessed. "What can I do for you?"

The French poodle had stopped yapping and was ensconced on the man's lap. He said, "Just stay there, that way, Dedee." Then he turned his attention back to Bardoni and said, "Man, you're in bad shape, what's with you?"

Bardoni recited the part of his travail that he thought was relevant.

The man crossed his legs under him, Buddha-wise, and considered Bardoni. "So the Count has vanished again, huh? It was about time." Reaching up behind him he took down a book. Opening it almost at random he read: "Shortly after Le Comte de Saint Germain had taught Cagliostro all that Balsamo ever knew, and directly after he had 'cured' the Sun King's diamond, le Comte once more vanished off the face of the earth, until just before the Revolution. He vanished when the Terror was at its height. This is the last authenticated appearance that is recorded until the time of the Citizen King, 1866, when he was seen in and around Paris. In 1870, he once more vanished, leaving behind him garbled tales of having lived for thousands of years, of having been alive in Caesar's time, or knowing the secret of the Philosopher's stone, and myriad other wonders.

"In 1912, he was seen and known to have been in Russia. Whether as Rasputin always claimed, the mad monk was actually a pupil of Le Comte's is not known for a certainty. He vanished just before the Revolution and there is no record of his having been seen until 1928 when he appeared in New York City, in the United States of America . . ."

"This was written by an Englishman," the man interpolated and then continued reading: "On the Saturday after Black Friday on the stock market in 1929, Le Comte once more disappeared off the face of the earth.

"Well documented evidence seems to prove that Hitler's court astrologer was one of his pupils and that Le Comte was often a visitor at Berchtesgaden. He was last seen in Germany just before the fall of Berlin. Later he was seen in America at Los Alamos, and White Sands, and there are reports that he showed up at Eniwetok.

"There is another long hiatus and then, he reappeared most recently in New York City, where, at last reports, he still resides."

The man with the drooping mustache said, "So you see, it was just about time for him to vanish again."

Bardoni said thoughtfully, "He appears, there is sudden strife, revolution, war, and economic depression, and then just as disaster strikes, he departs. Nice fellow."

"Many occultists have made that point," the pudgy man said, rubbing his crew cut hair like a brush. "They feel that he is responsible for everything from the atom bomb to the Cold War."

"But why would he involve me in his Machiavellian plans, and what has happened to me? And why does my magic seem to have changed overnight from legerdemain and sleight of hand to black magic, potions and spells?"

"As for that, I fear I don't understand what you mean by sleight of hand or that other term."

This was from a man that Bardoni knew published a biweekly trade paper devoted to sleights and subtleties!

"What can I do? Lou seemed to think you'd be able to help me."

The man pulled at one straggling end of his mustache and said, "As to that, it's highly irregular and all that sort of thing, but I could call a Coven for tonight and see if Dedee, my familiar, can help you at all."

So he was to pin his hopes on an irascible, highly strung French poodle bitch, Bardoni thought disconsolately. A fine state of affairs, but as long as his host was willing to laugh at the thought of the police coming here, the apartment did serve as a sanctuary, and that was all Bardoni wanted at the moment—a chance to sit still and think things out.

It took roughly four lifetimes for the day to drag its weary way into nightfall, and then another ten or twelve centuries before all the members of the Coven arrived. They were all friends of Bardoni's and under other circumstances, and if he could have talked his kind of magic to them, he would have had a fine time.

But their light chitchat, about the best spell to employ when making one's self invisible, and what possible twists could be devised in order to better exploit levitation, left him cold.

His host had his eyes on the clock, and as midnight approached, he said, "Better stop drinking now, gents, it's almost time."

The magicians put their highballs away and, sitting around a rather rickety bridge table, their little fingers interlocked, they waited while the host kept track of the time.

Bardoni felt really left out of it. He was sitting to one side of the circle of men, and he was smoking so much that his lungs were aching and his mouth felt as if an owl had been living in it for a couple of weeks.

Dedee, the poodle, sat quietly in the center of the table.

Their host yelled out to his wife, "Douse the lights, Bunny, it's time." And then they were all in a velvet blackness that slowly became more and more oppressive.

These men, his friends, who had just been sitting around chatting, telling dirty jokes, and drinking, were now strangers, unseen members of a secret conclave.

Their voices rose high in a chant that was completely unintelligible to Bardoni. It was strangely accented and dissonant, like Schoenberg's music, atonal, almost as if it were based on the twelve-tone scale.

The darkness pressed on Bardoni's eyeballs.

The host said, "The Coven is ready."

The center of the table—an ordinary bridge table, Bardoni thought uneasily, off which he had eaten dinner earlier—now had a spot of greenish light emanating from it. The dog seemed to have vanished.

The light faded, flickered, and then Bardoni gasped, as he saw the green luminescence coalesce and become a man's face.

But no, he was wrong. This visage had never, dead or alive, belonged to any member of the human race. In the first place, the fangs that projected from the corners of the thing's mouth were as inconvenient as a saber-tooth tiger's. And the blank sockets where eyes might have been were covered with scales. In the center of the forehead, a round, unpleasant, jelly-like eye seemed to look in all directions at once.

The stuff that covered the thing's head had never been designed as hair. Bardoni was sure of that. It had an independent life of its own, which made him feel queasy. And the two bone-like objects that struck out of its temples had never grown on a human's head. That was for sure.

The host, the leader of the Coven said conversationally, "It's about time you showed up, Alzebaran."

The thing contorted its face into an even more unseemly expression and said, "You guys give me a pain in the behind. It was a bad day for demons when you slobs found the incantations to make us do as you want us to."

"That's enough of that." The host rapped the demon on the high arched nose which then proceeded to elongate like an elephant's trunk and feel itself with the tip.

It said, "Keep your big hands to yourself, Buster, or you'll slip one of these days . . . and then . . ."

"You just wait till I slip. In the meantime a friend of ours, Bardoni over there, is in trouble, and you'd better tell him what to do or it's no more sacrifices you'll be getting!"

The demon said, "Spit it out, I ain't got all night. I got things to do. Important things. The Count is busy calling all of us to heel."

There was a long silence. Bardoni thought, the Count, always the Count. But this was at least a lead. The demon, Alzebaran, had been called on by the Count.

"That's very interesting. What does the Count want?"

"Come off it, adept, you know the Count ranks you by about ninety-nine degrees. You better study up before you step in on him!" The demon was contemptuous.

"Then tell Bardoni what he must do to find out what he wants to know."

The green lighted face turned and looked at Bardoni. The single eye rolled and moved around as though capable, if it felt so disposed, of leaving its socket and going where it wanted to.

Something thick and liquid was pouring down its fangs, Bardoni could see, and collecting in a puddle in the middle of the table. A stench like nothing Bardoni's nostrils had ever encountered emanated from the little puddle.

"Make me," the demon said challengingly.

The host sighed heavily, and said, "All right boys all together—one, two, three."

At the count of three the seven men seated in a huddle around the table began to chant. It was in no language that Bardoni had ever heard before, and the heavy gutturals fell like blows from a whip on the demon's head. The hair on its scalp rose and fell, the skin crawled and it wrinkled its face agonizingly. Finally it said, in broken desperate tones, "Aw right, aw right, awready. You made your point. Now I have to obey you, cut it out."

The voices fell silent.

The single eye began to project outwards from the socket, and Bardoni felt malevolence like a live thing strike out at him.

The demon might be doing what it was doing because it was forced to do so, but it bloody well didn't like doing it. Bardoni wondered how much credence he could place in what the thing was saying under such duress. It said:

> "One time three, no fiddle dee dee.
> To the museum and you will see
> Carnavon's scarab, a petrified tree,
> The mouth of Adonis, tee hee hee . . ."

The host said, "I wish you demons didn't all try to be Edgar A. Guest."

Then, much more immediately than it had appeared, the demon head vanished and the poodle leaped off the table, ready to be petted.

"Lights," the host roared, and his wife turned on the electricity, and suddenly the room was like any room, and the people were once more all his friends. But for the pool of viscous fluid in the center of the shabby bridge table, Bardoni would have felt that he had been dreaming.

One of the men at the table took out a handkerchief and began to sop up the liquid. He said, "Mind if I take this? I'm almost out, and I want to try some teleportation in my show tomorrow night."

"Take it with my blessing," the host said. "I've got gallons."

Bardoni asked timorously, "Did that gibberish mean anything?"

"Mean anything?" The host was incredulous; he chewed at his scrubby mustache. "You are in a bad way, Bardoni. Why even a beginning first degree quid nunc would know that you better hustle your bustle up to the Magic Museum and get hold of the scarab and the petrified tree—and by the way, don't let that lousy curator try to palm off that puny little twig he tried to stick me with; get the whole tree. And when you make obeisance to Adonis, don't forget any of the formula, or, brother, you're in for trouble. Lay people may think that Adonis was just a pretty boy, but he was a mean bastard all the same. Whew . . . some of the ritual to him makes even me sick at my stomach."

"You don't seem to realize I don't know any rituals!" Bardoni almost whimpered. "What's more I don't even know where the Magic Museum is."

The host stood up and said, "As much as I loathe putting pants on, I guess I'll have to take you up there." Taking a small book off the bulging shelves, he said, "Take this with you."

Then hurriedly, dressing, he said, "Don't go 'way boys, I'll teach him the ritual in the cab, drop him off at the museum and be right back. I've got a cute idea on transmutation that I think you'll all like."

Kissing his wife good-bye, and telling her to put the coffee on, he accompanied Bardoni out onto the street.

Bardoni's mind kept heaving sickly. What the hell did he know about Adonis worship, or petrified trees and scarabs? . . . if only he could be back performing his kind of magic, even in front of the drunkest audience . . .

The man with him said, "We better go to the grocery store first and pick up a black rooster and some of the other things you're gonna need."

## IV

The cab drove off into the night and Bardoni was all alone. In a paper sack he had a live black fowl. In his right-hand coat pocket he had a curiously curved knife with the most obscene carvings on it that he had ever seen. In his inner breast pocket, he had a packet of herbs that his host had also given him. His mind was repeating over and over the meaningless words that he had had to memorize in the short taxi ride to the museum.

In any other circumstances, Bardoni would have considered the building in front of him interesting. But the fact that it stood on Fifth Avenue in the Eighties right where he knew the Metropolitan Museum of Art should be was disconcerting, to put it mildly.

Ascending the stairs, muttering the words he had been taught over and over to himself, he suddenly wondered how he was going to get into the museum at one o'clock in the morning!

Rapping on one of the glass panels in the door in front of him, he waited.

It was a long wait, and the guard, when he came, aged and cranky, was not much help. He said, "You magicians! You give me a pain. Why don't you go to bed like other people!"

But finally after much muttering, he opened the door and allowed Bardoni to follow him into the cavernous recesses of the museum.

"Mr. Charlier? The Curator?" Bardoni asked.

"Yeah, yeah, I'll go wake him. A lot you magicians care who you disturb."

Then Bardoni was alone in the darkened room that stretched as far away as he could see through the gloom. Nearest him, a devil mask, primitive in construction, but ghastly to view in that somber darkness, leered down at him. Under it a voodoo drum seemed to sit and wait for a Papa Legba to come and pound it and call out for Damballa to appear.

What little he could discern of the other exhibits made him a little glad that there was as dim light as there was. He had no desire to investigate any more closely.

In the distance he could hear a tap, tap, tap, tap.

His stomach muscles tightening, he waited, his hands sweaty with fear, to see who or what was approaching.

Some of the tension eased off as he saw a little man, no more than five feet tall, whispy and sparrow-like, coming closer.

Pince-nez on his nose, high forehead gleaming in the vagrant light from a street lamp that came through one of the windows, he asked, "Yes, what is it? Is it very important?"

Bardoni said, "Very."

"Who sent you here?"

Bardoni told him his friend's name.

The curator said, "Oh, that one! Wouldn't you know he'd think of some way to disturb my night's sleep! Between the police being here all day interrogating me, and magicians bothering me at night, I just don't know how I shall ever finish my bibliography of necrophilism. I do wish people would be more considerate. However."

He diddled with his pince-nez, and then said, "Just what do you want?"

Feeling like a complete and utter idiot, Bardoni said, as his friend had told him to, "By the name that is not a name, and that cannot be uttered, I direct you to take me to Carnavon's scarab and the petrified tree."

The man made a face like a prim old maid, and said, "Oh I say, you are dabbling in dark waters! It's your soul you're risking. Come along, come along."

Through corridors that seemed to stretch out into nightmare lengths, through rooms crowded with curiosa, past phallic statues that made Bardoni lower his eyes, the fussy little man led the way.

After it seemed that they had walked many city blocks, the little man said, "Do you want me to wait? This is your first stop."

The idea of being alone was more than Bardoni could bear. He said, "Would you mind waiting?"

"Would I mind? As if I could refuse after what you said. Do you think *I* want to be turned into a warty toad? I'm not that silly."

The curator sat on the lap of a small female idol in the far corner of the room to which he had brought Bardoni. Then, paying absolutely no attention to what Bardoni had to do, he whipped out a notebook and began to scribble in it.

The display case in front of Bardoni was open, unlike any museum case that Bardoni had ever seen. On black velvet reposed a shining, ruby red beetle.

As he had been told to do, Bardoni picked it up and tried to disregard the way the scarab's beady eyes glared at him. Putting it to his mouth, he said a long series of vocables, the only one of which he had ever heard before being Anubis.

When he had finished the ritual, he waited.

He looked at it.

It looked right back at him, unwinkingly.

Bardoni had been told that under the compulsion of the ritual the scarab would be forced to speak.

Resisting the temptation to heave the red stone beetle against the wall, he finally said, "Well talk, damn you."

The stone lips moved like a ventriloquial dummy, and the scarab said, "I hear and obey, master of me, who utters the words of power and wears the ring that once great Thothmes wore."

The ring of Thoth? Was that what Le Comte de Saint Germain had placed on his finger? Considerably impressed, Bardoni asked, "What must I do?"

"Clasp your fingers around me, pressing the stone in the great ring against me firmly, close your eyes, and I will do as I must."

Disregarding the little Curator in the far corner, Bardoni did as he was directed. It got rather boring and after a long silence, he heard the tiny reedy voice of the stone insect say, "Behold!"

There had been no sensation, none at all; as far as Bardoni was concerned, he was still standing like an idiot in a darkened room in an improbable museum, clasping a stone beetle in his hand.

But when he opened his eyes, he had to shut them fast. A noonday sun, white hot and brutal, slammed down at his eyeballs. He sustained a visual retention, even after he closed his eyes against that sudden assault of white sand; a tremendous building, and people—thousands of people, all milling around.

Eyes closed, he suddenly realized that the people were speaking, and that despite the oddness of their costumes, which ran to not much cloth, and intricate beards, and elaborate head dresses, he could understand what they were saying.

A man directly in front of him was drooling verbally as he said, "In all time, in all places, no woman has ever been so lovely as our queen, the exquisite, the incomparable, Hat Shet Set Sup."

Squinting his eyes, Bardoni risked another look. A palanquin, improbably decorated with ornate gold leaf and abortive looking figures, half man and half beast, was being carried past the vantage point where Bardoni stood.

Within the palanquin, reclining at her ease, was a most modern looking woman, despite the fact that Bardoni knew she and her mummy had long since been put on display in the Egyptological section of the museum that stood, he could swear it did, on Fifth Avenue in the Eighties, in Manhattan.

Her hair cut almost boyishly short, her finely chiseled profile familiar to him from all the reproductions that art stores sold, he was pleased to see that her body was as beautiful as her head.

All thought of her vanished from his mind as he looked into the gilded palanquin that followed her.

It, too, was carried on the burly shoulders of mammoth Ethiopian slaves.

In it was a human who was reclining as relaxedly as Queen Hat Shet Set Sup. However, this figure was that of a man, the features those that Bardoni knew as Le Comte de Saint Germain.

It was not hard to recognize that face even in the outfit that the Count was wearing, despite the sharp curled beard that projected nanny goat-wise from his chin, and in spite of the plethora of objets d'art with which the man covered his arms, his fingers and his costume.

He looked like a living junk jewelry display, Bardoni thought dispassionately, just as a hand grabbed his forearm and jerked him around so that he no longer faced the procession that was perambulating at a snail's pace towards a temple in the distance.

There could be no doubt, Bardoni thought, that the man who had grabbed him was, in one form or another, a law officer. Things might change, costumes give way to other costumes, a cop might wear a blue uniform and carry a night stick, or a white sheet and a sword as this man did, but a cop was a cop.

The man's heavy, beefy face was contorted in a snarl.

"Just watching the procession," Bardoni said innocently.

"Just watching the procession." The man mimicked. "Just happened to be standing where only the high priest and his acolytes are allowed to stand, eh? Come along." Jerking Bardoni's arm, he forced Bardoni to accompany him. It was only then that Bardoni realized that he himself was suitably accoutered, for the officer of the law had hold of Bardoni's bare forearm, above which a heavy gold bracelet cut into his biceps.

The officer snapped in the Egyptian equivalent, "Ya jerk! Ya realize that this brings you up before the ecclesiastical authorities? This is nuthin' for the magistrate's court. You're guilty of blasphemy. It's the sacred crocodiles for you, Mack."

That did not sound too pleasant and Bardoni tightened his grip on the red scarab as the officer dragged him through the colorful throng, away from the procession, towards a temple much smaller than the one to which Hat Shet Set Sup and the Egyptian Count de Saint Germain were going.

The inside of the temple was relatively cool. The aisle was set up between towering stone figures; Bardoni looked up at one whose jackal head, set on a human body, seemed to be sneering down at him, and then studiously avoided looking at any other of the animal heads that hovered above him.

In the middle distance a very old man in priestly vestments was rubbing his parchment-like hands together in glee, as he saw the officer drag Bardoni down the aisle towards him. His high-pitched voice called out, "Today is my lucky day, I knew it, I knew it, ever since I cast that dog's intestines over my shoulder at daybreak. Entrails never lie. It is a blasphemy case, is it not?"

The officer nodded. "Sure is. Got him dead to rights, too."

The old priest did a little jig of impure happiness.

Bardoni said, "Hold it, boys, I don't like to ruin anyone's day, but don't you think you better take a look at this?"

Instead of being quelled by the sight of the Ring of Thoth as Bardoni had thought the priest and the officer would be, they were delighted.

The priest chortled, "Entrails *never* lie. Oh, happy day. The stolen Ring of Thoth. Oh we shall be able to make an example of this one. Blasphemy piled on blasphemy."

The officer said, "You'll have to cook up a new torture for this guy, won't you?"

"Oh, my dear," the priest said in his thin voice, "I have devised torments undreamt of by the common run of humanity, and all my ingenuity will be able to express itself on this man!"

He danced around Bardoni, feeling his muscles, looking at his skin, and then said, "Oh, you'll last a long, long time. Perhaps I will even be able to employ the torture of tortures . . . the one that even Ptolemy said was too horrible . . ."

Putting the hand that held the scarab to his ear, Bardoni asked it, "What do I do now?"

"Tell him you demand the test by chance," the little reedy voice whispered. "He won't do it fairly of course, but that's up to you."

Bardoni cleared his throat, and roared in the silence of the temple, "I demand the test by chance!"

The priest was overwhelmed with delight. "Oh, you are a knowledgeable one, aren't you? You know all the rules." His titter was really almost all that Bardoni could bear. The little priest hurried to a flat stone set in a niche in the wall, and took up a piece of papyrus.

Then scribbling rapidly, he seemed to write two words on the little bit of papyrus. That done, he tore it in half and folded up the two pieces.

Holding them in his hand so that Bardoni could not see them, he walked to an urn nearby and dropped the bits of papyrus into the urn.

"What's all this?" The officer wanted to know truculently.

"This wretched blasphemer must have trained well in the diabolical arts. He knows that he must be allowed to throw his case in the lap of the merciful God Ra." The priest's giggle gave the lie to the word *merciful*. A pause, a giggle, and then the priest said, "According to the rules of the test, I have written innocent on one bit of papyrus and guilty on the other. If Ra directs his trembling fingers to the papyrus with innocent on it, then I dare take no action against him and must release him.

"But!" The priest chortled again. "If Ra directs his fingers to the guilty slip, as I am sure merciful Ra will, then he is mine to torture with all the rare and elegant devices that I have saved just for such an occasion."

The priest stopped giggling, and his senile old face was cruel as a sword blade as he said to Bardoni, "Impious one, choose your fate, at Ra's direction."

Bardoni walked slowly to the urn. The papyrus lay at the bottom of it. There was no conceivable way to determine which slip was which.

The scarab seemed to stir in his sweaty wet hand and he put it to his ear.

The little reedy voice said, "You realize, of course, that the old faker has written 'guilty' on both the slips."

The floor beneath Bardoni's feet slipped and swayed. His mind turned over, and he almost retched at the unfairness of it all.

"Can you help me?" he asked the scarab in a thready tone.

"Of course not. You are on your own." The little thin voice tittered like an obscene echo of the priest's own giggle.

**V**

Looking down at the urn, Bardoni could not help but wonder at what he was doing here, and why he was doing it, and whether if he were tortured to death here it would be a real death. In any event, the idea of physical torment was not appetizing, and the prospect spurred his mind.

There was complete and utter silence in the shadowy temple as Bardoni stood with his back to the priest and the officer of the Pharoah's law, and suddenly he darted his hand into the urn.

When he turned to face the two men, his jaws were working rhythmically as though he was chewing gum.

"What have you done?" the priest demanded indignantly. "Which slip did you choose?"

Gulping, Bardoni swallowed the bit of papyrus that he had been chewing with some difficulty and said airily, "Oh, I chose the slip that said innocent."

"Where is it, you lying blasphemer?"

"I swallowed it," Bardoni said innocently. "Why?"

"Swallowed it? Grab him guard, and I will . . ."

"You'll do nothing," Bardoni said truculently, feeling that he had been pushed around just about as much as he intended to allow himself to be manhandled. "Officer, remove the other slip from the urn, and if it says guilty on it, that will prove beyond doubt that I chose the innocent slip."

The priest's face was a study in baffled fury. The officer obeyed directions and, opening the slip before the priest's dancing eyes, he said, "The blasphemer is not a blasphemer, sir. See, he is right."

The priest sputtered.

"But, sir," the officer said, "you said that mighty Ra would decide the man's guilt or innocence, and He had done so."

"Tcha!" The old priest's claw-like hands were vibrating in a dance of rage.

Bardoni put the scarab to his ear, and said, "How'm I doing?"

"Fine," the little voice said. "But now pursue your advantage. This is what you have been brought on this perilous journey for. Demand from the priest the information you desire. Since you have bested him, he must tell you that which you want to know."

Turning to the raging priest, Bardoni snarled, "Simmer down, you. I want you to tell me something. But first get rid of the flatfoot."

The priest with very bad grace dismissed the officer of the law. "What do you want to know?" His rage was seeping away, but Bardoni could tell that he and the priest were never going to be buddies.

"Tell me all you know, or can find out about the man who was in the palanquin following the Queen."

Shuddering, and taking a few steps backwards, the little man spluttered, "Has your audacity no end? How dare you ask about the Queen's lover?"

Bardoni snapped his finger irritably and said, "I don't want a song and dance. I want information. Get to work."

Shaking his head dubiously, the priest said, "I must do as you will, but I want you to know that I am doing so only under duress, and will not be responsible for anything that happens . . ." He gulped. ". . . to either of us. I shall skry for you."

It sounded like a popular tune, and Bardoni hummed to himself as the priest picked up a flat, saucer-like object and poured inky black fluid into it. *I skried for you, now it's your turn to skry over me . . .* But then the priest was ready, and his gnarled finger was moiling the black liquid in the flat plate and his eyes were focused on the surface of the fluid.

Bardoni stepped to the man's side and watched over his shoulder as the little priest muttered an incantation and kept tracing cabalistic signs on the surface of the jet-black fluid.

Suddenly, as though projected on the stygian surface, Bardoni saw a picture begin to take shape.

The priest was quite unhappy about the whole thing and kept moaning as the picture cleared, and he and Bardoni could see quite clearly a scene wherein the man that Bardoni knew as Saint Germain, but dressed in hierophant's robes, stood facing an identical twin. The two Count de Saint Germains stared deep into each other's eyes for a long moment, and faintly indicated, above their identical faces, could be seen the outlines of Ra's face.

With no warning at all, one of the twins suddenly flashed a knife. It flickered and then was rammed deep into the chest of the other Count Saint Germain. The face of the god vanished. Then the living Count, a wild exaltation on his face, used his foot to roll the corpse over onto its face.

The priest whispered, "Oh monstrous blasphemy! He has murdered his Ka!"

Then the picture shifted and to Bardoni's incredulous surprise he was now looking at a representation of the whole earth. The ball spun around on its axis in space. It was as though he was looking down at the globe from the moon. What happened next caused Bardoni to rub his eyes, for like a double exposure, there gradually appeared still another earth, this one inextricably interwoven with the first one, but slightly off to one side so that parts of it were enveloped in the other.

Two planets, he thought in fuzzy bewilderment, co-existing, one within the other, neither visible to the other . . .

The picture became clearer and it was as though Bardoni was in a rocket ship on the way from the moon to the earth. But suddenly the priest's hand shook and he dropped the plate to the floor. The black fluid ran in random shapes over the temple floor.

The priest gasped, "No more, I conjure you, no more. I will not, I cannot show you more . . ."

Before Bardoni could realize what had happened, the little man ran off behind a statue.

Putting the scarab to his ear, Bardoni asked, "What now?"

The scarab whispered, "Look at the entrance to the temple."

The blood in Bardoni's veins didn't really freeze, it just seemed that way. Framed in the doorway stood the man he knew as the Count Saint Germain, his Egyptian clothes all awry, his face a mask of menace.

His hands wove together in a series of gestures that Bardoni knew instinctively were inimical to his welfare.

Bardoni said to the scarab, "Let's get out of here!"

He closed his eyes, not knowing whether he was surrendering to those horrid hand gestures or whether he was making good his escape. He knew, beyond any shadow of a doubt that what the Count was doing was not good . . .

When he opened, his eyes the first thing he saw was the little curator, Mr. Charlier, still seated in the corner of the room in the museum, still busy scribbling in his notebook.

Breathing a sigh of relief, Bardoni said to the scarab, "What now?"

There was no answer.

Opening his hand wider, Bardoni looked closely at the little eyes on the stone scarab. They no longer seemed alive. As a matter of fact, the red stone suddenly seemed just that, a red stone, crudely carved into the shape of a scarab beetle.

The fussy curator snapped, "That's all you'll get out of the scarab." Then under his breath, he muttered, "The very idea! Next thing I know they'll be saddling me with kiddies."

Uncertainly, Bardoni replaced the scarab in the museum case, and wondered what to do next. Then he remembered the injunction contained in the absurd doggerel that the demon had chanted.

He had used Carnavon's scarab for what that was worth; next he had to use the petrified tree . . . and then, and only then, the mouth of Adonis. He resolutely put out of his mind the way the demon had giggled after reciting the poem.

Picking up the paper bag containing the black rooster and feeling his pockets to be sure he still had the dagger and the package of rare herbs, Bardoni said, "I'd like to be taken to the petrified tree now, Mr. Charlier."

Adjusting his pince-nez, the curator said, "Anything you say, mine not to reason why, mine but to do or die . . ."

Another long walk through corridors where their feet left behind them resounding echoes, and then they entered a room whose walls were hung with flaming crimson drapes on which were embroidered some rather indecent possibilities in the way of men with maids.

Averting his eyes, Bardoni said, "The tree?"

The curator pointed to a raised podium. On top of it was a long sort of bolster, or mattress, which, like everything else in the room, was covered with the eye-searing crimson cloth.

Resting on it was what might once have been a tree, a living thing, but which the process of time had calcified. Bardoni found it rather doubtful that even the vagrant whim of playful Mother Nature could have contrived such an unlikely shape for a tree to grow into.

But that was none of his business.

Pretending that the shape of the tree was fortuitous, Bardoni looked around till he found a vessel in the shape of an open kettle. As a matter of fact, he thought dully, it looked rather like the kind of cooking instrument that cartoonists draw when they want to show a missionary being boiled for the delectation of epicurean cannibals.

The kettle was heavy, but he managed to move it the way garbage collectors maneuver garbage cans and, when he finally had it right in front of the tip of the tree, he reached into his pocket and opened the bag of herbs and sprinkled them into the pot, chanting as he did so the obscure syllables that he had been taught in the taxicab on the way to the museum.

As he crushed the herbs in his fingers the odors began to seep out into the air, and he found them singularly unappetizing.

Next he took the sleepy rooster out of the bag and held it over the kettle. He didn't like what he had to do next, but he used the wicked looking dagger as he had been directed to do, and dropped the defunct fowl into the pot.

Then, weaving his fingers together as he had been shown how to do, he began to mumble the meaningless words that he had learned.

If the tree, he thought in a section of his mind that was not concerned with what he was doing, came to life the way the scarab had done, it was going to present a rather unlikely picture.

Then, as he continued the formula, a thought occurred to him. This was all the ritual that he had been taught. What happened next? What was he to do to call on Adonis, or was this ritual with the petrified tree part of the Adonis worship?

His second thought was the correct one, he found as the smell of the herbs co-mingled with that of the rooster's fresh blood.

Whatever function the smells, the death of the bird, and the words of the chant were supposed to perform was in the process of happening.

All around him the unseemly pictures wove into the crimson cloth began to move, at first slowly, then more rapidly. It was as though they were beginning to come alive. The result was a little overwhelming.

The curator paid no attention to the process that was going on around him, which struck Bardoni as being odd, since directly over Mr. Charlier's head a sort of daisy chain arrangement was proceeding apace.

Bardoni came to the end of the formula that he had memorized. That left him with nothing to do but stand and watch bug-eyed the proceedings in the embroidery.

From nowhere and from everywhere, a deep bass voice, organ-like, overwhelming in its sheer virile masculinity said slowly, "One assumes that one has not been appealed to in vain."

The very words carried menace.

Stammering a little, Bardoni gulped and said, conscious of the fact that in comparison his own voice suddenly seemed thin, and almost falsetto, "Oh, no, mighty Adonis." At least he hoped it was not to be in vain. "By the powers that invest me," he said hesitantly, "and by the acts I have performed, I am empowered to ask Adonis three questions."

"You are." The deep rumble was almost deafening.

"Why did Count de Saint Germain, or whatever his name really is, murder his Ka, his other self, his soul, back in ancient Egypt?"

"In order to have life everlasting, fool! Why else?"

"Those two worlds I saw in the blackness of the skrying bowl. What were they?"

"The two worlds that *are*, idiot mortal." Then in a deep grumbling aside, the booming voice said, "To wake mighty Adonis for childish prattle . . . would that I were not constrained . . ."

One question . . . and only one question left.

Bardoni tried desperately to make sense out of what he had seen in the skrying bowl and the comparatively cryptic answers that Adonis was so grudgingly giving him.

He had to, he must take a chance and try to get two answers from one question.

Aloud he asked, bluffing mightily, "Since I am not in my own world, how can I return to it?"

A hoarse bellow of rage was for a moment his only answer.

Then, "To disturb me for these moronic questions!" Then silence. Finally the voice said, "Imbecile, you strain my patience! Know you not that all you need to do is remove the ring from off your finger?"

This time the silence was not disturbed.

That is, not until the curator said, "Well, really, how long are you going to stand there with that dumbfounded look on your face? Come along, come along, I have done all I can for you."

But the man actually had to push petulantly at Bardoni before he could make Bardoni begin to move.

Outside on the steps of the museum, Bardoni still stood thunderstruck, looking down at the curious ring on the middle finger of his right hand. Behind him the curator angrily slammed closed the museum's door.

And then Bardoni was alone in the night, on the steps of a magic museum, in a world that he not only never made, but in whose reality he did not quite believe.

All that mumbo jumbo and what had he really learned?

Down on the sidewalk a passing patrolman sauntered by.

The police!

And they wanted him for questioning as to the whereabouts of a man who had been alive when Hat Shet Set Sup lived . . . a man who, if Bardoni was to believe what he had learned, was immortal.

It was a little hard to take.

In his pocket be could feel the primer of incantations that his friend had insisted he take along with him. Waiting till the policeman was gone from sight, Bardoni flicked through the pages of the book. Hoping that by some chance there might be an inkling, some kind of clue in the printed words, he skimmed the pages.

A chapter heading caught his eye: *The Three Easiest Methods of Levitating a Human*. Interesting, he thought disconsolately, but hardly relevant at the moment. Shoving the book back into his pocket, he stared at the ring on his finger.

If there were really, which he doubted, two worlds existing side by side, with no one suspecting the existence of the other, or the way they interpenetrated each other extra-dimensionally, then all he had to do, according to Adonis, was to slip the ring off his finger and he would be back in the other world, the earth that was to him the only reality.

Timorously, he touched the ring, tried to pull it off his finger.

Instantly, he staggered as though hit by a blackjack.

Inside his head he heard the Count de Saint Germain's voice warning him of instant death if he removed the ring.

A fine how do you do, he thought angrily; if there were two earths and this ring was the way of getting from one to the other, how the hell was he going to make the trip if he couldn't take the ring off?

Suddenly he was vastly irritated with what had happened to him. Angry at the way he was being put upon. He did not doubt for an instant that the Count was using him for some fell purpose, but he did not want to be the cat's paw in a complicated inter-worldly plot. He didn't want to remain in a world where real magic worked, where there were pet demons and assorted cabalistic gestures that worked wonders. He wanted to get home. To rabbits that didn't talk, and nightclub audiences who, while they might be drunken bums, at least were the kind of bums that he understood. And he didn't want to meet any more simulacra of his friends who looked and acted like people he knew but were simultaneously capable of setting physical saws at nought.

Realizing that he was enjoying a rather childish rage, he nevertheless managed to work himself into a fury about the unfairness of it all.

Why in the name of all that was holy, or unholy, had the Count selected him on whom to work this hugger-mugger? Why couldn't some other sucker have been employed?

Descending the steps slowly, feeding fuel to his anger, trying to work himself up to a pitch to where he would be able to overcome the compulsion not to remove the ring, he was conscious at first only vaguely but then more acutely that the silence of the night was being disrupted by what seemed like an orderly riot.

Fifth Avenue stretched away from him serene and quiet, its streets tree lined, the fancy apartment houses clean and handsome, but keening his ears was the sound of many police sirens.

A tramp, disheveled and unkempt, staggered to his feet from his bed on a park bench nearby and said, "Wha's goes? Hah? Wha' goes any old how?"

To Bardoni's right, he saw a dolly-car racing towards him. To his left, a paddy wagon rolled through the night. From the north, a phalanx of policemen on foot; from the south, more dolly-cars.

The passing patrolman, the one who had sauntered by, must have recognized him, Bardoni realized. There would be, after all, no trouble in finding publicity pictures of him . . . and with his face known, they had spotted him.

But why all the hustle and bustle? Anyone would have thought that he'd robbed a bank, or assassinated a president, the way they were calling out the reserves.

The tramp staggered drunkenly towards Bardoni, saying, "I'll go quietly offisher. If I'd known you wanted me, I'da come to the station house. You didn't have to send out all the boys for me . . ."

A policeman, whose gold buttons and badge proclaimed him to be a sergeant, yelled out, "Bardoni, don't move! We've got you covered!"

What had he done? Or what did they think he'd done to warrant all this? The Count de Saint Germain, he realized must be pretty big potatoes in this world to warrant all this fuss.

Turning towards the sergeant, Bardoni called across the intervening twenty feet that separated them. "I'll go quietly officer, but why do you want me?"

The sergeant bellowed, "Ho, ho, that's rich! The President's adviser and right-hand man vanishes, and this punk was last seen with him, and then wants to know why we want him!"

The tramp lurched into Bardoni as the encircling police came closer. The sergeant roared out, "Careful everyone, he's a magician you know . . . get the detective from the Magic Squad up here, fast! Before this guy pulls anything!"

The order was sent back through the ranks of the police.

Bardoni swung towards the tramp, and said, "How'd you like a present?"

The tramp's eyes gleamed. "Me, I'd like it fine," he said.

Extending his hand, Bardoni said, "Here, I'm going to jail anyhow. You can have this ring, if you can pull it off my finger!"

## VI

The tramp's dirty fingers grappled with the ring, and it slipped right off. Bardoni closed his eyes, exulting. It was off, and he had not died. And with it off, supposedly he was no longer in the insane world of magic, but back in his own world where tricks were tricks and he was a working magician, and where he was not involved with the envanishment of the President's right-hand man, and he could just open his eyes and walk home to his rabbit that didn't talk, and maybe call Judy and go out and have a bite to eat, if she didn't have a date with the damned sax player.

Opening his eyes, with an exultant grin splitting his face, he instantly reclosed them.

The tramp still stood next to him looking at the odd ring which he held.

All around the tramp and Bardoni, the police came closer, and closer.

Behind them—Bardoni swiveled his head—behind him, the museum still stood like an ancient, gigantic sarcophagus.

The tramp said, "Jeeze, thanks, mister, but do you think the cops are gonna let me keep it?"

The nearest policeman, the sergeant, had a pair of handcuffs out, ready to snap them on Bardoni's wrists. In sheer and utter frustration, Bardoni looked about him frantically. Was there no chance at all for escape? Nowhere.

But as he rotated his head, exploring every avenue, he saw a sign on a lamp post. A sign that had not been there a moment ago. Bardoni's heart leapt up in gratitude. What if the police were after him. What if he were thrown in jail?

He read and reread the words on the sign, the sweetest words he had ever read. *The Metropolitan Museum of Art*, the sign said.

Then the handcuffs closed on his wrists and no detective from the "Magic Squad" made his appearance and Bardoni was thrown into a patrol wagon and carried off into the night.

The tramp watched thunderstruck for a long, long while; then, shrugging, he turned the ring on his finger and admired it in the light from a lamp post.

The tramp who had appeared in front of the Metropolitan Museum of Art was not even aware that he had been moved to another world. Merely aware that the disturbance was dying down, he shrugged and returned to his hard bed on the park bench.

Bardoni was considerably confused when the patrol wagon drove, not to police headquarters, but out to Long Island to La Guardia Airport.

The handcuffs remained on his wrist, the sergeant who sat next to him in the plane seat was uncommunicative, and all that Bardoni knew was that he was being flown to Washington, D. C.

His handcuffs were not removed until he was seated in an ante-chamber outside the room in which the President held weekly press conferences.

A terrific babble of voices was coming through the doorway and without trying to eavesdrop, Bardoni was able to hear the president say, "Gentlemen! Really, it's not as if I were alone in this. You must remember that Mackenzie King, for so long a capable and just administrator, for so many years the Premier of Canada, was a sincere believer in spiritualism. Now while I am not willing to say that I am a believer, I do say that I will wait till the Count de Saint Germain has shown me what he calls his proofs."

There was another outburst, quelled by the President saying, "And don't forget gentlemen that I have been for years an amateur magician. No corny tricks of the average fake spirit medium are going to deceive me!

"Besides that, I have called in a council of reputable men of science and they, too, will sit in judgment on what Count de Saint Germain has called complete and final proof of the existence of spiritualism.

"I know," the President said, "that must strike all of you as bizarre beyond compare; I have kept this quiet up until now, for fear of what the public's reaction would be. But now, in half an hour, the Count has promised a demonstration that will make converts of the most doubting.

"If five of you gentlemen of the press can be selected by lot, they may join the committee of scientists and me, when the Count shows us whatever it is he wants to demonstrate."

Another outburst of many men's voices and then the President's voice, which Bardoni knew so well from the radio, from newsreels and from television appearances, roared out, "Gentlemen, do you think for one moment I would have precipitated this affair, had I not seen the Count perform certain things that are beyond all explanation? Well then, wait and see what transpires at the seance, before you condemn or make complete and utter fools of yourselves!"

Bardoni sat looking off into space. When Le Comte de Saint Germain had been high in favor in France, the Revolution had come close on heels. In Russia, another revolution. He showed up in New York, the Depression followed. His seamed face was seen, and suddenly Hiroshima and Nagasaki. But that had been on the other world. Or had it been on both worlds. Anyhow, now . . .

Shuddering, Bardoni wondered what new horror the incredibly aged man who had murdered his Ka had up his sleeve.

Let him put this across; put him in the position of controlling the President of the United States . . . and who could guess what devastation, destruction, death and despair might follow?

It was a case of think-of-the-devil.

A small door to one side opened and the Count entered. He dismissed the sergeant of police, who seemed happy to leave such an elevated atmosphere and return to his more mundane spheres of activity.

As soon as he was gone, the Count snapped, "You idiot!"

It was bad enough having Adonis call him names, Bardoni felt, but he didn't see why he had to take much nonsense from the Count.

"To jeopardize all my plans, because in your imbecilic fashion you thought you could return to your own world!" The nictitating eyelids flashed up and down as the Count brought his accordion-pleated wrinkled face close to Bardoni and whispered, "Understand this, you lunatic, there is no chance at all for you to return to your world, unless and until I send you there and bring that other Mongolian idiot back to this world."

He was being called an idiot in both of his persons, Bardoni realized, and didn't like it. But he was cheered to find that the Count was not omniscient, that he did not know that the Bardoni who sat in front of him was not the real magician, but was the trickster, the hanky-panky man.

But the Count went on, "Now listen to me. As I have told you and even you in your dim-witted fashion should be able to understand, once you have come from your world to this, your real magic powers fade inside of a fortnight, or three weeks at the most. I have been back and forth so often that my powers are, at the moment, and until I can go back home again for a while, at very low ebb. They must be recharged occasionally. Your powers are fresh and will stay so long enough to do what I want done.

"Therefore, in twenty minutes when I put on the seance that I have promised the President, you will bring about the manifestations that I need!

"Understand me? Or else you will never be able to return to your world!"

The Count turned and walked away from Bardoni, exulting aloud, as he paced back and forth, looking like an evil Cardinal Richelieu, "With the President of these sprawling states in both worlds in my power, what horrors can I not wreak! I shall build up enough evil so that I can walk between the many worlds, free, the master of all I survey. Not all the evil that I have banked through all these myriad years can hold a candle to what I will be able to do now . . ."

To be able to put evil in the bank seemed like an odd kind of bookkeeping to Bardoni but he kept his mouth shut as the ancient man said, "Never, not since the birth of this ridiculous pair of matched planets has there ever been, or will there ever be, anyone to come up to my shoulder as far as power is concerned.

"To think, with success in my grasp, I will no longer have to return to that other world to recharge my magic, but will instead be able to wander where I will, to far Alpha Centauri and beyond the most distant planetary systems known to man . . . that crawling insect befouled by his own short sightedness . . ."

There probably would have been a lot more in that vein, Bardoni thought, but at that point one of the President's aide de camps entered the room and said, "Whenever you are ready, Count."

The Count snapped his fingers in irritation and then said,

"Presently. I shall be ready in two minutes." Then he stepped close to Bardoni and whispered, "You remember my instructions? Follow them or you risk my eternal displeasure."

"You'd better run over them once more," Bardoni said, realizing that he hadn't the vaguest idea what the Count meant.

Tensely, irately, the Count said, "I don't want to risk transporting any real demons from our world, therefore, you are, by the aid of your magic, by incantation and spell, to give the appearance of a spiritualistic seance. Got it, stupid?"

"Umm, I guess so," Bardoni said hesitantly. "But just what effects do you want me to perform?"

"Cretin!" The Count was close to the edge of a maniacal fury. "With all the magicians in our world why did I pick you?"

That was a good question. "Why did you?" Bardoni asked.

"Just at random. What earthly or unearthly difference did it make as long as I chose a competent master of enchantment?"

Bardoni realized it had been just his lousy luck that the Count had picked his identical twin in that other world . . . and therefore had to transport him to switch the other guy here.

Le Comte de Saint Germain whispered, "Now remember, you are to levitate, to conjure up wraiths, and to force them to speak in the voices that the President expects to hear them use."

"I gotcha," Bardoni said. "But you'd better stall for a couple of minutes. And get me the use of an official car. I forgot some of the mystic herbs I'm going to need!"

This time it really looked as if the aged man was going to have a stroke. His face turned blackly red, then he caught his breath, and said, "I will not lose my temper, I will not lose my temper!"

But, against his will, he was forced to accede to Bardoni's request.

Moments later, racing through the circuitous streets of Washington, Bardoni prayed that another magic dealer friend of his, Harry Baker, would have his shop open. Luckily it was not far from the Presidential headquarters, and, leaving the official car parked at the curb with its motor running and its obvious Secret Service man chauffeur looking puzzledly after him, Bardoni rushed up the steps of Harry's shop.

Harry was not in the shop, but Bardoni saw Dolly Snow in back of the counter, and he prevailed on the blonde assistant to get him what he wanted.

Then, smiling his thanks, he left her looking baffled, as he ran out of the shop and back to the car.

Three minutes later, he was dashing back into the antechamber, his pockets bulging with his new acquisitions.

The Count snarled, "Are you ready now? Finally?"

Bardoni nodded. He was ready, all right!

There was a lot of protocol involved in the seating arrangements, and the President was tapping his fingers impatiently on the long mahogany table long before everyone, scientist and reporter, was seated properly as high echelon etiquette demanded.

The Count seemed removed from all worldly considerations as he stood in a corner of the room looking impassively out the window, out toward the imposing building that houses the Congress of the United States.

Bardoni could imagine what wild rampaging dreams of evil power the Count was allowing himself.

But then, at long last, all was ready.

The President said, "Gentlemen, Le Comte de Saint Germain."

Barely nodding, the Count acknowledged the introduction; and then indicating the lights that flooded the room, his strange voice husky with strain that did not show in his impassive face, he said, "If any of you has ever gone to fake spirit mediums, you know only too well that they demand darkness and hocus-pocus with much singing of hymns and grunting and groaning. You will note, that I demand none of these aids to deception.

"This will be a full-light seance."

Nodding to Bardoni, the Count continued, "My assistant, Mr. Bardoni, and I will now prove beyond any shadow of doubt that spirits live."

The scientists at the long table were still, their faces avidly turned to the Count; Bardoni realized how much they wanted to attack and tear the Count to shreds. He hoped he wasn't included in their plans. Newsmen, on the other hand, preserved their reputation for impartiality and sat, one and all, with cynical smiles on their faces, a show-me attitude that challenged everything the Count said and did.

Only the President, Bardoni saw, was really concerned with what was going to happen. With the President in the Count's vest pocket, Bardoni thought, what horror could be expected . . . World War III with destruction unparalleled in the history of the human race; or perhaps, since the Count expected so much of all this, perhaps he was planning on the complete destruction of the world.

That raised a puzzling question. Would the destruction of one world end the other intra-dimensionally woven world?

No time now for any further mental questions.

Holding his hand up for attention, which he need not have bothered to do, since every eye in the room was glued on him, the Count said, "Spirits, I would ask indulgence of you. Manifest yourselves for these gentlemen, give them any and all proofs that they, in their doubts, demand."

Bardoni's hands were busy under the table at which he sat, off to one side of the big conference table. No one was watching him, any more than any member of any audience ever watches the magician's assistant.

They sat and watched the Count, just as all audiences watch the man in the spotlight, the performing magician.

Eerily, a tenuous finger of what spiritualists call ectoplasm slowly meandered across the room, fragile as a child's dream; incoherent as a drunken nightmare, it floated, and assumed various shapes as it came closer, ever closer to the President.

No one in the room moved a muscle.

All eyes were frozen on the "ectoplasm."

The President sighed a breathy sigh of relief, and said, "See, gentlemen, didn't I tell you?"

The Count said, "Silence, please, Mr. President. Just keep watching."

The very tip of the grayish impalpable substance split and became many fingered, then these seemed to weave together, become more and more solid.

Then and only then, the Count said, "Now, gentlemen, I will force this extension from the 'bourne from which no man returneth,' to open a way for anyone that you desire."

A babble of voices, fear-filled mutterings, and then the President said, "I don't know about the rest of you, but I have always admired Benjamin Franklin. Would you have his spirit put in an appearance?"

"Certainly, sir," the Count said, his odd eyes turning briefly to Bardoni as though warning him to do as he was told. "I admire your choice of the illustrious dead.

"Franklin of all people, this young republic's choice of ambassador to France. Franklin the last universal genius, but for me." The Count smiled immodestly, then continued, "You might Mr. President, considering Mr. Franklin's intellectual achievements, ask his advice on that knotty problem you spoke of to me."

"Good idea," the President's lean bony face smiled. "Let's see if he agrees with you, Count."

The cloud of grayish material was circular now, hanging in the center of the room, and it seemed to Bardoni, who eyed it dispassionately, that any outsider looking into the room might well imagine that the cloud was being held there by the intensity of the glances that the scientists and the reporters were according it.

The pivot of all their eyes, it hung like one's breath on a crisp wintry morning.

Bardoni was really busy now, his hands racing to each of his pockets in turn, manipulating certain devices, making certain adjustments.

The Count said almost threateningly, "Franklin, appear." But Bardoni knew that the words were directed to him, and not to the cloud of "ectoplasm" that was the magnet for all eyes.

Hoping against hope that the President was a better amateur magician than most, Bardoni proceeded with the dangerous game that he was playing. The stakes were high.

The fate of the world.

## VII

At first the cloud of gray material was merely round, but then slowly, exceedingly slowly it began to assume a shape that might, by a stretch of the imagination be considered humanoid.

What could have been lips slowly opened, and a heavy voice said, "Who calls?"

There was no doubt about it, Bardoni thought, it was a hell of an effect. The reporters gasped and the scientists were now exchanging uneasy glances.

The Count said, "Hurry it up! Mr. Franklin, arrange yourself."

The Voice that might have been coming from anywhere said irritably, "Keep your shirt on, Count. It's not easy to pull one's ectoplasm together."

Those nictitating lids came up, Bardoni saw, as the Count sent a glance of raging fury at him. Bardoni's face was completely immobile, his lips unmoving as the voice that the audience seemed to think belonged to Benjamin Franklin said, "Break it off, Buster, you can't push me around! I'm dead!"

Tottering, the Count walked towards the pall of gray, smoking material and, his hands raised as though to disperse it, he cried to the President, "I regret, sir, that seemingly a poltergeist has interfered."

The President explained in an aside, "Poltergeists are very difficult, they are rather like imbecile demons, the spirit of the insane. They are given to breaking dishes, and making noises in untenanted houses. Very irritating."

The Count's wrinkles seemed to become more wrinkled, if that was possible. Staring at the "ectoplasm," he said, "Poltergeist, begone, Franklin, appear!"

From the center of the gray cloud, a voice seemed to say, "Nuts to you, you old faker! Why don't you go back to where you belong?"

There could be no doubt about it, Bardoni thought, immortal the old boy might be, but close to an apoplectic stroke he was. The Count pretended to be speaking to the grayish cloud, but his words were directed to Bardoni.

"Go back, poltergeist, beware my wrath. Begone, or you will rue the day that saw you born of woman!"

Since poltergeists were never born, let alone of a woman, Bardoni knew the threat was directed at him.

Insolently, the disembodied-voice snapped, "Go roll your hoop, Count, you've had it. Who do you think you're kidding with this cornball routine?"

The President was turning his head one way and then the other, like a spectator at a tennis game, from the "ectoplasm" to the maddened Count.

Stepping directly through the gray cloud and dispersing it, the Count tottered towards Bardoni, his white hands looking like claws as he reached for Bardoni's throat.

"Come what may," the words came thickly, "I'm going to kill you for this!"

Then two men, who up till that point had seemed like reporters, kicked their chairs back, and in that one move revealed themselves to be Secret Service men.

Just as they grabbed the Count's fragile body, his hands reached Bardoni's throat.

Bardoni said, "How far did you think you could push me?"

Then the President's guards were holding the Count. They had to lift him off the floor, for like a child gone berserk, he was kicking with his feet, flailing his arms around, screaming at the top of his lungs as he said, "You're not the right Bardoni . . . you're the one I sent to the other world!"

Bardoni rose to his feet, and bowed mockingly. He said, "You're post-hypnotic command not to remove the ring didn't work."

"Adonis must have told you!" The Count said, and then there was a slackening in the mad fury that writhed across his face, and suddenly his body went limp.

One of the scientists left the conference table, and took a quick look at the Count. Then he said, "I'm afraid this old gentleman has had a stroke."

Maliciously Bardoni thought, so go on being immortal, you old louse . . . live forever, but with a brain that no longer functions in all its parts. Let's see how much trouble you can stir up for my world now, you ancient reprobate!

And then the Count's unconscious body was being removed, and the President was at Bardoni's side while all the other men in the room were busy talking to each other. In the little area of quiet around the President and the hanky-panky man, the President said, "Thank you."

Smiling, Bardoni "So you almost fell for that charlatan, eh, Mr. President?"

"I recognize you now. You're Bardoni the magician, aren't you?"

Nodding, Bardoni waited.

"You're right. I did almost fall for him. But, Bardoni, the first time he performed for me . . . I swear he did things that magic and trickery cannot account for . . . that's why I called this meeting . . . if he had performed today what he did that first time, I assure you that the world would have accepted his chicanery as proof of life after death . . ."

Lucky, lucky day, Bardoni thought, that had allowed him to be present at this meeting.

The President said, "That was very cute, the seance you rigged up." Then, like any amateur magician anywhere, the President of the United States added, "Look, Bardoni, I have a little card effect that's fooled everyone I've shown it to. I'll swap it with you for the secret of how you managed to control that fake ectoplasm."

"You knew I was ventriloquizing the spirit voice?" Bardoni asked, trying to change the subject.

"Oh, surely, surely, as soon as I spotted what you were doing under the table I knew what was up. But tell me, how did you control the chemical ectoplasm?"

Poor President, poor amateur magician, Bardoni thought. That was the one thing he could not reveal. He had bought the fake ectoplasm in the Harry Baker magic shop. But he had controlled it by a spell he had read in the little book that his friend in the other world had given him.

Aloud he said, "I'm sorry, sir, but that was given me by an old Hindu fakir, and I had to swear never to reveal the trick or he would not have taught it to me."

That the President was disappointed there was no doubt, but Bardoni managed to do some close-up impromptu tricks, three of which he taught the President, and that seemed to take care of the matter.

Then there was a long harangue in which the President asked the reporters to keep the whole unseemly seance off the record, and then finally Bardoni was free to leave.

He flew away from Washington with the President's words of gratitude ringing in his ears and a letter signed by the President, praising his skill, which was going right into his advertising brochures the following day. It was only when he was sitting at his ease in the special plane that the President had commandeered for him that Bardoni was able to relax and wonder how long the Count's stroke would completely incapacitate him, and whether it would end forever his ability to do evil.

That, Bardoni decided, was in the lap of the gods. He had done all he could, he had given his little all; and only now could he heave a vast sigh of relief as he realized how grateful the whole world should be to him . . .

For that he had saved the world from destruction he did not doubt. The fact that no one was ever going to know it was irritating, but .. . his hand touched the primer of magic spells. But there were going to be rewards at that.

A beatific smile on his face, and he fell asleep, dreaming of how he was going to baffle the hell out of the boys in the magic shops and his audiences, when he performed *real* magic for them!

And the reality if anything surpassed his dreams.

When he entered Tannen's magic shop, bowing, and calmly proceeded to float up into the air, reclining at his ease as he did so, the expression on the other magicians' faces was worth every bit of the trouble through which he had gone. That and the way they sneaked up to him and offered him everything in their power, if he would only reveal his secret.

Gloating, he worked out a routine that took him and Judy right out of the honky-tonk nightclubs and to the stage of Radio City.

Dwarfed by the immensity of the largest stage in all the world, he made his entrance, the tremendous symphonic orchestra playing his music, Judy at one side of him, her eyes wide with amazement, as he tossed his hat to one side, where it floated, while without his even touching the levitated hat, a bunny appeared out of it by magic.

And not one rabbit, but a stage full of them, a plethora. An over-abundance of them, hundreds of rabbits, thousands of rabbits, which at a gesture from the Great Bardoni, suddenly merged and became one huge gigantic rabbit that wavered for a moment and then vanished.

Then at a muttered incantation from Bardoni, Judy became invisible.

What a gasp that brought from the four thousand people in the audience!

Wonder piled on wonder and, there in the front tow, Bardoni could see every magician in America sitting with their faces frozen, their minds a blank as they tried to imagine what conceivable gimmicks he was using, as piling Pelion on Ossa, he proceeded *really* to do every magic effect that every magician had ever done by means of gimmicks, gadgets, mirrors and sundry other devices. In the front row, Harry Blackstone, his white, white hair a beacon, watched as amazed as any layman, and around him magicians, amateurs and such professionals as Walter Essman, Bill Simon, Frank Garcia, Rickie Dunn and all sat stunned.

Never in the history of the entertainment world had there ever been such an overnight sensation.

It got so you could not turn on a television set without seeing his smiling face, without seeing him do something completely baffling, completely inexplicable. One day he was on television more than Arthur Godfrey!

His agent was almost insane with joy.

He was able to take an ad in *Variety* that bragged, *The Great Bardoni, Booked Solid Till 1966!*

Those bookings came in handy when, two weeks and three days after he had prevailed on the drunken tramp to remove the mystic ring of Thothmes, he made his entrance on the Radio city Music Hall stage, levitated himself fifteen feet in the air, then, sitting cross legged on nothingness, as he had begun to do for an opening, floated casually out over the audience, throwing bonbons as he went. Behind him on the stage, Judy, as baffled as any member of the audience, watched with baited breath as he showed off a bit and did barrel rolls over the audience, smiling down at their upturned faces; then, not satisfied with that, he straightened out his body, floated over the loges, a spotlight following his every move, and, poising on the rail of the loges, he did a swan dive over the orchestra.

Judy was the only one who realized that something had gone wrong, for suddenly, when he was halfway down from the loge's, he seemed to quiver.

Losing altitude, he fluttered his arms, like broken wings, and then everyone realized that something had gone wrong, for his face contorted with despair and he fell the last fifteen feet, to land in a crumpled heap in an aisle.

It was only when he had picked himself up and felt his limbs to reassure himself that nothing was broken that he knew what had happened.

As he had feared, the magic was gone. It had worn off at last.

He finished his act with his usual gimmicked magic tricks, displaying his virtuoso sleight of hand, but gone were the days of emulating Apollonius of Tyana. He was once more a hanky-panky man.

Audiences in the hinterlands wondered, but not too audibly, why a year earlier the papers had been full of Bardoni's exploits, when all they saw was a fairly stock stage magician performing pretty run-of-the-mill tricks for them; but publicity has a real magic of its own, and Bardoni was able to stay on the crest for much longer than the average ten-day sensation.

And when it was all over and he was once more just a regular magic act, back working nightclubs and battling hecklers, he never let it bother him, for he had had his heart's desire.

And how few men, magicians or not, ever have that?

With Kit Marlowe's Dr. Faustus, Bardoni could say, "'Tis magicke, magicke that hath ravisht me . . ."

# The Man Next Door

*Papa's in the study, involved in giving birth;*
*Junior's in the basement, blowing up the Earth;*
*Mama's in the bedroom, making up her face,*
*While the guy next door saves the human race.*

Bennet Barlay sat in front of his typewriter and gazed with anguished eyes at the white paper on the roller. He had a work block. The longer he sat and looked at the blank paper, the less he seemed to be able to think of a story idea. For a tremendous word producer, this was an impossible thing to have happen. Here he had written, and what was more important, sold, millions of words to the pulp science-fiction market. His name, or rather his many names, since his production was so high that he was forced to use pseudonyms, was a household word to those peculiar people who called themselves fans, an ugly neologism that had caused him to dislike all science-fiction fans, and yet . . .

And yet, he could not force his weary brain to conjure up a single story idea.

Perhaps, he thought, looking dully at the calendar, not really seeing the date, March 14, 1953: perhaps he was written out. It had happened to other writers he knew.

Or maybe, he hoped, the work block was brought on by the desperate need he had to raise some money to pay his income tax.

Leaning forward, his two middle fingers and thumb became busy at the keys of the typewriter. The sound of the machine rapped out through the quiet room.

Down in the cellar, Bennet Barlay junior heard the rat-tat-tat of his father's typewriter, but it was so usual a sound that he paid no attention to it. It was part of his conditioning, just as his father's type of writing had practically forced him to be interested in science. The gadget he was working on looked like one of the peculiar illustrations for any of his father's stories.

Wires, oddly angled braces, lights that seemed to flick on and off for no particular reason, a pulsing sound that was on the off-beat to the sound of his father's tap-tapping, all combined to make the machine the boy was working on seem like the product of some unearthly science.

Pressing a particular sequence of buttons, the boy's face became drawn with adult strain as he waited. He had kept his research a secret from his father because he wanted to surprise him. But if this worked....

Walking away from the machine, the boy opened a hutch. From it he took a hamster. The tiny animal seemed more like a Disney drawing than a real mammal. It looked up at him with its round, brown eyes, its pathetic stub of useless tail frozen into immobility.

The boy placed the animal on a platform that was an integral part of the apparatus on which he was working. Biting his lower lip, the boy pressed the last button.

Then he waited . . .

Two floors above ground level the sound of the typewriter was so muted as to be almost inaudible. Mrs. Barlay, standing in front of a three-fold mirror on her vanity table, considered herself and her body. She was pleased with it.

Naked, fresh from the shower, she felt a glow of happiness that bearing her son had left so little sign on her young body. Her face needed makeup before it would match the body which it surmounted. After all, she thought, Benjamin Franklin had been right when he had recommended an older woman for a mistress. The vital fluids *did* descend very slowly, aging first the face, then more slowly, the rest of the woman.

Franklin, she thought, had been so right when he had listed all the advantages of older women, particularly the last sentence he had written for a younger friend's amorous guidance. "Besides," the American Ambassador to France during the Revolution had said, "they (older women) are so grateful . . ."

Gratitude was only one of the emotions she felt for her next-door neighbor. With her fortieth birthday only weeks away, she had been feeling just a trifle sorry for herself. Her connubial relations had slid into a once-a-week affair as automatic as eating. But all the glamour and romance had gone . . . so many years ago. Until the new man had moved in next door, she had resigned herself to the imminence of her menopause. She had felt and acted like a middle-aged woman, with all love long behind her.

And then, running her hands over her naked body, she preened herself for her own regard, admiring her multiple reflection in the full-length mirrors, and then he had come. Striking looking as a matinee idol, avaricious, eating her up with his eyes, wooing her with his silences as much as with his words. She hoped dispassionately that she had not been too much of a pushover—for like an over-ripe apple, she had fallen from the tree of rectitude at the first touch. Not regretting it, she wondered a little at herself, for in so many ways she had considered that kind of thing revolting. She had never had any difficulty in rejecting any other of the ten or twelve men she had had woo her since her marriage. Of course, most of them had been messy, and their passes had been made at the end of drunken parties . . . but even so, no one's touch had ever so moved her.

Then too, he was odd. Very odd, so unlike anyone else she had ever known. Underneath the passion which he had for her there was something else, a goal he seemed to have, one that she could not understand.

He was, it seemed to her, as she wriggled into her brassiere, much more interested in her son, than the boy's father was.

Why?

But even if the question was never answered, she was full to overflowing with gratitude to the man who had made her young and desirable again. Her blood pounded as she prepared to meet him.

The man who had worked this miracle in the mind of a woman approaching middle-age did not look like a lover preparing for an assignation. He was peering through the tightly drawn curtains of the window in his house which faced out on his neighbor's domain. He could not hear the clatter of the typewriter, but he could see Barlay frantically tapping at the machine.

Looking away from the writer, the man glanced down at his wristwatch. It was peculiar. Divisions, much too many of them, divided the face of the watch into myriad sections. A sweep hand, one of six, raced around the dial. The man watched it, and waited, sweat pouring from his almost too high brow. Runnels of perspiration ran down from the widow's peak of his hairline. He brushed the back of his hand across his eyes, clearing them.

So soon!

His heart jumped.

From his window, he could see into the other house. The door behind the writer was opening. Now the boy, Bennet junior, was entering his father's sanctum sanctorum.

So much depended on the next few minutes . . . so very much. In the room that was dedicated to writing, Barlay almost leaped over the desk when he heard his son's voice.

"Dad . . . I . . ."

Turning around in his chair, Barlay snapped, "How many times do I have to tell you, never, never, come in here when I'm working?"

The boy retreated a little at the anger in his father's voice.

"I know, Dad—I wouldn't have come in—but I think you should know . . ."

"Know what?" The father shook his head. "No, don't tell me! Get out. Get out and leave me alone . . ."

The boy tried once more to open his mouth, but when his father saw this, the man half rose from the chair. "Out!" Fury spilled from him.

The boy left.

Bennet Barlay sat and looked at the paper in front of him which no longer was white. Type covered it. However, the words were repetitious. All they said over and over again, was "Now is the time for all good men to come to the aid of the party." Sometimes when Barlay was stuck badly, just the mechanics of typing would get his brain working again. It had not helped this time. This was a real block.

Not a shred of a plot idea, not an iota of a story line had occurred to him. As the door closed behind him, and his son left the room, he began again to try and force his tired brain to work.

Time travel? Done to death. A fourth-dimension story? How to make the most cornball of science-fiction ideas palatable? He had pulled so many switches on time travel and the fourth dimension. . . . One more?

Scowling with concentration, he put another piece of paper in the typewriter. Was it possible to squeeze just one more story from these hackneyed elements? He needed a story so badly.

Across the lawn that separated the two houses, the man who was watching let the pent-up breath out of his lungs. One crisis was safely past . . .

The boy had tried to tell his father about the success of his experiment and had been rejected.

Next . . .

From his vantage point he could see into the mother's room. She was dressed now, at least the top half of her which he could see. His hand went to the phone that rested on a table near him.

He could see her turn as at a sudden sound.

In her room, Mrs. Barlay was putting the last touches on her makeup. Now her face seemed to match the youthfulness of her body. "Come in," she called in response to the light tap on the door.

Her son came into the room. His lower lip trembled a trifle. "Mommy . . . I tried to tell dad, but he got mad because I interrupted him when he was working."

"Yes, dear?" She was not really very interested. Until her affair with the next-door neighbor the boy had been almost the whole of her life. Now . . . he was just an interruption, someone to be gotten rid of as gently as possible.

"You know how long I've been working down in the cellar on my idea."

She was paying him very little attention, a wisp sticking out from the bottom of her coiffure had caught her eye in the mirror. She busied herself in trapping it and making it join the shining helmet of her hair. "Yes, dear?"

"Well . . . Mummy . . ." The twelve-year-old boy ran to his mother, threw his arms around her and said, "It worked . . . it worked!"

"What worked, dear?" She still was only paving half a mind to his childish prattle.

Across the way, in that other house, the man dialed the phone frantically.

The boy said, " I put a hamster in it . . . and . . ."

The shrill ringing of the phone interrupted him.

His mother held up her hand for silence and said, "Yes?"

The man on the other end of the phone said, "My darling, dearest, I cannot wait till tonight! Somehow you must come to me now. Never have I wanted you so desperately . . ."

Holding her hand over the mouth piece of the phone the mother said, "Run along, dear. You can tell me all about your little experiment tonight at dinner."

Shoulders sagging, the youngster left the room.

As soon as the door closed, the woman pitched her voice low and almost whispered, "But, darling, is it safe? In the day time . . ."

He said almost angrily, "Why do you fear love? Come to my house, now this instant—I beseech you!"

She said, ". . . he's working . . . maybe I can . . . I'll say I went into town to buy something . . ."

"Good. I'll be waiting, my very dearest," the man lied. He hung up the phone. More sweat was beading up on his forehead. Now he must get into her house, sneak in, get down to the cellar and supply the little boy with the listening ear he so desperately needed.

He went to the back door of his suburban house; which was extraordinary to him since he had never seen one before except in pictures, until the day he had arrived, unheralded in the one house that was near his objective.

The woman called through the closed door, raising her voice to make it heard above the clatter of the typewriter keys, "Bennet, I'm going in to town . . . be back soon . . . dinner . . ."

He mumbled something that could have been anything.

He stared reproachfully at the new sheet of paper which was also covered with "Now is the time . . ."

She left the house, looking around, making sure that neither her son nor her husband could see that the route she was taking would curve around and back to that of the next-door neighbor—the only bachelor in all that suburban area.

In the cellar the boy looked at his machine. It had worked . . . and no one was interested, no one was willing to listen.

From the top of the stairs he heard a voice. It was warm, friendly, it expressed interest. The man at the head of the stairs asked, "How's it coming, laddy?"

Mr. Gardner, as he had chosen to call himself in this particular time continuum, descended the stairs. He smiled at the boy.

"Gee . . . Mr. Gardner, you know the idea I had?"

The man nodded. How well he knew. How important the boy's idea had bulked in the time that came after…. He knew.

"Well," shyly, but bursting with pride, the boy said, "It worked, sir. It worked. I put a hamster in it and it disappeared!"

The man walked to the machine. Such a silly looking object, a boy's plaything, and yet . . .

"Have you tried to bring the hamster back?"

The boy gulped. "I'm a little afraid to. I was hoping dad, or mommy would come down here with me when I pressed the last button. You see, all the time I've been working on my invention, I never really thought it'd work. It was a kind of hobby . . . like when I was a young kid, and played with my Erector set."

A child's toy, Mr. Gardner thought, and what a result it had had! As though it was yesterday instead of three hundred years in the future, he remembered the amazement that he and his confreres had felt when the tiny hamster had appeared in the middle of the conference table.

Consternation was the mildest word that fitted what they felt. An aperture in time, a fourth-dimensional device which allowed travel through the unresounding corridors of time, in his time it had been believed that the device had been invented by one of his contemporaries. They had just begun, he and his fellow workers, to explore the possibilities of the machine. And then, right in the middle of their plans, the hamster had arrived, throwing everything into confusion.

Someone had been needed to go back through time, nip this thing in the bud, prevent its too early application. He had volunteered, much to his own disgust, because he had felt the gesture was a little too romantic, too heroic, the kind of thing he had hoped he had outgrown.

But here he was involved in a series of shabby stratagems, making love to the boy's mother, interfering with the boy's father's mental processes, all to the end that it would be he, and not they whom the boy would show the device and how it acted.

His plans had worked but that did not prevent him from having guilty feelings about what he had done. He hoped the shame would wear away, when he was successful and again back in his own time.

"If you're a little afraid," he said, measuring his words carefully, "and I can't blame you if you are, I'll try the gadget for you . . ."

The boy felt reassurance flow from the man to him. He smiled and said, "Golly—would you?"

He showed the man the simple series of operations that he thought would reverse the action and return the hamster to its own time.

In the neighboring house, the woman was distraught. Why the sudden call from the man? Why had she come here? What had possessed her to risk fouling her own nest? Had she been insane? She loved her husband very dearly, the years they had shared were precious ones—and she had risked all that for a cheap flirtation and momentary gratification . . .

Pressing her knuckles into her forehead, she thought of the way her husband worked, the way he chained himself to his typewriter, hurting himself, working when he was tired, forcing himself to think when his brain was exhausted, and for what? Just to care for her and their son . . .

The thought of the boy made her flush. He had tried to tell her something and she had been so full of "love"—of lust—that she had rejected him!

Alone in the empty house she considered her actions and was revolted by them. They would never know, and her love would have to make up to them for what she had done.

She left the house, never to return to it. But a strange thing happened as she walked across the lawn. Full to overflowing with what she now thought of rather medievally as her sin, she felt her emotions go through some odd kind of change as she neared her own house.

In the cellar, the man who called himself Gardner, said, "I just press these buttons and that's all there is to it, eh?"

The boy nodded, his eyes glued to the frame of the device. If he was right, the hamster should appear on the platform as though by magic.

He watched as the man pressed the penultimate button. Next . . .

Mr. Gardner vanished and with him went the machine. In the hutch nearby, the little hamster nibbled on a lettuce leaf, its tiny pouches, from which it got its name, full to bursting.

On the lawn, Mrs. Barlay paused, trying to remember what she had just been thinking, a vagrant shred of a thought, gone, forever. She looked about her, eyed the privet hedges. Bennet would have to get to work on them as soon as he took a breather from his writing. A warm feeling of fulfillment made her glad to be alive, love for her husband and her son made her grateful for her womanhood. She was happy that she had never had any other lover but her husband; sometimes, almost wistfully, she had thought it would be nice to know another man, but now in the full glow of the sun, with the sweet smell of the cut grass coming up to her nostrils, she knew that this, her way, was best.

In the cellar, young Barlay, mind idle, wondered what to do with himself. He had come down to the cellar for some reason which he had forgotten. To play with his old trains? No . . . His Erector set, now rusty from disuse? No. Now he had it. He wanted to make a model plane.

Getting out some balsa wood he went happily to work whistling as he carved out a fuselage.


In the room with the typewriter, the man facing the machine smiled suddenly. An idea had come to him finally. Good old brain, it always came through in a pinch. He had thought of a twist.

Tearing out the type-covered paper with its foolish repetitive "now is the time," he crumpled up the paper and threw it in the overflowing trash basket.

He typed "THE MAN NEXT DOOR" halfway down the white page. Then rapidly, as fast as his fingers could move, he wrote, "Bennet Barlay sat in front of his typewriter and gazed with anguished eyes at the white paper on the roller. He had a work block."

THE END

BRUCE ELLIOTT BIBLIOGRAPHY
(1914-1973)

**Novels**
You'll Die Laughing (1945)
One is a Lonely Number (1952; abridged as *The Cocktail Jungle*, 1956;
   reprinted as *A Woman*, 1961)
Asylum Earth (1968)
The Rivet in Grandfather's Neck (1970; originally published as "The
   Planet of Shame", 1961)

**The Shadow magazine novels as written by "Maxwell Grant"**
The Blackest Mail (1946 #306)
Happy Death Day (1946 #307)
Seven Deadly Arts (1946 #308)
No Safety in Numbers (1946 #309)
Death on Ice (1946 #310)
Death Stalks the U.N. (1947 #311)
Murder in White (1947 #312)
Room 1313 (1947 #313)
Model Murder (1947 #314)
Svengali Kill (1947 #315)
Jabberwocky Thrust (1947 #316)
Ten Glass Eyes (1948 #317)
The Television Murders (1948 #318)
Murder on Main Street (1948 #319)
Reign of Terror (1948 #320)

**Short Stories**
All Ready for Framing (*Mobsters*, April 1953)
Asylum Earth (*Startling Stories*, Oct 1952)
Carnage in Calossa (*Sea Stories*, Nov 1953)
The Case of the Melting Artichokes (*The Shadow*, July 1944; Nick Carter)
The Cocktail Jungle (*Justice*, Jan 1956)
Crime Goes to College (*The Shadow*, June 1944; Nick Carter)
The Darkened Room (*Popular Detective*, May 1953)
The Dead Doll (*Triple Detective*, Winter 1953)
Death Lives in Brooklyn (*Thrilling Detective*, April 1953)
Death Paces the Widow's Walk (*The Shadow*, Oct 1944; Nick Carter)
The Devil Was Sick (*The Magazine of Fantasy and Science Fiction*, April
   1951)
Do You Know Me? (*Thrilling Detective*, Feb 1953)
Fearsome Fable (*The Magazine of Fantasy and Science Fiction*, Feb 1951;
   vignette)
Going, Going, Real Gone! (*Thrilling Detective*, Summer 1953)

House of Horror (*Keyhole Detective Cases*, March 1942; as by Walter Gardner)

Jungle Jazz (*Doc Savage*, June 1944)

The Last Magician (*The Magazine of Fantasy and Science Fiction*, Jan 1953)

The Man Next Door (*Amazing Stories*, Dec 1953/Jan 1954)

Meet Me on 47th Street (*Popular Detective*, Jan 1953)

The Ninety-Sixth Hour (*Alfred Hitchcock's Mystery Magazine*, July 1957)

The Planet of Shame (*Amazing Stories*, May, June 1961)

"So Sweet as Magic..." (*Fantasy Fiction*, Aug 1953)

They're Hustling You (*Shadow Mystery*, Aug/Sept 1948, as by Walter Gardner)

Vengeance Is Not Enough (*Stories Annual* v1 #1, 1955)

Wolves Don't Cry (*The Magazine of Fantasy and Science Fiction*, April 1954)

You'll Die Laughing (*Five Star*, 1945; *Triple Detective*, Summer 1952)

### Non-Fiction

Magic as a Hobby: New Tricks for Amateur Performers (1948)

Behind the Magic Wand (*Black Book Detective*, Winter 1952; article)

Houdini—Escape as a Fine Art (*Escape* #1, 1953; article)

Great Secrets of the Master Magicians (1953)

Classic Secrets of Magic (1953)

The Best in Magic (1956)

Magic 100 New Tricks (1957)

Professional Magic Made Easy (1959)

### Magazines

The Dude (editor)

Gent (editor)

Phoenix (on stage magic; editor 1946-1954)

Picture Week (editor)

TV Girls and Gags (editor)